Mr. DARCY'S DECISION

Mr. DARCY'S DECISION

A SEQUEL TO JANE AUSTEN'S
PRIDE AND PREJUDICE

JULIETTE SHAPIRO

Ulysses Press

Published in the United States by
ULYSSES PRESS
P.O. Box 3440
Berkeley, CA 94703
www.ulyssespress.com

ISBN10: 1-56975-682-1
ISBN13: 978-1-56975-682-9
Library of Congress Catalog Number 2008904130

Cover design: DiAnna Van Eycke
Cover illustration: George Goodwin Kilburne/Fine Art Photographic/Getty Images
Editorial: Jennifer Privateer, Kate Allen, Abby Reser
Production: Tamara Kowalski

Printed in Canada by Transcontinental Printing

10 9 8 7 6 5 4 3 2 1

Distributed by Publishers Group West

for
Michael, Zoe Elizabeth, Emma Charlotte and Cameron Elliot
and
Yasmin Alice, Carmen Grace, Tristan Rhys and Alissa April
delightful creatures all

INTRODUCTION

This continuation of *Pride and Prejudice* alludes to both Jane Austen's original story and the popular British television adaptation of the work (starring Colin Firth and Jennifer Ehle). Its intention is to entertain those who wish to know what happened to Darcy and Elizabeth after their marriage, and how the lives of those around these favorite characters unfolded.

CHAPTER 1

"Pride," observed Mary, who prided herself upon the solidity of her reflections, "is a very common failing I believe."

Though it may not be universally acknowledged, it *is* a truth that the creation of one man's pleasure is oft the reason for another's grief. Amongst others, this truth is well fixed.

On first coming into Hertfordshire, Mr. Darcy was a single man, he possessed a large fortune and, although he may very well have overlooked the fact, these two defining features dictated that he was in want of nothing more than a wife.

When he married Elizabeth Bennet in the autumn of 1812, it was the cause of a great flow of feelings. The bride and groom were elated, the intricacies of both their natures entwined so naturally now that recollection of any previous dislike of each other was avoided by the pair and discouraged in others. Oh, what a disagreeable and thoroughly inconvenient facility memory, particularly a good one, could be. Elizabeth often pondered on the sharpness and clarity with which acquaintances could summon up each detail of the past and, despite one's blushes and discomfort, warm up stale moments of embarrassment to be offered around for refreshment.

"To think, Miss Eliza, how thoroughly objectionable you once found the fellow," remarked Sir William Lucas, the father of her dear friend Charlotte, on hearing news of Elizabeth's engagement. How she, Elizabeth, had tried to argue, struggled to affirm the faults as all her own and contrived to persuade all cynics of her true affection for Darcy. Her elevation in status from country girl to mistress of Pemberley had the effect, she often felt, of giving others the idea that she had married first for money and second for love. That she should be so misunderstood! What mercenary, feeble minds could think that she could fall in love with fortune? Oh! Such blindness was unforgivable. They had only to look at Darcy to understand her better, for how could she not love him and had not she begun, just a little, to love him before she had found the good sense even to like him.

It was unacceptable to her that others could make the mistake she once had in misunderstanding him. For in every way that his appearance was pleasing Fitzwilliam Darcy was in equal part a genuine spirit. Elizabeth could have designed him no better. He was as handsome as he was good, he stood as tall in stature as he did in sound judgment and his particular tenderness, of which she was the only recipient, astonished her, took her breath away and warmed her heart. No one could think, if they only knew the value of his affections, that the price for her soul could have been paid in pounds. Even ten thousand of them a year was too small a fee for a heart that had proved so hard to win as Elizabeth's. But think thus skeptical minds will and Mrs. Darcy—how strange and thrilling that new title—wished sometimes that the only fortune she had gained was that of her husband's love.

But she adored Pemberley; the house so much a reflection of its master; the exact formality of its architecture and the natural freedom of its grounds in every way depicted him. The trees, the streams, and the very earth were steeped in memories of the boy he had been, the air itself seemed to have soaked in the potent essence of his being so that even in his absence a sense of him could be felt. In his presence, the house and the parkland came alive but appeared rested. All was reassuringly safe under his governing eye. It was there, in the grounds that had formed the picturesque backdrop to his boyhood, that Fitzwilliam Darcy had introduced himself again as the man he had become. It was under the old oak that Pemberley first saw its master place a gentle kiss on his wife's cheek; by the stream she had coaxed his laughter from somewhere deep within and gradually Elizabeth's own ready laughter had filled the fine rooms. United they were, Elizabeth and Darcy, by love, undeniably, and by being, in equal part, complicated, intelligent creatures who, they both conceded, were well suited, if only because there was no one else who could tolerate either of them so well as they did each other!

It is, however, folly to assume that perfect ingredients make for pictures of perfection. Where the united couple was at first reserved and subtle in any outward show of feeling, the fervor of the bride's mother provided ample compensation. Fervor of such enormity is best avoided if it cannot be extinguished and in certain cases, where there appears that little would be gained by attempting to induce composure, evasion of the enthusiast is advised.

Mrs. Bennet's fickleness was never more sharply evident than during this time of excitement. Fortunately, the two faces of her nature never met head on for she might have been humiliated to be put in mind of her former uncharitable opinions of her daughter's new husband. Six weeks after the wedding had taken place, she was still in the habit of regaling her acquaintances with every detail of how it was *she* who had first considered Mr. Darcy to be a suitable match for her Lizzy. Although, as she said once in mixed company, "Lizzy did not appear so fond of *him* in the first instance. I scarcely dare to mention it but I feel I can claim some small credit for maintaining his interest in her. You know, I have always had a genuine affection for the dear man. Indeed, my goodwill was very well received."

Twenty years and more of marriage had made Mr. Bennet so accustomed to his wife's capricious tendencies as to respond with no thoughts other than to vex her and he countered his lady's assertions in his irrevocably distinct style. "Indeed my dear, Mr. Darcy's admiration and respect for you very near exceed his affection for our own dear Lizzy. Considering the intensity of his feelings for you I am incredulous of the fact that the entire winter has passed and you have, as yet, not received a formal invitation to

Pemberley. The Gardiners, of course, have the benefit of every luxury there."

Mrs. Bennet's countenance was not so agreeable now. How loathsome the reminder of her exclusion from Darcy's estate was and how widely known it was that her brother and his wife *and* their four children had been most graciously favored. Indeed, they had taken almost permanent residency at Pemberley upon the master's insistence. This was a blissful existence for Mrs. Gardiner and her young family. She was a woman incapable of conceiving that even Heaven could be more beautiful than Derbyshire and, as was her lifetime's habit, delighted in repeated sentimental reminiscences about the nearby village of Lambton where she had spent an idyllic childhood. She and her husband rarely returned to their address of Gracechurch Street in Cheapside, London, when they did it was in order to attend, firsthand and only with eager thoughts of their departure, to Mr. Gardiner's matters of business.

Mr. Gardiner now had the chance of fishing to his contentment in the streams and lakes on the Pemberley estate, a pastime that had always gladdened him when he had the opportunity of enjoying it. The Gardiners, in similarity to Mrs. Bennet, also professed that their part in the romantic attachment of Elizabeth and Mr. Darcy had been instrumental. There the similarity ended though for there was truth as a base for the aunt and uncle's proclamations. For had it not been entirely due to them that their niece had been persuaded to visit Pemberley during their respite in Derbyshire? Mercifully the unflawed manners of Elizabeth's Aunt and Uncle Gardiner dictated that they were only ever boastful of their achievements in each other's company. Theirs was a quiet sort of pride.

The youngest Bennet sister Lydia, whose own marriage to George Wickham had only recently preceded her two sisters' unions, was delighted, outwardly only, that Lizzy should have secured so handsome a husband. But young Mrs. George Wickham was inwardly rankled by an increasing awareness, despite her naivety, of her sister's good fortune. Elizabeth had indeed married extremely well. Lydia's own husband's expertly fashioned gentleman-like manners and good features were little recompense when compared to Darcy's recommendations in appearance, fortune, and status. Of the latter two attributes, George Wickham was noticeably bereft. Young Mrs. Wickham's displeasure was further fueled by the absolute belief, despite all history suggesting the opposite, that Elizabeth truly adored her love in a way that was only equaled by Darcy's undoubted worship, in turn, of her.

It was with reluctance that Lydia renounced her conceited declaration of being the only married Bennet sister so soon after her own nuptials had taken place. To have been obliged to relinquish the brief position of superiority that this afforded her over all four of her siblings caused a good degree of dissatisfaction for her. Lydia's disposition was partly inherited from her mother and had, in part, been honed by the woman. Misdemeanors, her own, were quickly forgot and she made no reference during reflection to the scandals and improprieties that surrounded her alliance with George Wickham.

She was, as ever, inconsistent in her beliefs and maintained her frivolous outlook on life. With her husband's regiment quartered in Newcastle she relied upon the post as a means to keep contact with her family, but she did not write often. Unless she could relate tales that would affirm her popularity and promote her hunger for enjoyment then she did not see fit to pick up a pen. She had made a couple of brief visits to both Netherfield and Pemberley whilst Wickham spent some leisure time in Brighton and London. He was as audacious as ever he had been in his attitudes and thought nothing of encouraging his wife to appeal to Elizabeth and Darcy to suggest that their position might be used to the advantage of securing him a respected situation in society. Congenial though they were, neither Mr. nor Mrs. Darcy saw fit to acknowledge the request.

It is disappointing but not at all surprising to learn that not everyone took pleasure in Elizabeth's ascent in standing to mistress of Pemberley. It was particularly well accounted and widely known that Darcy's aunt, Lady Catherine de Bourgh, was woeful and inconsolable about the union. It had meant the destruction of her hopes, and her dreams, that her own daughter Anne would one day be united with Darcy. The enormity of Lady Catherine's fury remained constant and her undisguised disdain for Elizabeth and the Bennet family in general was unyielding. That the name of de Bourgh and her personal social standing might risk being marred by what she judged to be an afflicted connection was insupportable to her and she declared quite publicly never to visit Pemberley despite her nephew's attempt at reconciliation.

"That is if they should deem to insult me with another of their invitations, or intensify their offense with any expectation of being received at Rosings Park."

Poor Anne de Bourgh remained, by demand as much as by any real malady, as infirm physically as ever she had been, she displayed very credible symptoms of anguish over Darcy's having been purloined from her by one so insignificant as Elizabeth Bennet, but the magnitude of her torment never once matched the magnitude of her mother's.

Felicitations from the Collins household were sent to Elizabeth and Darcy with more than a little misgiving. While Charlotte Collins was all gladness, and had no reason to be otherwise, her husband was not so easily persuaded to put forward any heartfelt and genuine blessings to the Darcys. Mr. Collins could not comfortably accept that the previous November Elizabeth Bennet had refused, with untoward obstinacy, to become his wife. There was little recompense to be had after this violent rejection so he contented himself with drawing a picture of Elizabeth as a hard-hearted and difficult girl. As a means to restore his own composure he became entirely persuaded that she would most certainly end a spinster. If he, Mr. Collins, a respectable clergyman, with all his well-contrived charms and affable ways, could not win her regard then it was a certainty, he decided, that no one would.

He had also boasted the advantage of being the sole beneficiary of her family home of Longbourn. But even the glittering prizes of the entailment and the relief and stability the circumstances would have afforded her family were not enticement enough for Elizabeth to betroth herself to him. It had taken Mr. Collins a shockingly short time to steady himself from Elizabeth's rebuff and his former smugness was reinstated with astounding velocity once his offer of marriage to Charlotte Lucas had been accepted. The foundations of Charlotte's friendship with Lizzy had the required strength to withstand such a blow. It is true to say that Elizabeth found it an uncomfortable thought that she had no entitlement to her own home whilst her friend had acquired certain rights in connection with her husband. But, as was Lizzy's nature, she wished them well and what had once been the very important question of the entailment soon became a matter of little consequence to her after her own worthy marriage. Her concerns, indeed her astonishment, on hearing of Charlotte's engagement came from her own inability to see any desirability in Mr. Collins herself. But she understood that Charlotte was practical before being sentimental and knew only too well that her friend could be satisfied with a marriage state that offered security and respectability even if there was very little else besides to recommend it.

Charlotte Collins was devout to be sure, she made as honorable a wife to a clergyman as could ever be wished for. In addition, she was able to enjoy Lady Catherine de Bourgh's patronage, though not quite so ardently as did her husband. She soon found herself resignedly content with life at the rectory at Hunsford and accepted, in the grateful way of a woman quite reconciled to not being in love, that the garden, ecclesiastical duties, and their patroness's demands kept her husband fully occupied. They lived in reasonable style, savoring the social enhancements created by their connection to the high ranks of the de Bourgh family, and had the reassurance that their future was by no means undesigned. Their contentment, however, was short-lived; Lady Catherine's wrath was unbearable and all beneficent attentions to Mr. Collins were withdrawn once Elizabeth's engagement to Mr. Darcy became widely known. Lady Catherine's previous views of Mr. Collins and his wife were dramatically altered by her rage. Her belief that the undesirable Bennet family, including those members of it so distantly associated as Mr. Collins, posed a very real threat to all that was good and principled became more fixed. William Collins and his wife fled Hunsford but as a result of their hasty escape to Lucas Lodge in Hertfordshire an unusual friendship was born.

Familial loyalties dictated that it should fall to the Lucases and the Bennets to each play a part in assisting the rejected clergyman and his wife. Sir William Lucas arranged a carriage—Mr. Collins's own much boasted of equipage being too modest for the task of his complete removal. Mrs. Bennet sent Mary to help. Her choice was limited as she now had three daughters married and taken from Longbourn and, although fanciful in nature herself, she deemed Kitty too fragile in composure to be numb to Lady Catherine's vitriol and derision, so concluded that Mary's plain looks and predisposition for moralizing and reflection would be least likely to cause offense. And so it was that Mary Bennet, viewing the task as an important personal crusade, accompanied Sir William Lucas and his daughter Maria to Rosings Park.

Lady Catherine would agree to no conversation with either Mr. or Mrs. Collins. Mary, much to her own astonishment, was the appointed mediator, her first undertaking being the examination of an inventory, provided by Lady Catherine, stating quite clearly a brief list of items that were permitted to depart from Hunsford, and an extensive catalogue of those which must be seen to remain. By this means Mary Bennet had assisted in ridding Lady Catherine of the unwanted clergyman and his wife and had therefore inadvertently begun, tentatively at first, a process of redemption.

Lady Catherine, finding herself noticeably afflicted with weakness due to the disagreeable nature of recent events, conceded against her better judgment but in deference to her poor health, to permit Miss Mary Bennet, and the inventory that had been placed in her care, to be brought to Rosings Park. Once informed of the invitation Mary Bennet, seeing the clear implications of such a privilege, set off on the short journey across the lane from the Hunsford Parsonage where she had thus far been accommodated.

The completed inventory, which emphasized the importance of the Collinses leaving Hunsford exactly as they had found it, was now complete and to be conveying it to Rosings Park when most everyone else in the world was denied access to the place allowed Mary to indulge in a good deal of self congratulation. But the girl's expanded mood was soon diminished by her finding Lady Catherine de Bourgh to be a most disconcerting woman to be face to face with. Her discomfort was not made easier when, having been subjected to a more prolonged inspection than the inventory, she was obliged to hear out the woman's misgivings.

"You can be under no misapprehension that I admit you here at Rosings Park by choice, Mary Bennet. I am guardedly aware of the perils of acquainting myself so intimately with the likes of your family." A brief but distinctly unsettling silence followed, then she went on, "I concede it goes in your favor that you have not the slightest sign of the arts of enticement that your contemptible sister displays. No, your ungarnished appearance is of encouragement to me now I take the trouble of observing it closer. It gives me pain to admit it, but my own dear daughter comes to mind. She has her own frailties, which I daresay render her a less desirable catch for a brutish type of man. You have little to boast of in the way of beauty, although in your case such an ill-favored appearance can certainly be put down to your poor line of descent."

Mary's spirits were lifted by what she deemed to be inverse flattery, for rather than seize upon the offense intended by Lady Catherine's remarks, she elected to view the opinions offered appreciatively. So long had Mary been accustomed to viewing herself as plain; she was wholly and miserably aware that her commonplace looks appeared more so in light of all her sisters' more becoming features. She always dressed modestly for fear that highly fashioned garments would throw her plainness into stark relief. Now, in the light of what she chose to read into Lady Catherine's observations, she could consider her modest presentation a virtue, a quality that at last afforded her a measure of superiority over her sisters. To be plain was not necessarily a shortcoming.

Lady Catherine continued to address Mary in a patronizing manner but her tone soon softened. She had, despite her dedication to finding anyone with the name of Bennet unbearable, found nothing significant to dislike about the unaffected demure young woman other than her unfortunate family.

That same afternoon Mary became acquainted with Anne de Bourgh who she had heard described as a "cross, disagreeable looking thing" by Lizzy. Between Anne and Mary there appeared to be no underlying feelings of threat or unease, as both could seem pallid and inspirited, favoring the pursuit of serious reflection and theological debate. As a result of these and other common interests a firm rapport developed with a rapidity that astounded those who observed it; though quite why the swift development of a friendship should be thought astonishing in a world where the instantaneous nature of love affairs, proposals, and marriage was readily accepted is a question that may well remain unanswered.

Eventually, when Lady Catherine was unable to deny the delight Anne took in the friendship, she began to recognize the advantages of her daughter having a devoted companion who was near to her own age and gave her consent to the acquaintance with limited reluctance. Mrs. Jenkinson, who had previously attended Anne and Lady Catherine, graciously obliged to let Mary take her place and it was settled that she would dedicate herself to Rosings Park and Lady Catherine in any way that would prove favorable to her mistress.

Later, having suffered the indignity of making a formal request to Mr. Bennet to propose that Mary attend her daughter's needs Lady Catherine managed, but not without being properly impressed by the humility she was showing, to swallow some of her pride. But this was not without a final and most definite assurance to Mary that she still thought very little of her family. "Mary Bennet, I am not in the habit of expressing gratitude to those so far beneath me as yourself. There is rarely if ever an occasion when such indebtedness should arise. However, I am fair in my judgments and I have noted that my dear Anne takes a liking to your morals and company and I myself, if my unstinting devotion to my daughter is to be sustained, must acknowledge this. I am, as you must by now realize, inordinately attentive to Anne's every need. It is this consideration that leads me to accept you... despite your low connections." Looking at Mary guardedly, she went on, "Although you probably would not bear detailed scrutiny, the examination I have made of your character thus far causes me less displeasure than I expected. I suppose I must be accepting of the relationship. I am prepared to take you on as a companion to Anne," she said. "And should you prove so loyal to her as Mrs. Jenkinson has to us all here at Rosings I shall have no cause for regret." She observed Mary closely and continued, "Take heed of this advice though, Miss Mary Bennet, should ever an inkling of resemblance to the improprieties of your family members ever manifest in your personality you will feel the withdrawal of the benefit of my attentions most sharply."

Thus was Mary's position at Rosings Park settled upon and secured with none doubting the conditions which had been laid out so succinctly. She had scant contact with Longbourn and wrote more to Mr. Collins than she did her immediate family, choosing to correspond with the clergyman with the purpose of her own religious advancement in mind. In every conceivable way Mary Bennet was loyal to Lady Catherine and intended, wholeheartedly, to show that one Bennet girl at least could be trusted to employ her time in a worthwhile way. Mary was no reprobate; she was rarely tempted to break rules or conventions but her continuing contact with Mr. Collins was a matter on which she chose to remain silent.

Jane and her dear Mr. Bingley were as mesmerized with each other as ever. From their first moving to Netherfield Park after their marriage, they decided to investigate the possibility of purchasing a fine estate not thirty miles from Elizabeth and Darcy at Pemberley. One happy consequence of this would be the endurance of fewer visits from Mrs. Bennet. The woman's manners and intrusions tested even Charles Bingley's placid nature. Mr. Bingley's sister

Caroline could do little to relieve her undisclosed grief at Darcy's marriage. How she had scorned Eliza Bennet. In keeping with young women of her kind she was quite comfortable with recollections of how she had asserted herself in her efforts to fuel dislike of Elizabeth in Darcy. That Caroline Bingley's social accomplishments were refined goes some way to explain how she could, whilst harboring feelings of utter disdain and envy, adopt an attitude of sincerity towards Elizabeth. Few considered Caroline genuine but she gave such a convincing performance that she was accepted at Pemberley, occupying her time by paying a great deal of attention to Darcy's sister Georgiana who now resided there.

Bingley's other sister, Mrs. Hurst, was no longer inseparable from Caroline as had been her previous form. This had little to do with choice, for she would much rather have engaged herself with Caroline in the shared entertainment of belittling Elizabeth. Mrs. Hurst's absence from Pemberley had nothing to do with her not wanting to be there and everything to do with Mr. Hurst's self-induced ailments. The results of his indulgence kept her retained at Netherfield. There she felt, with acute bitterness, that an ill husband proved an insurmountable obstacle to the enjoyment of life. The inevitable demise brought about by too much wine and too little fresh air did not seem to take effect rapidly enough to be thought convenient.

There are others to be considered here, pitied perhaps. Although not bitter or jealous or shot through with malice like some poor creatures, there are those for whom the marriage of sisters brings an emptiness. Alone at Longbourn, Kitty Bennet was obliged to take the full force of her mother's excitability. This was gravely frustrating for her as she had already spent some weeks at Pemberley and knew too well that there was much to be missed. There, her manners and character had improved, this advance was partially accounted for by Kitty's being in such fine company although it must be acknowledged that her detachment from her wayward sister Lydia also played a part in this favorable development.

So it was with true suffering that she returned to Longbourn in order that her mother could demand attention and receive it as and when she so desired. Mr. Bennet now imposed a strict and unsociable regime for Kitty who was stricken by the isolation she felt; the situation was worsened by his adamant convictions that the girl should enjoy no balls or assemblies until her responsibility in character had been proven. She felt overwhelmingly aggrieved that her character was forever to be judged by her sister Lydia's shocking conduct but could see no immediate way to appease her father. With the regiment gone from Meryton she no longer felt she had even the remotest chance of securing an officer for a husband, or even for an afternoon's distraction.

"God has been very good to us," Mrs. Bennet said, when three daughters were married the same year. Her boundless pride, gloating, and superiority consumed her. Jane and Lizzy's situations in marriage had long been her favorite talking point, but of late her inclination was to elaborate upon Mary's acceptance at Rosings Park. Kitty was vexed to hear of Mary being so highly praised, although she had not married, and Kitty privately believed that she never would, her residency at Rosings Park and the potential of such an association seemed to raise her to an unduly high pinnacle in her mother's estimations. Mrs. Bennet, in keeping with her selective view of things, would not concede that the position of companion was generally considered very lowly indeed.

With happy feelings of release Mr. Bennet took satisfaction from the situations of all his daughters. The relief on his finances that their positions afforded him was particularly valued. He had been no stranger to self reproach and had bitterly regretted not beginning, early in marriage, to make provisions for his family, but, as he so often recalled, in an attempt to justify his apathy, he had expected to have sons, or one son at least. That his wife had not obliged him in this expectation had not been his fault and he very kindly concluded that it was not entirely hers either. Bad fortune must be responsible for a house bursting with females.

When daughters came swift and fast there was no real cause for regret on Mr. Bennet's part for he loved all of them despite their silliness. It would be untrue to say that he loved them all equally, as he perhaps should have done; he did not, nor could he. His little Lizzy held the greater share of his affections. This unequaled love was due, not to defects in the father, but to merits in the child. However much Mr. Bennet lacked sense he had sensibility in abundance. Oh, the joy of having Lizzy settled and set so well. The relief! Enough to allow him the opportunity of journeys by carriage to Pemberley. There he enjoyed everything with full relish, but most particularly his wife's absence. Although they were not cruel, Elizabeth and Darcy were very properly impressed, in the early days of their union, by the fact that they had a considerable amount of recovering to do from the furor that had surrounded them. Tranquility was impossible with Mrs. Bennet near, she was not a woman most suited to inspiring calm in others. So, she awaited her invitation to Pemberley with a mix of conviction that it would come and anxiety, for she privately feared that it would not.

CHAPTER 2

"Your conjecture is totally wrong, I assure you. My mind was more agreeably engaged. I have been meditating on the very great pleasure which a pair of fine eyes in the face of a pretty woman can bestow."

Though she would claim to enjoy many amusements, Mrs. Bennet was never easier than when immodestly entertaining others with tales of her married daughters. One afternoon she set about diverting her sister Mrs. Phillips. "Of course Jane is excessively well catered for at Netherfield my dear and every attention is paid to her by all of Bingley's family. You know, I have always said that Jane has about her such an air of elegance that none could dislike her." She rubbed her hands together. "I can only describe it as the style of a person worth the attention of a man who has five thousand a year. Yes indeed, I knew all along that Jane at least would marry well."

Mrs. Phillips, whose appetite for gossip matched her sister's, replied with a smile. "Then your pleasure must have been twofold at the news of Elizabeth's unexpected alliance to Mr. Darcy?"

Mrs. Bennet always felt a degree of discomfort when forced to admit that this particular love affair had been a surprise to her, feeling it showed a neglectful streak in her own personality that she had not detected the growth of their passion. When the subject arose, as it invariably did, she would allude to being far more knowledgeable and informed than her restricted view of life had allowed her to be.

"Oh yes, my dear sister, you are quite right, but there was nothing in the affair that was unexpected for me. I was aware all along of even the finest developments. You know I have a particularly close bond with Lizzy and Mr. Darcy could scarce

17

conceal his obsession with her, well, not from her own mother he could not, no matter how accomplished his manners."

"But you allowed no one else to be party to your suppositions despite their importance, not even Mr. Bennet?"

Mrs. Bennet gave her sister a knowing look. "I can only say that my own exemplary manner of behavior prevented my exposing particulars of my daughter's budding liaison. I feared that sudden baring of a matter so delicate may have endangered the feelings of those concerned. I was not about to announce it! What are you thinking? They are both proud sorts you know and it is my belief that where a man has ten thousand a year it is worth all the caution in the world. That is in part why I always took such trouble to be agreeable to the man. Though as you know, sister, I am as good a judge of character as can be found and would have liked him very well if he had not had any claim to wealth at all. There was the little matter of the poor opinions others had of him but of course, this meant nothing to me. No, I was always very well pleased about the arrangement and I only wish I could have included Mr. Bennet in the secret when I first had suspicions about it, but my husband knows so little of romance that the notion may well have been lost on him."

Mrs. Bennet spent many a happy hour idling to her sister, who had heard all this news ten times over at least but nevertheless took delight in relishing it as if for the first time. Enjoyment of Mrs. Bennet's re-told tales was natural, for with each portrayal some little detail or other would have altered, an opinion, an account, a verbatim quote, all minor matters such as these were guaranteed to have changed, sometimes beyond recognition.

"I expect by now you must have word of a request to wait on them at Pemberley," said Mrs. Phillips. And, knowing full well the negativity of the answer, yet anticipating the enjoyment her sister's contradiction would provide, she went on, "You have regaled me abundantly with such stories of your visits to Netherfield Park, but I still hear nothing of Darcy's estate, when is your visit to take place?"

Mrs. Bennet flushed and retorted sharply, "The unfortunate positioning of Pemberley prevents my visit, you of all people will appreciate that with my delicate constitution I was not ready to withstand the rigors of extensive travel to Derbyshire. In winter! My nerves alone may not have held up. No, sister, I am afraid that Pemberley will have to be patient and expect my attention once I am in full health again, for as you know, I have been very ill of late."

"But now that spring is upon us you will be better set for such a journey." Mrs. Phillips concealed a wry smile for she was indeed well aware of her sister's nervous condition and how it was selectively adapted to suit the occasion. How sly of her to twist the realities to imply that she was refusing to visit when it was widely known that her summons had not yet arrived.

Mrs. Bennet countered her humiliation with further news of Netherfield and of Mary's situation at Rosings Park. Although she was adept at speaking at length on subjects she knew little of, she felt Mrs. Phillip's scrutiny acutely and decided that a hushed approach to matters of Pemberley would suffice for the moment. She mentioned Wickham and Lydia only in passing, the degree of her eagerness regarding that union had paled once she had the glory of Jane and Lizzy's marriages to bask in.

Of the gravest of her daughters she went on to confide, "Mary's opinions have always fatigued me, but she is in ideal company at Rosings. It is most suited to her because she is as serious and studious a girl as you could wish to meet." After a while she looked around, as if afraid of eavesdroppers and whispered, "That girl is as miserable and unaffected by merriment as I daresay poor Anne de Bourgh is. Now there is a creature who, I am led to believe, is the only other girl alive plainer than Mary herself."

Mrs. Phillips, whose vulgarity usually matched her sister's, nevertheless viewed the criticism of her poor niece dimly. "I must speak kindly on Mary's behalf, Fanny. You are not complimentary to your daughter. After all, it is not every woman's salvation to procure a husband by beguiling him. Mary, if given the chance of marriage, will suit a studious type of man I imagine."

Mrs. Bennet did not take well to being corrected and she certainly did not appreciate her harshness towards Mary being emphasized and was therefore obliged to feign an attack of the palpitations. Shortly afterwards Mrs. Phillips said her goodbyes and set off for Meryton. Her express purpose was to savor her connection to the Bennet girls' good fortune by repeating her sister's tales firsthand to her own acquaintances.

Only those fortunate enough to be in the favorable situation of being within the walls of Pemberley would have been in a position to satisfy Mrs. Bennet's curiosity. Elizabeth, in keeping with Jane, was attended to with such reverence and care that she scarcely recognized herself. All in the employ of Mr. Darcy welcomed her and accepted her as their mistress without the slightest difficulty. Their affection for their master and Elizabeth's innate charm meant that their feelings towards her would be warm. Despite the responsibilities of being the mistress of a large estate, Lizzy wrote frequently to Jane. Long letters, sometimes, writing as fast as she could, which was never as fast as her thoughts came, Elizabeth would quite forget herself and note, with frustration, that her hand had sprawled, that she had left wasteful gaps between lines and generally penned an altogether untidy epistle. The mixture of eagerness to convey everything to Jane and the hitherto unknown situation of being able to afford good paper in good quantities meant that efforts to discipline her hand were often abandoned.

Pemberley, Derbyshire

My Dearest Jane,

I am sure this letter finds you as happy with life as ever, though I cannot conceive that there is anyone alive in the world who can lay claim to being happier than I am. Oh, you must think back to my often contrary nature and wonder how I have made this transformation, but you will believe me, I know, when I tell you it is all down to my husband. Jane, I am sure you cannot accept that there is any man more obliging, more handsome or loving than your own dear Charles, but here we must consent to disagree, for my own Fitzwilliam is such a man in my eyes. He is so attentive, so supportive of me in ways I could never have imagined. We have had many tranquil weeks alone here at Pemberley during which time I have come to love it. I find myself quite at home here.

But, it was not long before social commitments had to be honored. You know me well, Jane, that my character is not easily frightened. But allow me to confess my nervousness when Fitzwilliam announced that a large party of more than a dozen of his highly esteemed associates was to be received at Pemberley. Oh Jane, you must have endured feelings of hesitation when first arranging events of such importance at Netherfield. I know I can count on your empathy and your praise when you learn that I have now succeeded in entertaining at this height myself. The arrival of my husband's fifteen guests was to constitute my first endeavor to exhibit my competence as mistress of Pemberley. Amongst the party were dignitaries of every kind imaginable, including a close acquaintance of Fitzwilliam's, described to me as the second Earl of Liverpool. Only now do I regret my refusal to educate myself better in matters concerning our country. But I have always struggled to immerse myself fully in the weightier subjects, usually finding folly and amusement where others see only serious things. Any history of England, as penned by me, would show me to be little more than partial, prejudiced, and ignorant. I would include few dates and could probably cover Henry IV to Charles I in a very few pages. On political matters, I am sure I would do no better. Have I perhaps had a propensity to see the world as too light, bright, and sparkling?

You have conscientiously labored at the improvement of your mind, Jane, and will have noticed the joke already. I am sure I do not need to tell you that the Earl of Liverpool is Robert Jenkinson. How could I have been so naive? You may worry that I have shown myself to be ignorant. Pray, do not concern yourself, Jane. Fitzwilliam seemed only to take delight in my innocence. Thankfully, he would not have me appear a simpleton in company. He is clever to be sure; for he informed me of his guest's identity just hours before we were due to receive him. I am glad of this, my sister. Imagine the consequences, had I dwelt too long in advance on the idea of entertaining our own Prime Minister! I think I should have generated a great deal of nervousness about the matter. As it was, I had little time to think even of an appropriate gown to wear. I had even less time for strategy and could therefore hope only to rely on my inherent ability to commune with all people. I prayed that I would not be the cause of disappointment or the subject of derision.

Jenkinson is a man of influence and prominence responsible for a great many portentous issues. You would have laughed to hear him engage in lively discourse with me about popular dances and, above all things, the fashion for long sleeves. Do not fear that I spoke only of frivolities such as these! All nervousness was lost, I cannot explain it but I was relaxed in the company, not too opinionated as to show disregard for my place, but assured enough to display "the mind of an accomplished and intelligent woman who has the added advantage of attracting attention to her laudable observations by her exquisite beauty." Those are my husband's words. I shall never forget them, and know they can never be lost as I have committed them to paper in this letter to you in order that you may share my delight at my small measure of success. Astounding, is it not, that a simple girl can talk on a great number of subjects without appearing too much of a bluestocking.

Please write to me with all your news, Jane, I long to hear of your days at Netherfield, you must tell me how Charles is and I insist upon your next correspondence being longer than your last. You must oblige me in this, there is no excuse, send me a novel if you wish, I can bear the charge at this end.

I leave you now and pray you will write soon only not so neatly as to cause me too much disgrace at the abominable state of this letter. I would blame the pen if I thought you would believe it to be at fault, but, sister, you know me only too well and will see I am sure that my words run across the page just as my feet are inclined to race through woodland.

Your loving sister Elizabeth

It was impossible for those around Darcy and Elizabeth to be blind to their ardor and its influence seemed to have a wholesome and curative effect on almost everyone. Although Darcy had always enjoyed the advantage of being well liked by his staff and those who knew him well, he had, on numerous other occasions, caused offense elsewhere with his aloof manner. From the very first he had not been liked in Hertfordshire, his pride and arrogance and others' misinterpretation had painted a very dim portrait of him. But he was a man so secure, so well-set, and so very assured that he had done little to attempt to brighten the picture and had gone about the world, Hertfordshire proving eventually to be an important part of it, without employing any means to disguise the faults he had then viewed as his virtues. So it was noted that with his love for Elizabeth came a softer, more tolerant aspect to his character.

One afternoon, Caroline Bingley, who had taken to assisting Georgiana at the pianoforte regularly, felt the need to raise the subject of Darcy's transformation to his sister.

"It is not totally unbecoming, this unveiling, but it is astounding I suppose because in the past he was a man who revealed so little. But then dearest Elizabeth is graced with her own peculiar charm and this seems to have the effect of unleashing your brother's feelings most publicly. The pair of them are rarely in the same room without some hand-holding or other sentimental contact being apparently necessary. They gaze at each other an awful lot."

Georgiana puzzled over her companion's comments but attempted to ignore the scornful tones, replying thoughtfully, "They are very much in love. I am sure it is no less than my dear brother deserves."

Miss Caroline Bingley had a unique way of cloaking derision in sweetness and this allowed her the exorcism of her own misgivings whilst saving her from contempt. She went on, "Their feelings are in no doubt. With such obvious displays how could anyone question them? You mistake my meaning, Miss Georgiana. I have no questions about the authenticity of their affection. Though I confess, it has occurred to me that the manifestation of their passions, being so liberal in style, may be judged imprudent in society. That is merely my opinion. Perhaps I am too correct, their warm glances and tender performances may be viewed as quite charming in polite society after all. It may indeed be the new way of fashionable conduct. After all," she concluded, "many an ugly fashion, with little more than the advantage of repeated exposure, becomes de rigueur and not because we like it, but because we convince ourselves that we do. It becomes habitual."

Georgiana, who adored the new sister she had in Elizabeth, was pained to detect Miss Bingley's resentful inflection, though it was reasonably well disguised. She dearly wished the conversation over and rather subtly contrived to have difficulty reading a passage of music that she had long since mastered. Miss Bingley said no more of Elizabeth and Darcy's passion. She pondered on it a while longer then triumphed in aiding Georgiana with the difficult passage, for she was very accomplished herself and made no secret of it.

CHAPTER 3

"She has nothing, in short, to recommend her, but being an excellent walker. I shall never forget her appearance this morning. She really looked almost wild."

Elizabeth would often walk the grounds at Pemberley for although she had reached one and twenty she still had the instincts of a country girl. Her manner when out of doors was as it always had been, quite different from the composed restraint she consented to display in company. She had no fear of the criticism her frolics may incite for she relished her freedom. She spoke of her delight in the outdoors to her husband when he joined her one afternoon in her beloved pursuit. He was inclined to accompany her when matters of business did not detain him.

"I think I would be quite beside myself with grief if I could not walk, nay, run even, through these woods," said Elizabeth looking about her to take in the scene. "Before I came here I had heard so much of Pemberley's grandeur and rich furnishings, and indeed it is exquisite, but I think I shall always profess that its true beauty is exterior."

Darcy delighted in finding the opportunity to compliment his young wife. "Then in some way our Pemberley mirrors your own state, my lovely Elizabeth, for your beauty is in my eyes equal both inside and out." On his face was the merest smile of satisfaction, he was only newly accustomed to emotional liberation and though it pleased him to express it, a certain level of restraint was always exercised.

His lady laughed and mocked him a little. "Yes beautiful indeed I am sure, a woman scampering about the woods, though on this occasion my petticoat is not six inches deep in mud." Darcy laughed too; the couple quite often amused each other about past times though neither could bear to think of their former discourteousness to each other.

What things lovers talk of in the early days of their lives together. It seems that questions must be answered and curiosity succumbed to. Even in the throes of love and in the absorbent environment of a new and happy marriage there are those trifling little questions that demand answers. Elizabeth's curiosity was never more piqued than when she considered her husband's relating of his reaction to Lady Catherine's fury.

"It taught me to hope as I had scarcely ever allowed myself to hope before. I knew enough of your disposition to be certain that, had you been absolutely, irrevocably decided against me, you would have acknowledged it to Lady Catherine, frankly and openly."

Oh, to have been party to that conversation! Had not Elizabeth's own refusal to oblige Lady Catherine been insult enough? With what little tolerance his aunt must have heard her nephew's declarations and with what bitter sentiments toward herself. But curiosity had never yet been entirely satisfied, and much as Elizabeth truly desired details, she found that, for a moment at least, memories of her walk with Mr. Darcy and the renewal of his proposal of marriage were diversion enough to quiet even her inquisitive mind. What ensued that day is universally known. Their marriage and their wishes to avoid recollection of previous mutual misunderstanding were viewed with equal admiration by those who truly loved them. Prejudices and misplaced pride must all be forgot; sharp comments, aloof behavior and insults rarely dwelt upon. How perfect it would be to achieve such refrain yet how little inclined Elizabeth was to such severe repression.

Her spirit seemed to have grown evermore playful since matrimony. Knowing Darcy the better brought about a tendency to tease him a great deal more than she would have imagined herself capable of and the reward of his reactions did not induce her to resist the temptation. She was inexplicably fond of his reluctant smiles, endeared more by these than his readier ones. To tease him, to make him laugh at life and human folly, as she was disposed to do, was her great delight. Being naturally enquiring she could not wait long before asking her husband to give particulars of Lady Catherine's attempts to prevent their union. He is fond of faithful narratives! I imagine he could, if coaxed, give a detailed account of the meeting. Oh, I seem meddlesome, but if amusement were my only design I should not trouble him with it. It would be entertaining to hear without doubt, but moreover I think I desire to know in what manner he defended me, thought she. Elizabeth was at once surprised by her own character. What trickery is love that it induces such longing to hear of my husband's gallantry, of his declarations of love for me? Are not his hand and his attentions enough?

But gallantry and defense by a man on behalf of a woman are potent and favored forms of flattery and Elizabeth, like any young woman, might be forgiven for seeking such compliments.

Recognizing his wife to be in a pensive mood Darcy questioned, she replied and it was all decided upon in moments. To narrate the tale of his aunt's adamant opposition to their union could hardly be pleasurable to him, but his wife's insistence, her guileless yet persuasive ways soon had him relaying the tale as if the idea of doing so had been his own.

"Lady Catherine was so determined to influence me and so disgusted with my impertinence in refusing to oblige her that I need not ask what tone she adopted when approaching you," said Elizabeth.

Darcy smiled. "You need not ask, Elizabeth, but you are desirous to know it all the same. My aunt was hardly about to flatter the woman who was to be the means of destroying her hopes for her own daughter's future."

"Oh yes, the engagement, the one 'of a peculiar kind'! It seems to me that only a very peculiar kind of engagement indeed would rely so little on the approval of the proposed husband."

"My approval was of little consequence, my aunt and, I confess, my mother to some degree were set upon the idea when Anne and I were in our infancy. I daresay their whims were conjured even before then."

"With so little thought given to their children's happiness? It seems an extraordinary style of mothering."

"The securing of fortune, the marrying of wealth to wealth is happiness enough for Lady Catherine. For my own mother's sensibilities I cannot vouch entirely but I believe her to have been less likely to have frowned upon you than my aunt is."

"You told Lady Catherine you loved me? I hope with less reference to the emotion being against your better judgment than your first proposal to me contained!"

"Oh Elizabeth!" cried Darcy. "Agreements must be adhered to. I shall refuse to recount the tale if you persist in reminding me of my former misconduct."

"Fitzwilliam," said Elizabeth softly, "you do not frighten me, you know how little offended I am by that memory, do not be troubled by the recollection, it was meant in jest."

"And it was very funny indeed, Elizabeth, as a recollection only. The reality, in contrast, was the cause of great pain to both of us. It is best forgot. The distraction has led me from straight thinking." He paused to regain his composure, the color that had risen about his face receded and he went on, "You wish to know in what way I convinced my aunt that I was determined to make you my wife? Then know this; I am a determined character. A man used to my own way. I was decided upon you. My love and admiration for you were unconquerable. It is now quite inconceivable to me that I ever attempted to triumph over my feelings when to endeavor to suppress or deny them was entirely useless. Lady Catherine, even if she could not concede that my love was genuine, was forced to admit that my willfulness, at least, was to be respected. I believe on that point alone she resolved not to pursue me."

"It was a wise decision on her part but did you really appear so resolute to her? I know enough of your stubborn nature, but Lady

Catherine seems to be a woman little disposed to accept defeat."

"She began defeated, Elizabeth, she knew you would not oblige her in refusing me and I made it clear that I would not oblige her by refraining from pursuing you. There was of course the advantage of my excellent cousin's interest in you. Colonel Fitzwilliam had praised you very highly to our aunt, more perhaps than she could bear."

"Colonel Fitzwilliam?" asked Elizabeth, astonished.

"You blush, Elizabeth, yes, Colonel Fitzwilliam holds you in high esteem as you must be fully aware, I think his admiration for you can, in part at least, be held responsible for reawakening my own determination to marry you. The prize is never more highly valued than when the likelihood of losing it to another becomes apparent."

"I certainly will blush now, Fitzwilliam. I am astounded. I had thus far believed your decision to propose to me again to be attributed to Lady Catherine's revelation that I would not refuse you. But wait, for a man without fault, jealousy seems to me to be a very particular type of flaw."

"I consider it a most advantageous imperfection, I could not suffer the indignity of your having a preference for my cousin. The idea of his admiring you I fully comprehend. I do not resent it, but the very notion that you could be lost to another was never so emphatically brought to my attention than when I recalled the expression of his countenance at the sight or mention of you, Elizabeth," he said, grasping her hand in his. "If two of our family were to fall so easily in love with you then I was not safe, my position in your heart, if I had one at all, was by no means un-defended. The world is full of men, I could not stand the thought of another loving you, moreover I could not contemplate living in the world knowing you loved another."

Elizabeth's affections grew, her smile was irrepressible and her face was overspread with color. "I could never have contemplated loving another, you are exactly the sort of man I would have designed, your skill lay in having concealed it from me for so long."

"You really *did* despise me?"

"I was resigned to. You did little to persuade me to feel otherwise but I concede the severity of my dislike was, at times, a little extreme."

"The severity of your dislike was matched only by the degree of my own folly. For my part, I will confess to foolishness. I was on guard, embarrassed."

"And all this you would have continued to be had you not imagined your cousin to be falling in love with me?"

"You may condemn me for my envy, Elizabeth, it will not lessen my feelings."

"I should never wish to be the cause of decreasing your feelings for me, Fitzwilliam. In fact," she said quietly, "I am disposed to behave in a way that will further them." With a quickening step Elizabeth headed for a secluded patch of ground beneath a heavily laden oak. Darcy followed but was not inclined to run and called out to her, "Every word you speak furthers my feelings, Elizabeth."

"I cannot always speak in words," cried she, "where love is concerned it is not the only language." She settled on a seat. Darcy was soon before her. "Ah poetry," he said, "you know my feelings on that... and music... "

Elizabeth raised her finger to her husband's lips. "I must interrupt you, sir, for I believe no language speaks clearer than a kiss between lovers."

When, through some twist in their conversation as both had just experienced, Darcy and Elizabeth were forced to recall their previous misunderstanding of each other they recoiled from the memories and put both their past behaviors down to the fact that the violence of their feelings had made them both ill-tempered and judgmental. On happier notes, Lizzy's untidy arrival at Netherfield Park to attend Jane in her illness, although long in the past, was always a source of amusement. Elizabeth had never had any difficulty in finding amusement in the examination of her own personality and was always ready to laugh at herself. This was a quality not natural to Darcy but he was mastering it well enough.

When they had called their brief respite beneath the oak to a close they walked hand in hand to the lake where already on several occasions they had diverted each other about their most portentous if impromptu meeting at Pemberley when Lizzy's Aunt and Uncle Gardiner had accompanied her. Again, Elizabeth's laughter set the style of their discourse.

"What a meeting, both of us embarrassed, for our own reasons, I cannot imagine which of us more so, though I daresay your inappropriate state of attire caused you provocation. Ah, but all is fair for I believe your untidy condition at the time equitable to my own at Netherfield?"

Her husband smiled. "It is a just comparison."

"Then we are equals?" she asked.

He was too close now for her to maintain any composure and she felt herself to be very deeply impressed by his proximity. "In every way it is possible to be we are, as you put it, equals, but in other matters I cannot compete, yours Elizabeth is the fairer sex," he said.

They headed back to the house refreshed by the outdoors and their reflections. The intoxicating effects of love and fresh air combined to make them more amiable in character than ever and they conceded that they must delay no longer in requesting that Mrs. Bennet should come to Pemberley.

"Poor mama," said Elizabeth. "I fear two weeks will not be early enough notice of such an engagement. I am all too familiar with the lengthy style of her preparations for a simple invitation to tea. I pity poor Kitty for she will endure the impact of mama's frenzied arrangements."

Darcy smiled. "Indeed, it is not difficult to imagine the scenes at Longbourn. No one will be safe! But I wonder now, having recalled your mother's characteristics, if we would be better disposed to receive her in mixed company here rather than attempt to withstand her personality alone. I have it from Bingley that she has been at Netherfield several times more than his sanity can bear, and if his serenity can be shaken I daresay mine will be tattered in a third of the time." He watched Elizabeth carefully; she had caught his look of concern.

"I am not insulted by your views, for they are as my own. Mama is excitable to be sure, and I think if you can bear her presence in a small company then it may be preferable to dilute her effects so. Perhaps Jane and Bingley could be amongst the party also, I would dearly love to see them both and there is little for them to wonder about mama's nature that they have not already experienced," she said.

"The perfect scene, Elizabeth. If Bingley can withstand more of Mrs. Bennet then I must oblige also."

"I doubt that *Miss* Bingley will be so receptive as you, she has the greatest difficulty in these matters."

Darcy nodded. "Yes, we are giving her a good subject for criticism since she is no longer able to find fault with you, my dear."

Elizabeth was surprised and could not conceal it. "You are mistaken, I think Caroline Bingley is as able and as inclined to find fault with me as ever she was, her facade is an affectionate one but it does not fool me."

"I am aware that little does and that affords me satisfaction, but I am grieved to hear that you detect scorn on Miss Bingley's part. You are too tolerant! I cannot accept it, I will demand she take her leave." An expression reminiscent of Darcy's previous arrogance spread across his face.

Elizabeth sighed. "Allow me to appease you. Her dislike is of little matter to me and who knows, it may ease in time, it would be a great loss to Georgiana should Miss Bingley depart, for despite her curtness she is accomplished and refined socially, her influence therefore is not entirely ill."

After a long silence Darcy said, "Then let it be so, though to hear censure of you, my beloved, is to feel fire in my blood."

CHAPTER 4

It was a large, handsome, stone building, standing well on rising ground, and backed by a ridge of high woody hills; and in front, a stream of some natural importance was swelled into greater, but without any artificial appearance. Its banks were neither formal, nor falsely adorned.

———◦∞◦———

All was tranquillity until Mrs. Bennet received news from Pemberley. Before she had read the contents of the letter, she had already had a fit of the nerves. She was given the vapors twice over and took no breakfast but for a little tea.

On finally reading the letter she shrieked, "Listen to this, Kitty, we are all requested to spend a week at Pemberley. This is a formal invitation indeed, my dear, in the master's own fine hand. I do wonder at Lizzy that she could not write to her own parents with all the time her leisurely life affords her. Ah well, it is of little consequence. I daresay this is Mr. Darcy's notion for he has always shown a definite regard for me. What a gentleman, so well bred." Turning to her husband she said, "I have always said his manners are as elegant as his dress."

"You outstrip Brummel with your inclination to judge a man by the cut of his coat," said Mr. Bennet.

Mrs. Bennet ignored her husband's remark and said, "Mr. Bennet, you will write directly to confirm our acceptance."

With a feigned look of surprise Mr. Bennet said, "Oh I see no necessity for haste, your nerves will surely not be intact by the time of the visit, which is to take place... when?"

Mrs. Bennet aimed a look of exasperation at her husband. "We have but two weeks today to make the arrangements. The travel is not of our concern for Mr. Darcy writes that our dear Jane and

Bingley are to be amongst the guests. We have the opportunity of making up a party in one of their fine carriages."

"Then with so little to concern yourself with and a full fortnight to ponder the delights of this invitation I wonder that you insist on my replying, when you will have ample time to write yourself."

Mr. Bennet often lamented that Lizzy was not present to see his purposeful vexations of his wife, but still he satisfied his own voracity for humor with his wit.

Mrs. Bennet huffed. "Write myself? Have you taken leave of your senses, Mr. Bennet? No indeed, I wager you had no senses to begin with. I cannot write myself, as you suggest, it will not do! You must reply and follow the dignified method that Mr. Darcy employs. And I will not have you think my time shall be spent idle from now until our departure, for there is so much to do. I have not a stitch of clothing that is fit to be seen in elegant company. Poor Kitty is equally deprived, you know, so we have no time at all to waste. There are some fine new muslins in Meryton which will make up very nicely into suitable gowns. And do not forget, I have my sister to inform." To Kitty she said, "Your poor Aunt Phillips lives to hear all the particulars of my social sphere and I should feel guilty not to brighten her dull life by letting her have this news before I am gone to Pemberley." She sighed and went on, "Ah Pemberley, Netherfield is nothing to it I hear."

Mrs. Bennet's agitation soon ceased and she afforded her nerves little consideration but set about her plans in a chaotic manner. Kitty was relieved that her mother's humor had much improved on receiving the news from Pemberley and was excited herself to be returning there.

"I wish Lydia could be with us, she makes such a merry addition to a party with her spirits."

Mrs. Bennet agreed. "Alas, my poor Lydia will miss out on this occasion. Though they do invite Mary, who would not enjoy it a jot, but she is better able to travel from Rosings than Lydia is equipped to get there from Newcastle. I daresay the distance is the only reason she is excluded and Wickham also for he has links to Pemberley and is all that is charming. But we will not trouble ourselves over their absence, for I am now of a mind to visit Rosings Park to discuss the arrangements with Mary." She looked knowingly at Mr. Bennet. "I confess I shall relish this opportunity to let Lady Catherine de Bourgh know my news. I hear that she will not go to Pemberley and that they will not have her. If I can incite a small measure of envy in her I will not feel it unjust." She thought for a while. "There you see, the week ahead runs away with me, for there is yet another visit to add to things. Oh well, if my health should finally give out with all this effort I shall at least die happy."

"Indeed you shall, my dear," said Mr. Bennet wearily, "for I have seldom seen anyone so gladdened by self-congratulation as your goodself."

Mrs. Bennet was too enraptured with life at that moment to take any offense at Mr. Bennet's comment, which in turn partially deprived him of some of the satisfaction he gained from making it. The talk of Pemberley went on for the full day and the cries and shrieks from Mrs. Bennet were heard all around the house. By the evening she had entirely worn herself out which granted the household some longed for peace when she retired to bed with one of her headaches and a bottle of salts.

CHAPTER 5

"You mistake me, my dear. I have a high respect for your nerves.
They are my old friends. I have heard you mention them with
consideration these twenty years at least."

News of the Bennets' imminent arrival at Pemberley had reached
Lady Catherine before Mrs. Bennet arrived at Rosings Park with
the intention of revealing it. Lady Catherine was quite sure that she
would never find it easy to receive Mrs. Bennet but she was little
disposed to refuse her while Mary did such service to Anne.

Mrs. Bennet corrected her accent when in the company of
Lady Catherine, which gave spuriousness to her manner of speech,
her flattery sang of falsehood also. "Your ladyship is quite well I am
pleased to see, and your dear daughter is in good health I take it?"

Lady Catherine nodded, but there was no softness in her
address, she remained as brittle as ever. "Yes, Mrs. Bennet, I am
reasonably well, considering, and Anne's health shows no signs of
expected deterioration although I would not be surprised to see
such given her recent share of traumas." With this she glared at Mrs.
Bennet accusingly before continuing. "In light of family distress of
the kind we have endured it astounds me to learn that my nephew
is comfortable to be sociable and entertaining while others suffer."
She looked over to where her daughter was sitting with Mary close
by her side. "But it is of little consequence. Anne improves a little, as
I do, since our opinion of my nephew has altered with enlightenment. Were his morals as high as his manners he would show
compatibility with Anne, as it is, the reverse renders his union to
your daughter no great loss to us. In that way I justify my present
contentment, and my future satisfaction relies on the inevitable

36

woe that the pair will suffer on closer acquaintance with each other."

Mrs. Bennet's apprehension of Lady Catherine prevented her offering defense on Darcy's or Elizabeth's part and she was very nearly lost for words but she replied meekly, "I am sure, ma'am, that your present misery will soon dissipate on seeing your daughter so much improved, my Mary makes a good companion does she not?"

"Yes," said Lady Catherine, "which gives me reason to inform you that she shall remain here at Rosings. She is a sensible girl. It will not disappoint her to be denied Pemberley. Besides, Anne cannot spare her, her situation is too delicate."

"Perhaps ma'am, Mary may be permitted to voice her own wishes on the matter?"

"She is entirely at liberty to do so," said Lady Catherine looking at Mary expectantly.

The girl chose to address her employer before her own mother, "Your ladyship," she began in a somber tone, "it will be no deprivation for me to stay with Anne, for I see no virtue in the frivolities and entertainments at Pemberley." She paused before turning to her mother, then she said, "I am sure your enjoyment of the visit will be little sullied by my absence, please send my highest regards to my sisters and father and my apologies, they will understand I am compelled by duty and instinct to remain here."

Lady Catherine looked analytically at Mary then lifted her head back a little so as to look down her nose at Mrs. Bennet. There was a hint of a smile on her lips and it had been put there quite decidedly by Mary's confession that she felt more duty bound to her employer than she did to her family. That was as good a sign of loyalty as any.

Mrs. Bennet was not so surprised by Mary's resolution. In a small way she had gained some satisfaction from having achieved legitimate entrance to Rosings. In light of the subsequent claims she, Mrs. Bennet, would enjoy, Mary's movements were of little consequence.

Her nerves were in a heightened state as she delivered the news to Mr. Bennet. "Let me tell you of her ladyship," she said. "I have never met with such avarice I am sure, and my intent was to be all politeness, so as not to cause offense. Well, so be it! Mary, of course, is as drab as ever; in fact the three of them make a woeful picture. They are quite greyly appointed there in all their seriousness. It falls to the more pleasant of us to enjoy life to the full and I am glad of it, for Mary has spoiled many a gathering with her moods. Never mind, my dear, that is Mary for you, but Lady Catherine need not have shown her smugness so explicitly."

"Indeed not," replied Mr. Bennet. "But do bear in mind, my dear, that Lady Catherine has not your good example to follow and I daresay this misfortune leaves her manners somewhat lacking."

"Yes indeed," agreed Mrs. Bennet who was as ever unable to detect the sarcasm in her husband's comment.

No sooner had Mrs. Bennet distributed her news to her sister, Mrs. Phillips, and the Lucases, and further let it slip at the haberdashers that it began to multiply and be universal knowledge of an exaggerated nature.

The Collinses had their share of the announcements at Lucas Lodge. Charlotte Collins rejoiced at the news, but her husband still privately harbored feelings of humiliation regarding Lizzy's rejection of him and this discomfort was further worsened by the loss of Lady Catherine's patronage and in turn the loss of his connection to the entire family. The only compensation in his disillusioned life was that he had Longbourn to look forward to. Though he realized that his anticipation of taking up residency of the estate made him desirous of Mr. Bennet's death, he felt only a fraction of the guilt he perhaps should have. The fact that Mr. Bennet, newly relieved financially and in fine spirits generally, showed no signs of passing away perturbed Mr. Collins, but he did not mention it to Charlotte who maintained a genuine affection for all in the Bennet family.

CHAPTER 6

Mrs. Gardiner abused her stupidity. "If it were merely a fine house richly furnished," said she, "I should not care about it myself, but the grounds are delightful. They have some of the finest woods in the country."

On arrival at Pemberley Mrs. Bennet was awestruck, for it was all and more than she had dreamed of for her daughter. At once she was determined to do all she could to hone Elizabeth to Darcy's liking. Disturbed by Lady Catherine's words she feared that the destruction of the marriage could indeed become a reality if her Lizzy's oft-untamed manners remained unchecked. It was her maternal duty to succeed in advising her daughter of the perils of being overly natural.

Elizabeth was pretty enough, if not bestowed with quite the extraordinary beauty of her sister Jane, and, concluded Mrs. Bennet, the girl must have merits besides being acceptable to look at. After all, had she not managed to secure herself a situation in marriage to one of the most notable men in England? But Lizzy's predilection to muddy her shoes, jump stiles and run about, not to mention her outspokenness, could well cause offense in refined circles. Mildly distracted from her concerns by the idea that her trunks might be sent to the wrong room, Mrs. Bennet delighted in behaving very high in requesting her clothes be unpacked without delay. "For I have with me," she announced with affectation, "the finest silks and lace… and truly, I cannot bear the worry of their creasing." She cast a glance at one of Darcy's men.

Elizabeth, holding up her skirts, ran from the house to greet her family, heartily embracing her father, whose fondness for her was unyielding, then Jane, Bingley, and Kitty were received with equal enthusiasm. Finally, she caught her mother's grave expression.

"Elizabeth," whispered Mrs. Bennet sharply, before kissing her daughter's cheek, "it might be as well to adopt a more elegant way of behaving. Whoever would think that the mistress of Pemberley would make such an ungainly spectacle of herself? You forget yourself, my girl, dashing around with your petticoats rucked up for all to see."

Her daughter countered, "And who am I to impress, mama? To adopt any air of falsity in the company of my own family would be ridiculous and to do so in the presence of my staff would merely insult them." She glanced at Bingley and said, "I am sure my friend would demand no such pretension on my part."

Mr. Bingley engaged Elizabeth with a warm smile and bowed to her. "Indeed I would not, Mrs. Darcy. May I say that I have always found your manners most agreeable, and never more so than today, I might mention too that you are looking very well indeed."

"I thank you, sir," said Elizabeth with a brief curtsy. To her mother, whose eye was fixed with intent upon her, she said with good humor, "Now, mama, that your scolding is over, may I welcome you to my new home?"

Mrs. Bennet was all eagerness. "Of course, my dear girl," said she. And Elizabeth, who took a sudden delight in raising her hand in the direction of the house, said simply, "Madam, on behalf of my husband and myself I welcome you to Pemberley."

Mrs. Bennet's eyes were drawn to the perfect uniform architecture and the established grounds of the house once more, but it was not Pemberley's unique beauty that seduced her, moreover her view was impaired by the thought of the riches the estate represented.

The housekeeper, who informed Elizabeth that the master was expected downstairs directly, met the party in the hallway.

"Thank you, Mrs. Reynolds," said Elizabeth warmly, and touching the woman's arm briefly in a true gesture of affection she added, "please tell my husband I will be in the drawing room with my family, if you could be so kind as to arrange tea for us."

"At once, madam, shall I send for a servant to show everyone in?"

"No, no," said Elizabeth in a hushed tone. "Spare the trouble, I shall manage to lead my family through to the drawing room alone, for it is not such an unruly group as it may appear!" The two women shared the joke quietly and presently the party was quietly and happily settled in the comfort of the drawing room.

When all aspects of the furnishings and fireplaces had been extensively admired Mrs. Bennet seized upon the moment as a further opportunity to check her daughter's manners. "I noticed that you feel very easy with the servants, Lizzy," said she with a frown. "It did not escape my attention that you indulged in some quiet amusement with the housekeeper! Is that wise, do you think? My advice to you, my dear, would be to exercise a little reservation when dealing with those of lower rank. Your overfriendliness may do you damage by association. I know we have always been very good to our own dear Hill but that is different. I daresay you have three hundred times the number of servants here. It would not do to befriend every single one. Every grate-blacking maid, every French chef."

Elizabeth laughed. "Mama, you grossly exaggerate both the number of servants and my propensity to befriend them, besides which there is a very great difference between friendship and what I judge to be fair and decent treatment of those in my employ."

Mrs. Bennet began to respond but was prevented from doing so by Darcy's entering the room. He went directly to Elizabeth's side; there was a bow, as was his usual courteous manner, to the ladies on introduction and he shook both Mr. Bennet and Mr. Bingley heartily by the hand and when those formalities had been attended to he leaned and kissed his wife tenderly on the cheek. She colored slightly, as she always did at his nearness, which seemed at once to please him and give him the easy style of attitude which sets a man in love very much apart from all other more rational humans.

Darcy informed the party of his sister's imminent arrival, all this was done with a smile, a relaxed posture and, as far as Mrs. Bennet was concerned, a hitherto unknown inclination to behave like the friendliest man alive. Georgiana Darcy, according to her brother's information, was expected to return by the early afternoon with Miss Bingley who had accompanied her to take tea in Lambton with friends. He went on to mention that Mr. and Mrs. Gardiner's absence could be accounted for by pressing affairs of business in London. They were staying at their house in Cheapside, although it was known to all present that this was considered by them to be a hardship indeed.

Mrs. Bennet was exuberant in her expression. "What a disappointment that I shall not see my dear brother and his wife today, nor indeed my sweet little nephews and nieces. But I am delighted by the prospect of your dear sister's arrival. Will she play for us?" she asked. Then, having been put quite at ease by her son-in-law's apparent unaffected manner, Mrs. Bennet continued rather rapidly before the latter was afforded the opportunity to give an answer. She went on, in high spirits. "I shall insist upon her playing at least a jig for us, for I hear she has perfected the art of entertainment."

.Lizzy glanced at Darcy; her mother was too hasty in her insistence, too presumptuous to declare her intentions to press a performance on Georgiana. The ease with which Darcy had received them all was quickly gone. Where his sister was concerned he was governed by feelings so strong, so beyond his own control, as to render him quite the distant creature that much of his reputation had been built on.

"She will be delighted I am sure," said he with curtness, "but pray," he went on firmly, "I will not have her pressed to perform. I must confess to her being timid, it is best left for her to decide how inclined she is to endure inspection."

Mrs. Bennet became too familiar with Mr. Darcy. "Come now," she trilled, "every young lady likes the chance of showing off a little."

There it was! His expression of old. Firm, aloof, cool. His voice was measured, there was an economy about his intonation. "Self-exhibition is not just the preserve of young ladies, Mrs. Bennet. Sadly, I have witnessed it, in certain circles, in women of senior years."

If Mrs. Bennet had had any intention of reacting, she was

prevented from doing so by Mr. Darcy's ignoring her and seeing fit to do nothing more than turn his attention elsewhere. He was soon happily engaged in conversation with Mr. Bennet, whose admiration for his new son-in-law grew rapidly. Along with his own great love for his daughter there was an affinity for Darcy that the latter appreciated and the former welcomed.

The concluding part of the Bennets' first day at Pemberley passed without consequence, ending with dinner which was taken, as always, at a fashionably late hour. This was followed by quiet adjournment in the music room. Georgiana obliged the party by playing the pianoforte and Caroline Bingley exercised admirable control over her desire to be malicious towards the Bennets, so peace was maintained, but it was to be a fleeting tranquillity.

CHAPTER 7

*"Oh! Yes, the handsomest young lady that ever was seen,
and so accomplished! She plays and sings all day long."*

———

The following evening the party repaired to the drawing room after dinner. Georgiana played for the entertainment of the gathering, her decision to entertain in this manner had been quite her own. Mrs. Bennet, on becoming further acquainted with Miss Darcy, took heed of Mr. Darcy's declaration that his sister should not be put upon and she was therefore uncharacteristically quiet and far less peremptory than would usually have been her way. When she did elect to converse with Miss Darcy it was to congratulate the young woman, both on her ability and her choice of music.

"Ah, you play very well, Miss Darcy, and Mozart is always a wise choice for a young lady, although I daresay you have the desire for a jig from time to time." While Miss Darcy's musical preferences did not include jigs she was not disposed to declare the fact and commanded as always by her timidity she said nothing and began to play again.

"Andante Favori!" said Darcy with indulgence, reminiscences of a most passionate nature regarding the development of his infatuation with Elizabeth quite taking him over. He succumbed to the clarity of his memories, the expression of his countenance, as he directed his gaze to his wife, was as gentle, and probing as it had been on one of the first occasions of their ever having been in that very room together. Elizabeth could not fail to observe the sensitive nature of his examination and, much to his pleasure, she graced him with a look that had an equally rousing effect on his

44

composure as his had on hers. At once his countenance was flushed with a desirous rosiness but he noted the scrutiny of Caroline Bingley and so cleared his throat and his mind simultaneously. He then began a light discourse on the pleasures of the shooting season with Mr. Bennet who always reveled in masculine conversation when given the chance of it; the opportunity to savor such manly distractions quite simply never arose at Longbourn.

"Ah," sighed Mrs. Bennet, seeking and securing the attention of Caroline Bingley, "I am quite enraptured by Miss Darcy's playing but I confess it inspires a small measure of sadness in me for it puts me in mind of my daughter Mary, with whom you are acquainted. Now she is proficient in music, and on this occasion I lament her not having the fortune to cheer the party with her performance, for she is always very well received."

Miss Bingley responded in her cultured tones. "Such deprivation must indeed be trying for you, Mrs. Bennet, as I am sure it is for all of us."

Mrs. Bennet replied, "Yes indeed, Miss Bingley, you are too kind. Alas, I confess poor Mary's absence from Pemberley must be put down to my own generosity. I was recently at Rosings Park you know, with the express intention of insisting that Mary remain there to attend poor Anne de Bourgh."

Enchantment with Bingley limited Jane's contributions to the conversation for most of the evening but she spoke now with quiet determination. "Mama, it is in your favor that your kindness needs no more emphasis." Jane's assurance was not enough to quench Mrs. Bennet's thirst for continued elaboration; again she addressed Miss Bingley, and when Georgiana was not preoccupied with her music Mrs. Bennet occasionally directed a look at the girl as a way of including her. "Anne de Bourgh is, as you know, a sickly thing," declared Mrs. Bennet, "so feeble and without vigor, I could not bear to wrench Mary from her, for she is a loyal companion to the poor wretch and highly regarded at Rosings Park."

Caroline Bingley was no stranger to conceit as it was a trait she displayed herself and recognition of it in others required little effort. "Your good intention cannot be questioned, madam," she said to Mrs. Bennet, "but your daughter's acceptance of relinquishing the delights of this assembly at your request cannot have represented any personal sacrifice surely?"

Mrs. Bennet knew not how to answer. To own that Mary would find no enjoyment in the present company would be to indicate no deprivation on her part. To profess as much would therefore diminish her own claims of authority. Lost for a suitable retort Mrs. Bennet rapidly altered the point of conversation by introducing another of her daughters as subject matter, she again turned to Miss Bingley as a suitable recipient for her oration.

"You have met my youngest daughter Lydia have you not? Now there is a wholesome girl! She would add spirit to our little assembly here, but of course you are already familiar with her husband George Wickham and all of Derbyshire must surely know him as well as they know Mr. Darcy. Sadly his regimental duties detain them both in Newcastle."

The mention of his own and his adversary's name brought Darcy to his feet. Deflection of any unfortunate atmosphere was now his purpose; he attempted distraction and addressed his wife. Her full sympathy he could rely on.

"Elizabeth," he said with determination, "I see my sister tires of playing, will you relieve her?"

"But of course."

The two exchanged looks. His was one of caution, hers was one of alarm.

When the members of the party had all retired to their beds Elizabeth and Darcy rejoiced in their privacy but felt the advantage of intimacy to be quickly lost. Immersed in concern over Mrs. Bennet's unbridled reference to Mr. Wickham the two reluctantly discussed the matter and the man. Elizabeth was eager to ease Darcy's agitation when she spoke of her mother to him.

"Mama's very open reference to Wickham is a sure sign that she is mostly ignorant. She does not know the full extent of his sinister nature or I am sure she would not venture to mention him at all. That at least should be of compensation to you."

"Her ignorance does not make the mention of him any less painful for myself or, more importantly, my sister, though I notice Miss Bingley's eyes brighten on hearing his name," said Darcy.

Elizabeth could only wonder at the implication. "Do you allude to some desirous feeling toward George Wickham on Miss Bingley's part?" she said.

"No, not at all, though the pair would be deserved of each other in some respects. But that is a harsh judgment and one made under duress. Forgive me and forget I said it. My inference was directed more at Miss Bingley's propensity to revel in any subject that casts your family in a poor light. Although she has not all the details of Wickham's past, she detects our unease and I have no doubt that she feasts on it."

"You are sure she is so uninformed?" Elizabeth asked.

"She has knowledge of my original misgivings."

Elizabeth colored slightly. "Yes of course, she delighted in informing me when we were at Netherfield that Wickham had treated you in 'an infamous manner.' She claimed not to know the particulars, but knew very well that you were not in the least to blame, that you could not bear to hear George Wickham mentioned, and that although Bingley had seen fit to invite him to Netherfield, he was gladdened to find that he had taken himself out of the way. Oh!" cried Elizabeth, "how enraged I am when I remember her sneering, *'I pity you, Miss Eliza, for the discovery of your favorite's guilt, but really, considering his descent, one could not expect much better.'*"

"Her observation was accurate, but I believe her delight stemmed from your association with Wickham at the time."

"I am ashamed of it now, that I was so easily fooled by his pleasing exterior and manners."

The consolation of her husband's hand on her shoulder appeased Elizabeth.

Satisfied, Darcy continued. "You took an apparent gentleman at face value, that he proved himself to be otherwise reflects poorly on him, not you."

Elizabeth smiled but was quickly angry with herself again. "Yes, but my liking of him then is unfaithful to my love for you now, I cannot bear to consider it, the admission of my stupidity, my prejudice, and my misconception leaves me mortified."

"I will not have you so, your opinions were formed only by what you saw, hence your partiality to Wickham was as understandable as your abhorrence of me, I cannot not berate you for either, my love."

Elizabeth managed a smile. "Indeed, in my blindness I showed no fondness for you, but I believe I felt more than I revealed, your distance had some appeal I recall."

"I cannot imagine that I challenged you any more than you did me, I thought I should never win your approval and I knew I could never conquer the power of my love for you, despite my contemptible efforts to do so."

Elizabeth touched her husband's cheek. "I fear we are so taken over with emotion that we neglect the question of Wickham. I cannot see that it would in any way be prudent to inform mama of the full extent of his wrongdoing, but the necessity to silence her on the subject is very great. It would give Georgiana peace of mind for she cannot bear to hear that he is highly esteemed."

"I know you fear keeping countenance on his behalf but there is little else to be done. It is not worth your mother's distress to reveal his distant past now that she is so suitably recovered from his more recent improprieties with your sister."

Elizabeth frowned. "A recovery that her fickleness and ignorance affords her. My father knows of your involvement of course, but my mother has not the slightest notion that it was your intervention that forced Lydia's respectability. She is still of the impression that my Uncle Gardiner settled matters and had them marry, though she shows him scant gratitude."

"She would show me less, I am convinced of it. But I sought only your gratification in intervening. And there at least I have satisfaction. Our dilemma now is not so great as you imagine, we must remain silent and hope that your mother's predilection for Wickham as subject matter will fade."

"Indeed, she tires quickly of old news when there is new gossip to be had, time will pass and she will soon be occupied by fresh themes."

Darcy laughed. "Only a miraculous fresh theme could tear your mother from her favored narratives."

Elizabeth was quiet for a while before saying, "Would news of the conception of her first grandchild prove miracle enough to absorb her, do you think?"

Darcy now stared into his wife's eyes. "My loveliest girl, how long have you had this exquisite secret?" he asked quietly.

"I am newly aware of it myself," said Elizabeth, "but I am sure enough to date it from our first..." she paused and reddened before continuing, "...from our first tender moments."

That night when Fitzwilliam Darcy carried his wife to her bed-chamber he was lost for words but, such was the nature of their affection, they had no need of them as a means of expression.

CHAPTER 8

*"Excuse me—for I must speak plainly. If you, my dear father,
will not take the trouble of checking her exuberant spirits,
and of teaching her that her present pursuits are not to be the business
of her life, she will soon be beyond the reach of amendment."*

Love, and those who have the good fortune to be in it, will always be veiled in mystery. There is an indefinable air about two people engaged in the shared pursuit of mutual adoration. Thus were Elizabeth and Darcy viewed and the prospect of their having a secret that was to be kept between them was certain to increase the mystique. Darcy and Elizabeth's intention to conceal their happy news was based on the rather groundless belief that fate may be adversely tempted by an untimely announcement. Although Elizabeth was sure of her condition, she was determined to have confirmation from a physician once signs of her confinement were definite enough to allow a firm diagnosis. Somehow, concealment lent a precious quality to their shared secret, and though she was often bold of character, she felt a little unnerved at the prospect of revealing the news publicly. Her husband's concerns verged more to the practical; at once his wife was a fragile creature, a quite different being.

Darcy implored her. "My limited understanding of such matters leads me to note how a strong and healthy disposition can become vulnerable. You are healthy in body, Elizabeth, and quite frighteningly boisterous of mind but now is a time for great care."

Elizabeth laughed. "We are not yet married six months and I believe, my dearest husband, that I know you better than you know yourself. In knowing you thus I am able, by some magical quality bestowed on me by matrimony, to exactly determine your words before you have even had the first thought of them yourself."

Darcy frowned; it was so like Elizabeth to jest, so much the part of her nature that defined her and made him love her. "You might wish to explain Elizabeth, what kind of madness it is you are speaking of?"

Elizabeth reached for his hand and confided, "I imagined you would want to stop my walks when you learned my news. Pray, please do not worry unduly, I shall walk slower and not run at all, does that satisfy you?"

He nodded and looked at his wife affectionately. "I ask only that you make your own rules on this matter, it will not do to force me to reprimand you."

"No running whatsoever, you have my word, Fitzwilliam," she insisted.

The delightful, undisclosed knowledge of a future heir served to increase Darcy's attentiveness to Elizabeth and he was so often distracted by her and thoughts of their child as to induce concern in those in his employ who knew him well. It must be acknowledged that fatherhood, which will never demand the enormous veneration that motherhood has grasped as all her own, has an effect on men which often goes unnoticed. But there is a kind of value to it that merits observation. The man may not have the advantage of great claims of fortitude, bravery, or tolerance to all the pains and discomforts that accompany childbearing, but that is no fault of his own. The encumbrance of responsibility, provision, and education cannot be lightly borne. In preparation for fatherhood, a man might spend an excessive amount of time pondering the magnitude of the situation. Mr. Darcy, in this respect at least, was not wildly different from other men and his contemplations led him, eventually, to think of his late father and in turn his dear mother. Then with regretful inevitability his mother's sister Lady Catherine was brought to mind.

While the Bennets and the Gardiners were simultaneously welcomed at Pemberley, Darcy's aunt's misgivings and their mutual absence from each others' lives had the effect of troubling his mind now that it was so taken up with family themes. He reflected that Lady Catherine's heart could hardly be described as warm but he kept some measure of dutiful affection for her in his own for his memories of his mother, Lady Anne, were exceptionally fond. Raising the subject of his aunt with Elizabeth, he found her to be understanding, if naturally cautious. Love-induced instinct dictated that she always wished to act in a way that pleased him but on the subject of Lady Catherine, Elizabeth reserved the right be wary.

"If your wish is for reconciliation, then I support you, although I feel your task will be a difficult one. Lady Catherine gave no response to the letter you sent soon after our marriage and a violent reaction to the one you sent announcing it. I cannot imagine that anything other than my removal could ever please her and as my intention is one of permanence where you are concerned I fear she must await my death before feeling truly happy," said she with a smile.

"Do not speak of such tragedy in jest, I cannot bear it! But I do wish to make amends with my aunt for the sake of my mother's memory at least."

Elizabeth took the opportunity to learn more of Lady Anne Darcy, a woman who, after all, was responsible for many of the aspects of Pemberley that Elizabeth so adored. "Would Lady Anne have wished for a reunion, was that her character?"

"I believe she would have wished it, she had a softer nature than her sister, she was more forgiving."

Elizabeth was direct. "Would she have forgiven the supposed sin that is your union with me? Lady Catherine did not hesitate to inform me that your mother hoped that you would be united with your cousin Anne as much as she did," said Elizabeth with frustration. "I fear we are once again compelled to discuss the favorite wish of them both. With that in mind could your mother have forgiven you and in turn accepted me?"

"A truly loving mother would forgive anything if the reward were to see her son happy."

Elizabeth was again touched by a certain softness in his gaze. "And I consider it a loving wife's obligation to be equally supportive, shall you write to your aunt?" she asked.

"I shall," was all the answer he gave.

"You would be best advised to withhold any greetings from me until her ladyship is better disposed to receive them."

Composition of a letter to his aunt was by no means a simple undertaking for Darcy. He wrote with consideration, with careful attention both to what should be said and to what should not. A good deal of time was spent mending his pen which Elizabeth noted with interest seemed not to have required restoration at all.

When the letter was written and sent, both Darcy and Elizabeth were intrigued to know, if the recipient should reply, whether the nature of her response would be more congenial than her last correspondence.

Elizabeth, who had so relished the thought of Jane's visit, determined that she must spend as much time with her elder sister while she had the advantage of having her stay at Pemberley, though both passed so much of their time enthralled by their handsome husbands that they were barely aware of anything else.

One morning the two young women sat together in the drawing room. There was a peaceful ambience to the room; Darcy had arranged that Mr. Bennet and Mr. Gardiner, the latter having returned early from London, should take the chance of fishing while the weather was to their advantage. Their wives took tea in the breakfast room and Caroline Bingley took charge of Kitty and Georgiana in the music room where her propensity to hold court and give instruction was used to best advantage. Darcy and Bingley, never better friends than now, walked the grounds and indulged in their newly favored sport of flattering each other on their good fortunes in love. The two sisters' activities mirrored their husbands' while their conversation was interspersed with both's inherent, though occasional, desire to talk of Longbourn.

"Oh Jane, it seems a whole lifetime has passed since then," said Elizabeth on the subject of their former home.

"Yet it is like yesterday that we two were bemoaning the probability of ending as old maids."

"The memories have great lucidity, but *I* was always more likely to end the spinster than you. You are still the prettiest of us all. Mama has always declared it, as I have done. I remember estimating that you were five times as pretty as the rest of us, but looking at you now, I think I was a bitter spirit to calculate your beauty with such economy." Elizabeth took in the bloom of her sister's complexion, the brightness of her eyes, and her hair's luster. Oh, she had always known her sister to be fair but observed, with delight, that where matrimony often made other women plain it had enhanced Jane and she sat now before Elizabeth a polished, exquisite jewel-like reflection of her former self. "Oh Jane, mama was always right you see, you could not be so beautiful for nothing."

"Do you suppose she will think me so fair when she learns we intend to quit Netherfield?"

"You have not told her?"

"No, I think we need not trouble her until our plans are more definite. Charles corresponds regularly with his attorney about the purchase of an estate in Yorkshire. I understand there are some delays, but it is worth the waiting for it will bring us nearer to you by a good measure." The thought of relative proximity, for both the sisters, was a comfort.

"And removing yourself so far away from mama, is that your intention?"

"No Lizzy," said Jane with a smile, "it is but a consequence."

"I beg your pardon Jane, it is a happy consequence. There," said Elizabeth, "I have said it for you! You always had a disinclination to speak ill of anyone or anything, I for one am not so mortified to be living at such a distance from Longbourn. Mama will miss you I daresay, but any grievances she may have will soon be forgot. She can be quick to rise but she is diverted with equal rapidity. No Jane, she will have no grounds to issue complaint. She has been very generously received at Netherfield by you, and she will savor every moment of telling all her friends of your grand new home when she has news of it."

"Oh yes, it does not bear thinking about, my consolation now is that you will be the object of her discourse and that at least will afford me a rest," said Jane.

Talk of their mother and Longbourn brought the young women to think of Lucas Lodge.

"Poor Sir William tires of Mr. Collins's company I believe, but he welcomes having Charlotte back home, Maria does too, for she is maturing rapidly and has little in common now with her younger brothers and sisters, sweet children though they are." Jane reported this to her sister who readily heard the news of old acquaintances, being so far removed from them herself.

"So, no living has come Mr. Collins's way?"

"It would appear not, I believe there was talk of a vacant parsonage at Brook Green in Milstead but it is known that Lady Catherine is a forceful influence in Kent and Charlotte is convinced she took offense at the idea of them residing less than ten miles away, so nothing ever came of the offer."

"I can well believe it, Lady Catherine does indeed have influential authority, I've seen her wield it over mere mortals many a time, but it had not occurred to me that she had the potency to prejudice God."

Jane smiled. "No but his servants, at least some of those in Kent, seem vulnerable to her power, Charlotte is inclined not to underestimate Lady Catherine's control."

"Dear Charlotte," said Lizzy. "I would very much like to see her, but I think that Mr. Collins will not wish to confront me, I am convinced that he blames me entirely for the loss of his patroness."

The girls laughed. "It would be no penalty to be deprived of Mr. Collins's company," Lizzy continued mischievously, "or his handsome features."

Jane stifled her laughter and said, "Poor Mr. Collins, he is ill-favored to be sure, but Charlotte seems well pleased with her marriage, and all goes smoothly I gather."

"I have no current news, I last saw them together at Hunsford, Charlotte seemed well enough, theirs is not a passionate union, but Charlotte errs more to the practical so she does not miss out."

"No, how could she miss a man's tenderness if she has never known it or desired it?"

"She could not," said Elizabeth, "but for my part I know I could scarce stay alive now without it." She kissed her sister on the forehead and they continued their conversation on the happy subject of the fortunate circumstances that had led both to fall in love in so short a space of each other, and to such men, those so worthy of their affections and so receptive to them. Elizabeth and Jane could not have dreamed of more. Neither, even in stretching their imaginative capabilities, could have foreseen the romanticism that defined what was now theirs. Like the girls they had once been, but were fast growing away from, they sat for a while and shared secrets of kisses, of little particulars of their husbands' mannerisms and publicly unknown ways. Jane, with the assurance of confidence only a close sister could promise, was explicit in her depictions, diverting Elizabeth with the amusing, but little known fact that Charles Bingley always reacted to his wife's first application of scent, with a sniff, then a sneeze and a curse.

"Oh his poor dear face, Lizzy. It is never my intention to laugh at him, but I find him, with his nose red and eyes streaming, a most humorous sight and for some reason I am always reminded of our first meeting. When first acquainted with Charles I would never have imagined this human aspect."

"I understand you completely, Jane, our dreams of marriage are never colored by the things that make the reality of matrimony so much an adventure."

"You do not think it odd then that my endearment is increased by so mundane a thing as Charles's sneezing."

"No, not at all," said Elizabeth, "for all Fitzwilliam's looks and attributes I think I savor most, the way he frowns before laughing, and he always does it, Jane. Oh, I laugh all the more then, it is so like him to attempt to resist the pleasure of mirth and so rewarding when he succumbs to it, I do not think I ever thought him capable of it before. Oh and one thing I favor more than the last," said Elizabeth, enraptured, "he has perfected a look of disapproval which, for some inexplicable reason all my own, I find entirely seductive."

"Then we are enticed in such different ways, Lizzy. Can you imagine Charles adopting a look of disapproval?"

"Oh no, it could not be achieved, or if it were it would never be taken seriously. He is too open of countenance, so absolutely in character as he appears, he has not my husband's complications, but Jane, he is your perfect match, for you have none of mine."

The breakfast room, Mrs. Bennet observed, was quite the equal of the drawing room in comfort if not quite its match in grandeur. She was intent, now that Mrs. Gardiner was returned, on talking as if she had been at Pemberley all of her life. Mrs. Gardiner, if she had had any idea of joining in the conversation found that Mrs. Bennet was not about to allow it, she was ordered to keep quiet on account of having endured a journey and so late an arrival the previous day.

"For you look fatigued, my dear, but I daresay parts of town do that to you. I do not care for the fuss and bother of it myself, though my presence there is often requested. But I see no occasion to be anywhere but the country, the air is so curative on my nerves, and the company sophisticated enough for the highest taste. Besides, travel weakens me as you know." Mrs. Bennet liked to imply that she was familiar with the fashionable parts of town but the reality was that she had rarely been out of Hertfordshire and her interest in town extended little beyond knowing where the best warehouses were.

The English countryside in spring is made entirely of small patches of promise stitched together by nature's hand. The definitions of the seasons, which may lose something of their clarity in a town, are most sharply emphasized in sympathetically landscaped surroundings. Pemberley, which boasted some of the finest grounds in the land, was such an environment and that morning, with the swallows bearing low over the lake, the spring sunshine and the abundance of fresh leaves on the trees, it made a pleasing vista. Mr. Bennet and Mr. Gardiner congratulated themselves on the happy chance of their being at Pemberley together unencumbered by social obligation and they engaged in easy conversation by the water's edge. The latter's sons and daughters occupied themselves with paper boats and running games.

"We stand little chance of a catch today, Mr. Bennet," declared Mr. Gardiner, gesturing toward his boisterous children. "Unless we can both be satisfied with ensnaring a paper ship! Hush children! You will have Mr. Darcy's fish scared out of their wits." To his companion he observed, "They can have their fun and games outdoors this morning and when they are all four exhilarated by the air and the excitement I shall return them to their mother's care by which time they will be as skittish as horses on a windy day!"

"Quite so," said Mr. Bennet. "They have a mother and an aunt to see to them, between two grown women the office of taking charge of four children cannot be so impossible, it amounts to exactly two dreadful little creatures each!"

Mr. Gardiner was ready with a smile and in between moments when he was compelled to call out, "No, no, Alice, let your brother have a turn," or, "Come along, Henry, you cannot spend your life on all fours, your mother will faint when she sees your knees," he immersed himself with enthusiasm and contentment in Mr. Bennet's company. The subject of Mrs. Bennet inspired similar sentiments in both, Mr. Bennet sighed and alluded to his wife.

"Our visit here heralds the death of any alternative talking points you know, Mr. Gardiner, for we shall hear of nothing but Pemberley for the rest of our lives."

Mr. Gardiner, who knew well enough his sister's nature, nodded in agreement and observed, "She is bound to be ebullient, but I am sure you are better able to tolerate her nerves when they are the result of high spirits rather than low."

Mr. Bennet smiled. "My wife's seizures, whether glad or morose are amusing to me in equal measure and usually short-lived enough to be forgot quite easily. Their effect and regularity dictate much of what goes on at Longbourn."

"Your tolerance is admirable, sir," said Mr. Gardiner.

"Well, I flatter myself that though I have no control what-soever—'Oh careful, Francis, don't lean over the water like that, dear. Oh heavens, where was I?'—Ah yes, though I have no control whatsoever over my wife's fluctuations, I have made an art of entertaining myself with them and that has been my solace these twenty years or more."

Thus their discourse continued; they spoke only of light matters for neither had a propensity for gravity and the distraction of four high-spirited youngsters steered them very clearly away from serious subjects. Both, being affable in nature, found the bond between them to be further secured. At last Mr. Gardiner, once more disappointed to have reeled in an empty hook, turned to Mr. Bennet. "With the perch taking the bait and the children the attention we are unlikely to see a good specimen of trout today, I shall have a word with Darcy, he can do little about the rowdiness of the children but he might have the perch population reduced!"

Adopting an elegant stance, as was her usual air, Caroline Bingley stayed by the pianoforte where Georgiana was engaged in practice. Nearby sat Kitty who, without Lydia beside her, appeared less con-fident and more demure than was customary. Miss Bingley addressed the girl coolly. "Your accomplishments, Catherine Bennet, do they include music?" She did not see fit to await a reply but went on to reflect, "Your sister Eliza plays and sings tolerably well, and of course Mary derives her own pleasure from the activity, are we to assume that everyone in your whole dear family is so masterful?"

"Not everyone is comfortable with performing, Caroline," said Georgiana, whose timidity was not so extreme as to prevent her attempting to protect Kitty.

"I concede," said Caroline, "but in my honest opinion, the Bennets seem to be people who are quite at ease with exhibiting, whether it be their abilities or their shortcomings they display. I daresay their rather natural airs make it difficult for them to know the difference between the two."

"I like to dance," said Kitty, quietly relieved that Georgiana struck up once more on her instrument so the conversation and the uneasy atmosphere it created was, thankfully, halted.

Darcy and Bingley, their tour of the grounds now complete, were returning to the house but were still some yards from it when they heard a horseman arrive whose expediency indicated some urgency. Both gentleman added speed to their pace.

"To the house!" cried Darcy.

On return their hats and canes were given to a manservant awaiting them in the hall, by which time they were under no misapprehensions that news of a disastrous nature had arrived by express. Had there been any reason to doubt the gravity of the situation Mrs. Bennet's shrill tones provided ample confirmation of a crisis. "Oh, where is Mr. Bennet? I must see my husband!" she cried, fleeing the breakfast room in great haste and making a hurried arrival into the hall. Her handkerchief was taken up as a fan and the efforts made to cool her agitation seemed only to exhaust her further. She came face to face with Mr. Darcy and Mr. Bingley. Darcy sent his man to fetch the housekeeper, he spoke with urgency. "Fetch Mrs. Reynolds, have her bring a tonic. Mrs. Bennet is unwell."

Mrs. Bennet's nervous state was, as ever, heightened by attention and she reeled and swayed dramatically before settling herself on the lower treads of the great staircase. She looked desperately at Mr. Bingley.

"Oh sir, it is alarming news. Lydia is gone from Newcastle to Longbourn in my absence. I have had the account not moments ago in an express from Mr. Collins." Saying no more she indulged in a fit of noisy crying which went on long enough for all relevant parties to be present before she continued to relay all she knew. Her audience was obliged to stay in the hall. Despite Mr. Darcy's suggestion that she would better maintain her dignity and appease her distress by taking a chair in the drawing room, she pleaded that moving her from her present position may prove fatal. Her nerves, she insisted, had seized her bones and made them so rigid that she feared at the very best she would be confined to her bed for an eternity.

Elizabeth attended her mother, observing that Darcy kept a noticeable distance from the furor. Jane was at her side; Mrs. Bennet mainly addressed her elder daughters, only occasionally glancing at Kitty.

"We are forced to end this happy gathering, my dears," she said tearfully, "for Mr. Collins writes that your poor dear sister is in so dreadful a state that he can make no sense of her ramblings at all. This is sorrow indeed, my strength deserts me. Oh! My dizzy spells shall return now you know, girls, it is certain."

Elizabeth, who was all too aware of the certainty, spoke with caution, "Mama, try to calm yourself, I am sure Wick..." she broke off, avoidance of his name was imperative, once checked she continued in a lowered voice, "I am sure that Lydia's husband can be prevailed upon to explain her illness as she is not disposed to."

Mrs. Bennet glared at Lizzy. "If that were the case do you think I would get myself so heated up? No indeed, but that is the point! My poor Lydia arrived unaccompanied. Wickham," she spoke his name very distinctly, "is not in sight, heaven knows what has happened. I have a very definite prediction of doom in my being and you should know I am not the sort to think the worst but I fear he may even be dead. Why else would he not accompany her?"

Mr. Bennet interjected calmly, "Let us not bury the fellow before it is certain, Mrs. Bennet. I am sure no great tragedy can have befallen him. Mr. Wickham is a man who is naturally adept at eluding crisis. I advise you to comfort yourself, Mrs. Bennet, with that notion. I daresay this will all blow over and prove to be nothing more than a puffed up little disagreement between lovers."

Mrs. Bennet gasped and although her nerves and the sudden bout of ill health she claimed had overtaken her would have debilitated a weaker soul she went on energetically, "Little disagreement?" she cried. "You take a dim view of our poor Lydia if you think her so variable that she would come from Newcastle over a simple disagreement. As if she has such silly tendencies!"

Jane, who had been engaged in solemn conversation with her husband, addressed her father. "We should arrange to go back to Hertfordshire this afternoon, papa."

Bingley agreed. "I shall order that the carriages be made ready directly, Mr. Bennet. Leave it to me to have all our belongings prepared, it will be a later hour than advisable for travel, but the roads are good, we will spend one night on the road I am afraid, but we shall reach Longbourn before the next draws in."

All matters concerning this sudden departure were decided upon in moments. Mrs. Bennet, indisposed to endure further exertion, would answer no more questions but insisted on remaining where she was. She sobbed loudly while those whose departure was imminent went about their preparations.

At last, when Mr. Darcy could take no more hysterics he instructed his man. "Have that woman removed from the stairs," he said. His voice was cold and his expression aloof.

Jane and Elizabeth studied the correspondence from Mr. Collins. It was dated the sixteenth day of March 1813, addressed to Mr. and Mrs. Bennet and read:

Dear Sir and Madam,

I urge you to return to Longbourn posthaste. Your daughter Lydia arrived here alone today and is so indisposed I fear none can deal with her but her mother. Hill has her in her old bed with a tonic. I must take this opportunity to say that I shall, as a member of the clergy, attempt, in your absence, to impart a little of the good Lord's influence to the dear child while your arrival is awaited.

William Collins

All that Elizabeth could do now was wait.

Chapter 9

"There is something a little stately in him to be sure,"
replied her aunt, "but it is confined to his air, and is not unbecoming.
I can now say with the housekeeper, that though some people
may call him proud, I have seen nothing of it."

There are some, being so accustomed to travel as to view it as commonplace and even natural, who would not consider the journey from Derbyshire to Hertfordshire to be arduous in itself. The distance between the two counties is judged to be nominal and indeed there is plenty to support the argument. Miles of good road, the degree of comfort to be found in carriages and reliable horses have all served to ease the situation to such an extent that half the world has been encouraged to stray, with little more reason than a whim, from one end of England to the other as if doing so represented nothing at all. So long as adequate refreshment, rest, and air can be taken there is no reason why people should not enjoy being carted about the world on wheels, there is even an air of grandeur attached to being hauled hither and thither and it seems that, for the most part, the activity is enjoyed rather than endured. To be thus conveyed, on their outward journey to Hertfordshire from Derbyshire would, in reality, have been no more ominous an endeavor for the party than the incoming journey had been, but Mrs. Bennet's frequent outbursts along the way proved trying for Mr. Bennet's even temper. Kitty showed signs of mortification.

"I do not see why I have to go home, I could have stayed behind with Lizzy," she moaned, adding, "Lydia always ruins everything for me."

Her father forgave his daughter her sulks, for each of them was, in their own way, very troubled by the news.

When they finally arrived at Longbourn, Mrs. Bennet went straight to Lydia's side and for a while it was hard to see who was suffering the most. Lydia looked pale and her mother's distress and rapid questioning only served to make the girl withdraw and sink lower in spirits.

"Oh Lydia, what has become of your dear Wickham?" cried Mrs. Bennet. "No dear, pray hold your tongue and keep the truth from me a while longer for I cannot bear to imagine what tragedy has befallen my favorite son."

Lydia sniffed. "When you learn what has happened you will not favor him, mama, he has treated me very ill."

"Then he is not dead?" cried her mother clapping her hands. "Oh, I am so relieved, my dear, for I could not bear to see such a young bright girl as you made drab by mourning, I know I should break my heart."

Lydia sighed. "I should be glad to lose him, mama, I hate him." And true it was that at that moment, Lydia, poor, thoughtless, rash child that she was, craved the station of widowhood.

"There, there, my dear," her mother cooed, "things cannot be so bad as you say, what has he done that his wife cannot forgive? Oh stop whimpering, girl, I can make no sense of you at all."

Lydia seemed once again to lose sight of herself and failed to say anything more to her mother who quickly tired of other people's hysteria. She retired to her room with an attack of the palpitations. Later, in a calmer frame of mind, Lydia revealed all her misgivings to Jane who had insisted that her own husband return to Netherfield while she stay and do her share of the comforting at Longbourn. It was later again that evening that Jane spoke of Lydia's story to her parents.

Her expression was grave. Her disinclination to convey the unpleasantness that had befallen her younger sister governed her and it was not without due aforethought that she spoke.

"It is distressing news indeed, for Lydia has found Wickham out in a severe indiscretion," she paused before going on, "with a servant girl."

"I knew it," spat Mrs. Bennet bitterly, "he never fooled me, there was always that look about him." She glared at Mr. Bennet. "You should never have let him have her hand, Mr. Bennet, now look what has happened because you would not fight him."

Mr. Bennet gave a resigned sigh. "I will not argue the point with you on this occasion, Mrs. Bennet, blame me if you must, there are graver issues to concern us." He turned to Jane. "Is Lydia absolutely certain of this liaison?"

"Yes, sir, and she has spoken to Wickham, but he reacted badly to the confrontation. He was very angry and said a great many terrible things, I barely know how to speak of them myself but I must relieve you of this anxiety," she said and, more than a full hour later, when she had finished her sad account they knew some, if not all, of the situation. To deceive was never in Jane's nature but to protect was, her concealment of certain aspects of Lydia's dilemma was therefore meritorious in origin. She sat alone in her old room and wrote the facts that she had revealed and those that she had not, on two full sheets of paper in a long letter to Lizzy.

Longbourn, Hertfordshire

Dear Lizzy,

I will waste no time with formal pleasantries to begin this letter, for you will have guessed that Lydia's news is grave indeed. I scarcely know where to begin, the pain this will give you causes my hesitation, forgive me that I am not there to comfort you.

We arrived here at Longbourn to find that Lydia was indeed in a most fatigued state. She was pale and distressed and as we had learned from Mr. Collins's letter, she did arrive alone. Mr. Collins had been called from Lucas Lodge by Hill. It is unfortunate that he has been involved at all, but there it is, Hill could think of no one else to summon, our Aunt and Uncle Phillips being otherwise detained. You will agree that Charlotte would be all that is sincere and loyal, she is very concerned, but neither of them stayed at Longbourn for any notable duration. We must be grateful at least that they were able to send the express; the rest has been left to poor old Hill.

Many hours passed before Lydia's full grievance could be extracted but finally I had the whole story. I must tell you that no terrible fate has befallen Wickham; he is, it is revealed, as vigorous as ever in health. Yes, he is as alive as ever he was, but I fear, Lizzy, when you hear of his wrongdoings, you will wish him otherwise. How can I reveal this, knowing that the consequences are so far reaching? Alas, I shall give it to you as it is. Lydia had lately discovered her husband's indiscretion with a local maid. There is no doubt of the truth, she told me the shocking nature of her discovery and from the details of it there can be no mistake that a seduction has taken place. But Lizzy, I am grieved at myself for concealing what I knew of Wickham's character in the past. You see now that it is not such good fortune that I rarely think ill of people, when I think that I knew of his wickedness last May, but did nothing about it. Ah, but it is done and what benefit can be gained from self-reproach? I must therefore continue with this worsening narrative. On Lydia's finding out her husband's infidelity a vicious quarrel ensued, Wickham was demented with rage. Her poor heart, of course, was broken, how could she comprehend this behavior, this unfaithful act so destructive and inconsistent with their love? When she expressed as much to him he viciously denied that his love was true or that it had ever been.

Yes Lizzy, I know it will distress you to hear this. Wickham told Lydia that from the very first his attention to her was not the result of any particular regard on his part. He revealed that his actions were all design and no feeling whatsoever. It is hard to believe is it not? Wickham says that he did not choose to pursue Lydia, but claims the choice was made by someone in whose power he lies, and that this unknown party issued the instructions that resulted in his luring her into the elopement. Could there have been an easier victim than Lydia, Lizzy? But I fear I ponder too much because I dread the scandal I must write as this sad tale intensifies. Wickham told Lydia that his instruction did not include him marrying her, his payment, yes payment, was made in lieu of him scandalizing our family's name. That was the intention.

He was paid half of an agreed sum before setting about his allurement; it is thought to have been a substantial amount. That Lydia's and our respectability was salvaged by their marriage infuriated Wickham's employer and he was denied any further recompense. That he has revealed so much to Lydia is astonishing, but I can only conclude from what she says that he spoke of it in a further attempt to insult her. I do not know what to think, Lizzy, are we to be glad that our Uncle Gardiner sacrificed so much to pay for their wedding?

I wonder if it would not have been better to suffer the scandal, for now she is bound in a most miserable marriage. They suffer most dreadfully in cheap accommodation; it seems that Wickham's predilection for gambling has not faded. I do not have the details of how much money he received for the job of polluting Lydia's name, but whatever this fortune was, it is spent, likewise there is little to be said for the money our uncle provided. Wickham has replaced all his old debts with new ones. He is fond of the inn, not just for the liquor but the young girl with whom he betrayed our sister is employed in such an establishment.

I am ashamed to think of our own opulent style of existing now I am familiar with the destitution our sister endured. But what to do? We must be grateful that Lydia makes friends with ease, she was able to borrow the total fare to Longbourn from several of the officers' wives, I shall, of course, deal with their reimbursement as soon as Lydia is well enough to give particulars. Have you ever known such distress, Lizzy? I am all anxiety about whose hand guided Wickham, but I am not to be taken up with it. There are more pressing matters that need attention; Lydia says she is a good way into her first confinement, that soon it will not be hid. The comfort is that as time goes on we may explain Lydia's return to Longbourn with the idea that she rests here until the child comes.

I fear that she may not see her husband again and, as for the mystery of all his conduct, we may never uncover the truth. I must tell you I have withheld some details from our parents, so they concern themselves only with her health and assuring her that things can be resolved. I have not told them of the apparent corruption that lies at the root of this and have urged Lydia not to reveal it. I now have the distressing responsibility of speaking to Charles when I return to Netherfield tomorrow, you will not trouble yourself over this, you know he is discreet.

I deeply regret being the one to bring you this sad news when you are not so near as to be able to satisfy yourself of events but be assured I will write again.

I leave you now my dear sister. God Bless You.

Jane

Jane adhered to her vow of secrecy on the matter of Wickham's revelation and tried to assure herself that Lydia could be silenced. Situations that depend so much on secrecy cannot be lightly borne and although Lydia's loose tongue lay quiet in her mouth, it represented a risk that Jane was all too aware of. Even with the most distressing aspects of the matter withheld, Mrs. Bennet's agitation was as if she had known them.

Longbourn had not seen a full quota of hysteria since the three married sisters had left, for Mrs. Bennet, although always able to rise to the occasion with a bout of the nerves, never performed so well without an audience. With just Mr. Bennet, Kitty, and the handful of servants for spectators, her attacks had lately taken on a more melancholic note which usually resulted in her retiring to bed early with an ill head. Lydia's predicament gave Mrs. Bennet the happy opportunity to give way entirely to the palpitations whenever she saw fit.

Mr. Bennet reverted to his old custom of retreating to his library for hours on end. For what better way is there to obscure the evils of the world from unwilling eyes than to place a book in front of them? Little could tear him from his solitude apart from the increasingly frequent visits from Mr. Collins who seemed hungry to discover every detail of the scandals surrounding Lydia.

The girl herself improved slowly through rest and regained her voracious appetite quite rapidly but was still prone to tearful hours for, despite her husband's cruel claims that no love existed between them, she fancied that she was nursing a broken heart and feared it would not mend. Mrs. Collins, whose practical nature prevailed above all else, called daily from Lucas Lodge to inquire about

Lydia's well-being. Her interest and concern were genuine, she seemed not to seek out the disgrace of the matter but merely offered the hand of friendship in case it should need to be grasped. Her husband's philanthropy remained as transparent as ever and this did not go unnoticed by his wife.

Kitty tried her best to cheer Lydia's spirits but found that talk of fashions and dances and officers no longer held any appeal for her unfortunate sister. It was as if the girl had grown old long before her time and was taking Kitty with her, never before were there two young girls less youthful. Mary, who had never seemed young, learned of Lydia's traumas in a letter from Mr. Collins. She did not write to Longbourn, but replied directly to Mr. Collins quoting what she deemed some suitable bible excerpts. Jane came often to Longbourn but could not rest there or at Netherfield until she knew that Lizzy had her letter and its sad content.

A week passed before Elizabeth had the news of Lydia. It could hardly be believed, were it not true, that the arrival of two letters on the same day could be the cause of so much that is troublesome and wearying. But it was so, and on the morning that Elizabeth received Jane's correspondence, Mr. Darcy received a letter from his aunt, Lady Catherine de Bourgh. While Elizabeth's letter brought bad news Darcy's was, if not a profusion of glad tidings, something a little more promising. There was, at least, no discernable sign of Lady Catherine's famed resentment. She had consented that a reconciliation should take place and Darcy was relieved to hear of it. Discord of any sort troubled him, he was not a man who found it easy to put things to the back of his mind and his aunt's absence from his life had been worrying him. After reading his letter he looked at his wife who was engaged in re-reading hers.

She noted his stare and handed the letter to him, he took it and before examination of it said firmly, "I need not ask the theme of this, your frown tells me it is troubling news, Elizabeth." She said nothing. When he had read the letter from Jane and considered its contents he stood up and paced about the room, his breath quickening. "Damn

Wickham, I will not have him cast his curses over us anymore, I have done all in my power to rid Pemberley of his influence."

Elizabeth was shocked by this outburst. "Pemberley *is* rid of him and let us hope Lydia will be also, I fear the shame of abandonment will be preferable to a reunion."

Darcy could do no more than sigh for a moment, then he went on, "The mention of his name is like a poison to me. What of these further scandalous dealings, who can make sense of them?"

"I would imagine only Wickham himself, and this supposed conspirator of his could be prevailed upon to provide clarity but, as we are unlikely to have the opportunity of an address with either, it seems we are to be unfamiliar with all the facts." Elizabeth was near to tears. "What to do? I dare not consider traveling too long or too far in my condition, my heart tells me to go to Longbourn where I could be of some use, but I know I must not go."

"I would not have it, I cannot have you fatigued, Elizabeth, they must do without you."

With sadness, Elizabeth acknowledged this to be true. "I know it must be so, but how do I explain myself? This is no time for us to reveal our happy news." She thought for a while on the irony. "No indeed, how could I speak of my lucky situation when Lydia's so contrasts it, it would not do."

"You are all sweetness," said Darcy, picking up his aunt's letter from the breakfast table, "so sweet that even Lady Catherine may eventually succumb to you."

Elizabeth tried a smile. "She has condescended to visit?"

"A fortnight today, she does not say for how long."

"She will no doubt stay long enough to check my progress," said Elizabeth wearily. "If I could only be in better spirits, I shall impress no one with my gloom, nor melt any hearts."

"Only mine," said Darcy.

The two passed the morning writing in the drawing room. Mr. Darcy drafted a letter to his aunt confirming the arrangements for her visit and Elizabeth sent a letter to Longbourn.

Lady Catherine was due to arrive on the eleventh day of April.

CHAPTER 10

"But can you think that Lydia is so lost to everything but love of him?"

Keeping Lydia's predicament hushed was not so easy a task. All at Lucas Lodge were aware of her return to Hertfordshire but not the reason for it, thankfully. Everyone at Longbourn, even Mrs. Bennet, thought better of informing Mr. Collins of the limited particulars known.

A small measure of speculative talk began to circulate around Meryton and there was gossip amongst the servants at Netherfield. News of Lydia's unexpected homecoming had reached Rosings Park through Mary, but little was said of it there. Only once did Lady Catherine allude to the situation. "Such antics come as no surprise to me, a union that begins in an elopement must be doomed from the start. A man's propensity to rush into marriage must also be balanced by an equal tendency to rush out of it."

A week passed quickly at Longbourn, Netherfield, and Pemberley. At the latter, preparations for Lady Catherine's arrival were in progress, but before she was to get there another letter arrived from Rosings; Anne and her loyal companion Mary were also to join Lady Catherine. She wrote with regret that Mrs. Jenkinson would not be amongst the party and would remain at Rosings Park until their return.

"It is so curious to hear of Mary as if she were a stranger to me," said Lizzy thoughtfully. "Loyal companion! I wonder Lady Catherine could not refer to her as my sister, it makes Mary seem so remote."

Darcy agreed but was distracted. Elizabeth went on, "Oh well, I look forward as best I can to seeing Mary, but I do not relish the idea of her moralizing, she had better save that for Anne. Poor Anne, how is she of late? I imagine Lady Catherine will have instructions for her care, I should like to see that everything is as it should be."

"Yes of course, every detail will be attended to regarding my cousin's health," said Darcy, but this verification did little to ease Elizabeth's disquiet. The dreaded scrutiny, the very idea of being closely observed by Lady Catherine set her mind to imagine, in that instant, at least ten of a thousand possible mistakes she was likely to make. But she was quick to remind herself, *There is a stubbornness about me that never can bear to be frightened at the will of others. My courage always rises with every attempt to intimidate me.*

At Longbourn Mrs. Bennet tired of Lydia's slow progress and became increasingly aware of the idle talk that went on in the village. It was becoming a most unsatisfying drama for her.

"I wonder at people, Mr. Bennet, that they have nothing to concern themselves with but meddlesome talk of other people's business," she said one day at dinner. "I should be ashamed to have such an unvaried life that my only pleasures were malicious talk and gossip."

"Ah well, Mrs. Bennet," said Mr. Bennet, "not all are so gifted in their ability to rise above the temptations of tittle-tattle as you, my dear."

"No indeed," said Mrs. Bennet firmly, adding, "Lizzy keeps herself out of the commotion, I wonder she could not take the time to visit and help out. She knows all the strain falls on me in these difficult times. What of my poor nerves? She makes no mention of them in her letter and she knows well enough my condition. No, she is to stay at Pemberley and that is that. Of course, I knew this would happen, she has no time at all for her own dear family, I daresay because she fancies herself quite high now. I hear from Mary that she is to accompany Anne de Bourgh and Lady Catherine to Pemberley in less than a week, so there is your explanation, Mr. Bennet; Mrs. Darcy, as she is lately known, is too busy planning enjoyment, I have no doubt she congratulates herself on escaping the burdens that we now bear alone."

The husband, weary of his wife's espousing said, "I sought no explanation, Mrs. Bennet, I can see no benefit in Lizzy's returning here. Lydia has enough attention at present and dare I say, the less she has of it the better. A greater audience may encourage her to prolong the performance."

"Performance!" cried Mrs. Bennet, "And where would she get these dramatic tendencies? I sometimes wonder at you."

Kitty, who had been sitting wearing a sullen expression for the best part of the day, began to cry.

"It is not fair, now Mary is to go to Pemberley. Mary! Of all people. And I shall be stuck here with Lydia feeling sorry for herself."

Mrs. Bennet glared at her husband. "There you see," she said bitterly, "that is exactly what I mean. That is the result of Elizabeth's selfish attitude for you."

Mr. Bennet, who bore criticism of his little Lizzy with reluctance, retired to his library with the intention of staying there as long as possible.

CHAPTER 11

"Do you know who I am? I have not been accustomed to such language as this. I am almost the nearest relation he has in the world, and am entitled to know all his dearest concerns."

———————

At Pemberley the day of Lady Catherine's arrival came. Every kind of instruction regarding poor Anne's health had been adhered to on her ladyship's insistence. Mrs. Reynolds had undertaken to ensure that all particular kinds of medicinal remedies were at hand, and sterile sheets were to be hung at the windows in Anne's room.

"I have all the best herbals from the apothecary, ma'am," said the housekeeper to Elizabeth that morning. "The master tells me that Lady Catherine has expressed that the young lady's bedchamber be 'just so' for her arrival, she does not travel well I understand."

"I believe not, Mrs. Reynolds. Thank you. Do you know Anne de Bourgh well?"

"Not so well as I know the master and Miss Georgiana, ma'am, she did come here on and off as a younger child, when her health permitted, but I saw less of her than I did of Colonel Fitzwilliam and his brothers."

Elizabeth smiled, she had not seen Colonel Fitzwilliam since her marriage but apart from that it had been a year almost to the day since she had become better acquainted with him at Rosings. "I am fond of Colonel Fitzwilliam, I welcomed his company when I last really had the chance of it, he has a pleasing manner." She felt herself blush and hoped her color went unnoticed by Mrs. Reynolds, for her embarrassment had been caused by the sudden recollection that she had once viewed the Colonel in a light more generally cast upon lovers than upon friends. Ever since her husband's revelation that his cousin's regard for her was notable, she had contemplated the situation with mild discomposure.

The housekeeper smiled fondly. "Oh yes, Mrs. Darcy, ma'am, Colonel Fitzwilliam is a good man, a very good man." Checking the mantle clock she said, "I shall never be ready if I stand idle like this."

Elizabeth thanked Mrs. Reynolds again and tried to steady her spirits in anticipation of Lady Catherine's arrival.

By four in the afternoon a grand carriage drew to a halt outside Pemberley and it was with great ceremony that Lady Catherine and Anne were greeted, Elizabeth left her husband to welcome his aunt and cousin but she watched from a window—far better, thought she, to delay. Her sister Mary stayed close to Anne de Bourgh at all times and had about her the appearance of a sub-servient mouse.

"Oh my goodness, abasement suits Mary very well!" observed Elizabeth aloud.

There was a great commotion about the unpacking of clothes and the airing of rooms. Lady Catherine's exacting tones reverber-ated through the house and when all her orders had been adhered to, she consented to take some tea with her nephew and his wife. She had informed Mrs. Reynolds that her daughter should take some bed rest before dinner and that Mary should sit by her and read should Anne request it and be silent if she should not. Eliza-beth had no chance of seeing her sister.

Georgiana had the opportunity of accompanying Caroline Bingley to a recital, a distraction which she welcomed, for her Aunt Catherine had always rather frightened her, so she was content to delay seeing her again.

Darcy and Elizabeth sat opposite Lady Catherine who scruti-nized the room as if hoping to seek out some detailed change for the worse in its furnishings or atmosphere that Elizabeth might be blamed for. She sat quietly for a while but let her piercing stare engage the couple. Eventually she addressed Elizabeth, making no attempt to soften her tone. "Miss Elizabeth Bennet," she said, "you are very lucky that my excellent sister had all these rooms so well furnished, are you not?"

"Yes ma'am," Elizabeth said.

"Yes," said Lady Catherine, nodding thoughtfully. "I cannot imagine that you would have found the task an easy one had you been faced with it."

Darcy was quick to reproach his aunt. "My wife rises readily to any challenge."

Lady Catherine sneered at Elizabeth. "Before we go any further," she warned, "let me just say this, your sister's appointment with me and my family in no way gives you license to assume inappropriate familiarity, I would like to make that quite clear."

Elizabeth could sense her husband's discomfort but wanted to placate his temper so she spoke as calmly as her angry feelings would allow. "You could not speak plainer, ma'am, I should think we are both of us very far away from mutual familiarity. I certainly do not seek it, but I think we should both be ready to adopt civility in its place," she said, adding with a glance at Darcy, "for your nephew's sake, your ladyship."

Lady Catherine breathed deeply and looked at Darcy. "Fitz-william," she snapped, "it surprises me, but your wife has some idea of manners and with your interests so dear to me I concede that we must give the appearance of courtesy."

"We must indeed, madam," said Darcy. "I insist upon it and request your blessing and congratulations on our marriage."

Lady Catherine narrowed her eyes at Elizabeth then addressed Darcy again. "I agreed only to being courteous! That, for now, will have to suffice. If I should see the chance of liking your wife a little I shall not reject it, but I have known her to be headstrong in the past and that I do not approve of." She turned sharply to Elizabeth and studied her. "You do seem a little less forthright than I remember. Perhaps the dignified life Fitzwilliam has provided is proving correc-tive to your willfulness." She smiled but did not appear genuine. "You see," she continued, "I am not at all harsh on you, Elizabeth."

Darcy rose from his chair, his expression was firm. "I cannot allow you to be misled into believing that I am the kind of husband who will sit by and hear his wife insulted. Elizabeth, contrary to your opinion, is too sweet to endure such abuse and her love for me, I believe, is too strong to allow her to freely offend you in her turn. I suggested in my letter to you that we reconcile our differences. That, madam, is the purpose of your visit here. I demand an immediate end to this reunion if your intention was merely to dishonor the woman I love."

Lady Catherine laughed coldly. "Love? How whimsical you have become, Fitzwilliam. I care little for love and I care far less for its destructive heat. Our families have thrived due to more than mere fancy. As you are aware, an admirable mix of honor, duty, culture, and heritage is the backbone of Pemberley, that cannot be broken, but love," she said scornfully, "what will be left to you when its fickle flames die out?"

Elizabeth rose. "I fear, your ladyship, that we have started badly. I for one do not know what will give you recompense other than to know that the love you scorn is now as much the backbone of Pemberley as all the pompous, proud, and narrow rituals you uphold."

"How dare you abuse me with such language, Miss Bennet, what gives you the right to discredit the customs of our heritage, you who are little more than a fortune-seeking provincial girl. You should learn some respect for nobility and history; they are the things that represent true strength. Nothing can weaken their power."

Elizabeth flushed with anger. "If that is so, Lady Catherine, you can have no reason to fear that as simple a thing as my love could ever be a threat. As for my fortune hunting, I never sought anything but affection and in that I have indeed become rich."

Lady Catherine was tiring of Elizabeth's retaliations and she stood to excuse herself. "My journey has fatigued me, I wish to take a short rest. I trust my room is ready, Miss Bennet."

Darcy called for a ladies' maid and guided Lady Catherine to the door. "Some rest will benefit you, you are showing signs of exhaustion and confusion," he said.

Lady Catherine was very obviously insulted by her nephew.

She raised her voice and her hand. "I am merely a little overburdened from traveling but my mind is quite clear."

"Then you will, from now on, have no difficulty in remembering that my wife is no longer to be referred to as Miss Bennet."

Lady Catherine glared at her nephew but before she could concoct a fitting retort he interjected, from the hint of a smile that crossed his lips it seemed he took pleasure in doing so. "It would not do if you were to publicly address the mistress of Pemberley inappropriately, you are usually so attentive to these matters."

The suggestion of a smile grew on his face and took a considerable time to fade. Elizabeth, weary from the distressing conference, was glad to see it for she was filled with feelings of anxiety and her husband's good humor was a comfort to her.

CHAPTER 12

"Not so hasty, if you please. I have by no means done.
To all the objections I have already urged, I have still another to add."

It could not be said that the relationship between Lady Catherine and Elizabeth improved greatly over the first days of the former's stay at Pemberley, but the cool civility that both adopted was not seen as unexpected or felt to be unbearable. Elizabeth soon had opportunities to speak with Mary, though she had never been as close to her or any other of her sisters as she was to Jane. Mary, when afforded respite by Anne's regular bed rest, would take tea with Elizabeth or join her in a walk, though she was not so passionate about the outdoors as her elder sister and of late Elizabeth had resisted temptation and limited herself to strolling within a very few yards of the house. Her conversations with Mary rarely amounted to anything much for the girl's predilection for moralizing inevitably gave her discourse a reproachful flavor.

As much as was possible, given the contrasts of and the conflicts between the various members of the given company, a peaceful atmosphere reigned on the estate. Caroline Bingley took to entertaining Lady Catherine by day, for apart from Darcy and Georgiana, the elder woman considered the younger the only person present, excluding her nephew, who was worthy of her attention. Elizabeth felt only gratitude that both could tolerate each other as she had little time for either by choice.

An agreement, unspoken only but nevertheless quite fixed, that all parties should confine their meetings to dinner provided a polite method of avoidance that proved satisfactory to all concerned. Elizabeth fared well enough at these gatherings for she was at ease in her new home and always felt her husband's staunch support for her. She was not afraid of Lady Catherine, but she was uncomfortable in her company. Anne, when her various frailties allowed her to join them, rarely spoke. When she did, she did so quietly to Mary. Caroline focused her attention on Lady Catherine or Darcy but she was conscious that her gaze must not be perceived to be aimed in his direction too often. Georgiana stayed close to her brother and Elizabeth whenever she could. The Gardiners kept themselves quite hidden away and were seen so little as to raise speculation about whether they had returned to Cheapside. They infinitely preferred the intimacy and solitude of their estate cottage to Lady Catherine's company and were the only people present at Pemberley who could avoid the woman without condemnation.

Lady Catherine was as ever she had been; her penchant for fawning observers had not faded and Caroline, Anne, and Mary made an adequate if small band of admirers in front of whom she could hold court. She was mindful to abstain from overt verbal criticism of Elizabeth whenever Darcy was present, but she regularly took the opportunity to express her dislike by giving Elizabeth disdainful looks. Lady Catherine had made a study of giving disdainful looks and believed that they could be more effective and insulting than words, though she was notoriously adept at vicious speech also. Anne and Mary were, each in their own way, impervious to the tangled and bitter feelings that are so often prevalent in certain types of human spirit, so most of Lady Catherine's barbs to Elizabeth went unnoticed by them. In contrast to their oblivion, Caroline Bingley missed not a single tightening of the de Bourgh lips, she observed and relished every nuance. Not one of Lady Catherine's spiteful looks went undetected by Caroline, and it gave her immeasurable satisfaction.

By the time the second week drew near Caroline Bingley had formed a close alliance with Lady Catherine. Miss Bingley, never so inventive as now, formulated the means to enjoy private conversations with her ladyship. Mary and Anne de Bourgh took little pleasure in what they considered to be idle talk. Both preferred the occupation of moralistic debates which they would carry out in Anne's room in order that her weak body could rest whilst her mind was being suitably exercised. Darcy and Elizabeth went about their business, relieved that Caroline had taken the responsibility for Lady Catherine's daily entertainment.

"Miss Bingley," said Lady Catherine one afternoon, "I understand that your family also has the misfortune to be associated with the Bennets." Caroline looked quizzically at Lady Catherine who spoke again, "I hope I have not caused offense?"

Caroline spoke in a cultured whisper, "No, your ladyship, I assure you no offense has been taken. Indeed you are right, my brother Charles is married to Jane Bennet, Eliza's older sister. Admittedly, she is the prettiest of the Bennet brood and a sweet-natured girl. None of the other Bennets are so tolerable as Jane, she is quite set apart from the rest."

Lady Catherine sneered. "They make quite an art of beguilement these Bennet girls, two of them have negotiated their paths in life most profitably."

"Indeed they have, ma'am. I do not know how they can bear to congratulate themselves on their good fortune when it has been the cause of so much unhappiness for two other, dare I say, more deserving and well-bred young ladies."

Lady Catherine's surprise was obvious. "*Two* young ladies? Another poor girl has suffered rejection in the cruel way in which my own daughter was obliged to? Who is the unfortunate creature?"

Caroline Bingley smiled. "Why, it is Georgiana, your ladyship."

Lady Catherine made no attempt to cover her astonishment. "Are you implying that my *own* niece was to marry your brother? I heard nothing of this."

"Then you must allow me to elaborate; it was a plan as yet in its infancy, but it was generally thought, amongst those in our family at least, that it would be a most suitable match for all concerned."

"Indeed, it would have been, Miss Bingley, but tell me, Georgiana displays no signs of desperation, was she very attached to your brother?"

"The relationship had not yet begun to develop, your ladyship, which I concede is a kindness, for Georgiana is a delicate soul, one cannot imagine how she would have stood up to such a usurpation."

Lady Catherine, whose facial expressions could change swiftly, looked forlorn, then determined. "Tell me, Miss Bingley, what attempts if any were made to prevent your brother's entrapment? Surely he was warned off."

Caroline's mouth was set in a grim line, only her harsh words could prize it open. "Darcy did try at one time to persuade Charles that a better choice could be made, but it seems that once he had made his own pitiable selection he felt no compunction to prevent my brother doing so also. It is very sad, ma'am, but thereafter it seemed that interference would be pointless."

Lady Catherine gave a small laugh. "In circumstances of such severity, interference is never pointless and must always be thought acceptable. That the results of intervention are not always successful is something of a cruelty I confess. I went to great lengths to thwart my nephew's senseless plans and it cost me dear, but to no avail, there is little justice in the matter and no benefits at all can arise from the marriage."

"They speak of happiness and love, your ladyship," said Caroline.

"Oh yes, they speak of happiness and love, but self-gratification should not be the first consideration where marriage is concerned. I believe honor and duty should always take precedence, particularly over affairs of the heart. Oh yes, Darcy thinks himself in love, I am sure." She paused for a moment, then she went on, "But consider, there is always the possibility that he could be persuaded to think himself out of it."

Never were two women better practiced in the art of dramatizing the slightest impropriety or fault in others. The overexaggerated news of Charles Bingley's supposed intention of betrothal fueled lengthy conversation and debate and made a great occasion for the two to berate those beneath them with vigorous animosity. So triumphant were they in outlining all that was undesirable in the Bennets that they had not a second to spare where they may have had the inclination to examine their own inhumanity. Thus they spent their hours, two ladies of supposed good breeding, engaged in the shared and vulgar entertainment of giving vicious critical observation and harsh opinions of whichever Bennet made a ready victim. They showed the cruelest disregard for Elizabeth, each for their own very different reasons, and it united them further.

Lady Catherine always preferred the company of a well-bred woman with a vicious tongue to that of a commoner with a kind heart. She had never been truly kind herself, although she had often been materially generous, but at the root of her benefaction her need for worship and gratitude was to be found. It was unthinkable that Lady Catherine de Bourgh should be devoid of adoration. She had recently lost her most avid admirer Mr. Collins, and Caroline Bingley, although not obsequious in manner, provided a satisfactory replacement. Now, enchanted by Lady Catherine, her character seemed set to worsen.

Elizabeth happily indulged Lady Catherine and Miss Bingley in their soirées. She arranged for tea and every refreshment and delicacy to be taken to them as often as they liked. It was her suspicion that the nature of their conversation would be bitterly set against her, but she was willing to pay this small price and indulge them, for their absence was her reward. "I am quite happy to be the object of their scorn," said Elizabeth to her husband. "I am sure it gives me as much amusement to think of them pulling apart my character as it gives them to do so."

Darcy was concerned. "They have sense enough between them to keep their venomous opinions from me at least."

Elizabeth smiled. "Oh yes, only a privileged few earn their respect, and you are one of those few, they would not wish to displease you though they take delight in grieving everyone else."

"It is sad, Elizabeth, that Bingley, one of the most excellent men I know, should have such a sister."

Elizabeth stared at Darcy. "It is sad that you, an excellent man yourself, should have such an aunt, but such are the blessings of family where we have no choices and must be tolerant. At least we may determine who our friends shall be," she said.

"And our lovers," said Darcy quietly.

Elizabeth kissed her husband on the cheek. "And our lovers," she repeated thoughtfully.

CHAPTER 13

"This was a lucky idea of mine, indeed!"

Although it was not often spoken of, Darcy knew that Elizabeth was frequently preoccupied with thoughts of Lydia's dilemma. She was restless and concerned. No further news had come from Long-bourn. Darcy and Elizabeth bore between them the ominous quiet that settled around them like the barely audible breath before the scream of despair. At times Elizabeth wanted to return to Long-bourn, but knew that neither her presence in Hertfordshire nor her absence from Derbyshire would achieve much. She felt, so quickly into her marriage, the tight reins of duty constricting her. Should she flee Pemberley she risked alerting Lady Catherine to the scandals that were germinating within the Bennet family. She did not fear her husband's wrath for he was consistently supportive of her wishes. But she grew frustrated, her desperate need to prove their marriage a worthy one was made greater by the fear that it could be tarnished by her family. Oh, if Wickham had married Mary King there would have been no beginning to the disgraces and heinous scandals that tainted them. But Mary King was long gone, the girl and her fortune saved from Wickham and despair.

The past seemed to hold all the answers now that it could be viewed from the advantageous position of the present. If Lydia had not gone to Brighton. If she, Elizabeth, had revealed Wickham's true character. If her own dear husband had not thought so gallantly of her to effect such a generous rescue of her sister. Her thoughts gave her no comfort. She knew too well the fruitlessness of trying to prevent a disaster that had already happened. Lady Catherine was fixed in her disdain and Elizabeth feared that further revelation of her family's impropriety would raise that dislike to an irreparable level.

All the while Lydia kept to her bed at Longbourn, weakened by her confinement and her despair. Her mother spent her time equally between her own bed and Lydia's bedside, coming in when another worry occurred to her and distressing her daughter further. "Lydia, Lydia," she shrieked, waking her daughter, "if you are never to see Wickham again, which I suspect is the case, then we must keep things very quiet when the child comes."

Lydia groaned, "I am still a married woman mother, I am not ashamed."

"No indeed, but think of the child, what a life it would have with no father and a mother with no prospects in life." She made a point of thinking for a while. "We will keep this whole business quiet, I cannot bear to have it all around Meryton. I have thought about this, Lydia, and you must do as I say. I shall say you have been very ill and will soon travel to Derbyshire for the air," she nodded with satisfaction and went on, "and if anyone should suggest you would be better remedied in Bath I shall have a fit, anyway, you can stay at Pemberley. God knows your sister can spare you the hospitality and afford the expense without noticing it. We will say that Wickham insisted you be with your family while you recover. It vexes me not to reveal how ill he has treated you, but it will be best to hide the dreadful truth about the man, it will look better on you, child."

"But I can hardly keep the child secret forever, mama."

Mrs. Bennet rolled her eyes dramatically. "Do not be a simpleton, of course you shall not, you shall have the child at Pemberley, they will keep it quiet there, I daresay you could hide dozens of mothers and babies in that place before anyone noticed. I shall tell Lizzy she must take the infant. There you see! That will give the poor mite a chance. Then when the business is over, you can come home again, my dear, I will tell everyone you are much recovered and that will be an end to it."

"And what of my marriage, mama, how will you hide the scandal of its end?"

Mrs. Bennet huffed impatiently. "I will think of something, we should have you widowed I daresay, there is no shame in that, only misfortune. You will infinitely prefer to suffer sympathy than disapproval."

"If my dead husband should turn up, what of that possibility?"

Mrs. Bennet became more impatient. "Am I to work everything out at once? You should be grateful I have the good sense to have thought up any sort of plan. That is what a mother's duty is, but there, you do not appreciate me as fully as you ought. No Lydia, do not trouble yourself with thoughts of Wickham, I doubt he will dare show his face again." She stood and smoothed her daughter's bedspread looking satisfied, "There, there, my dear, I told you I would arrange everything, I doubt you have much of a future before you, but the church may take you. I shall speak with your father directly, he must make arrangements with Lizzy and you shall go as soon as possible." Seeing her daughter's look of protestation she went on, "Well my nerves are not strong enough to nurse you, I daresay I shall be dead before the end of the week and then who shall you rely on to sort out all your troubles, your father has not the first notion about dealing with things sensibly."

Lydia stayed in bed, too tired and confused to make sense of anything while Mrs. Bennet outlined her plans to her husband in his library, but he did not take well to her ideas. He removed his spectacles and put down the book he was reading. "Mrs. Bennet," he said solemnly, "let me see if I have understood you, Elizabeth is to take Lydia's child and raise him, or her, as her own?"

Mrs. Bennet nodded proudly.

"And have you thought, my dear," her husband went on, "what Mr. Darcy might say to this idea?"

Mrs. Bennet was clearly agitated, her cheeks flushed with indignation. "I do not care two sticks what Mr. Darcy has to say on the matter. It is all decided! Mr. Darcy will have to make the best of it, *he* saw fit to lure my Lizzy with his riches, *he* should be willing to share them with her family. Besides, we can hardly consider keeping a small child here, in our old age."

Mr. Bennet gave a weary sigh. "Faults though Mr. Darcy may have, lack of generosity is not one of them, Mrs. Bennet."

"Well, let him prove it by helping our poor dear Lydia," said Mrs. Bennet smugly.

Mr. Bennet thought better of revealing that it had been Mr. Darcy who had paid fully for Lydia's wedding to Mr. Wickham. He thought back to the day when Darcy had asked him for Elizabeth's hand in marriage. His reminiscence led him to recall the moment when Elizabeth had told him of Darcy's part in Lydia's salvation. With clarity, and a little embarrassment, his own reaction was brought to mind, *"…these violent young lovers carry everything their own way. I shall offer to pay him tomorrow; he will rant and storm about his love for you, and there will be an end to the matter."* Mr. Bennet was determined to conceal the truth from Mrs. Bennet despite a strong desire to defend his son-in-law, so he said simply, "Mr. Darcy is more helpful than you could ever know, Mrs. Bennet, now let that be an end to it, please."

"An end to it? I have scarcely begun! You must write directly to Lizzy and tell her what she is to do. I will send Lydia as soon as possible. We cannot waste any time, she must go while she is still fit for travel. Lord knows the time will come soon enough when she is not. And besides her condition will become noticeable."

"Heaven forbid," said Mr. Bennet, adding, "do you consider such conditions are in any way less noticeable in Derbyshire, Mrs. Bennet?"

"Oh, Mr. Bennet," cried his wife, "I ask nothing of you other than to write to your daughter, is that too much?"

"The writing itself, no, though the request is neither simple nor dare I say reasonable."

"Request indeed. It is not a request. I *demand* Elizabeth does as I say. Heaven knows it may do her good. I hope that the discipline of marriage has tamed her headstrong ways, for you never had the strength to check her."

"I can make no claims to strength, Mrs. Bennet, but when we look at Lydia, whose upbringing and shaping of character has been in your charge, neither can you."

"Oh! That is just like you to blame me," cried Mrs. Bennet, bursting into tears, "when it was you who let Lydia go to Brighton in the first place, you who consented to the marriage."

Mr. Bennet smiled. "And you wanted none of it, my dear?"

Mrs. Bennet continued to weep noisily. "I have only ever wanted, as any decent mother would, what is best for my girls. I only want what is best for them now, I see no wrong in that."

Rarely did Mr. Bennet raise his voice, but now he did so. "If you see no wrong in forcing one of your girls to give up her own child while another is burdened with it, then so be it, but let me say this now, I will happily accept the blame for all other misfortunes in our lives, but I take no part in this."

"You infuriate me for your own amusement, Mr. Bennet, I am quite sure you do, but in your heart you must know I am right, if only I were listened to more, half of these disasters would never have happened."

Mr. Bennet could bear no more of his wife's accusations. "But other tragedies may very well have happened in their place. You would have had my dear little Lizzy marry Mr. Collins, remember?"

Mrs. Bennet's face reddened. "Would that have been such a catastrophe? No indeed, a clergyman may have taught her some compassion at least, she may not have lived so high, I admit, but there we are, I do not wish to be reminded of unfulfilled dreams."

"And I thought Mr. Darcy's ten thousand a year was fulfillment enough for all your dreams, Mrs. Bennet."

"Oh! you make me out to be a hard creature. Fortune is not everything you know, besides, I refuse to waste time letting you argue with me. There are matters requiring attention, I have done more than my part in organizing everything, you will write to your daughter or I will never speak to you again." With that, Mrs. Bennet stormed from the library slamming the door shut.

Mr. Bennet chuckled to himself and spoke aloud. "If my quill should break and my inkwell run dry I should be pained to conjure up even the smallest feeling of disappointment." But, despite his irreverent attitude to his wife, he set about writing to Elizabeth with a very heavy heart.

Some days later the four o'clock post brought the scream of despair that Elizabeth had dreaded would break the quiet. Her hands shook as she read the news.

Longbourn, Hertfordshire
25th April 1813

My Dearest Lizzy,

Loathed to trouble you though I am, your mother insists that I write and tell you her demands. If I were a stronger man, I could endure her persistent fussing better, but alas, you know my character well enough, Lizzy, I cannot suffer much more of her ranting without going out of my wits myself. Your mother says you must take Lydia at Pemberley and you must take her soon before her confinement is the talk of Meryton. I know, my dear, that you must think there is no scandal in a married woman being with child, but your mother looks farther into the future. A fatherless child, with an ill-fated mother, has poor prospects indeed. We are too old to set about raising the poor wretch and your mother says Lydia would not manage it alone. According to her, your part in the matter will be to keep Lydia and her condition concealed in Derbyshire until the child is born. Thereafter you will take over its upbringing as if it were a babe sprung from your own happy marriage, and there we have the solution, Lizzy.

Oh, pray I have the required strength to deal with your mother, she behaves so demented she would put King George to shame—God save him. I do not need to outline to you the complications of this situation, and it is pointless my doing so to Mrs. Bennet as well you can imagine. Her heart is set on this arrangement and it pains me to put such demands upon you, my child, but there it is, I am too weak to defy your mother for too long and therefore know you will detect the tone of defeat in this correspondence. I take the cowardly course once more, Elizabeth, and rely upon your bravery, though Lord knows where you get it from, to sustain us. You must know also that Lydia is resigned to the decision, though none of it was of her making.

I do not envy you, my dear, that you have the task of asking your husband to consent to raise Wickham's child as his own. I dare not imagine that anyone could make a more insulting request of the man and therefore await your response to this letter with a solemn heart. For my part I have agreed to make this request of you on your mother's behalf.

Please note this, I place you under no obligation to comply or even consider the requests outlined. Your foresight should afford you some protection from the events that now unfold. Your mother is, of course, ignorant to your own previous anticipation of Lydia's ruin and remains unaware of your husband's role in her initial salvation. I outline these final details in order to detach myself from the intentions in this letter. I need not tire you further with lengthy explanations of the furor that blights the peace here at Longbourn only to say; to be in York amongst the Luddites would afford me respite.

You have, as always, my very dearest love,

Papa

Darcy paced while his wife read the letter but could not contain his concern for long. "What of Longbourn, Elizabeth? Your sister? I hope you have not had more bad news."

Elizabeth held back tears. "I do not know how to explain it," she said.

"What has happened? You cannot shock me, I am accustomed to expect the worst where Wickham has an association," he said.

"This is the very worst. It is ridiculous, insulting. I fear it *will* shock you," she said walking to the window.

Darcy turned Elizabeth to face him and put his hands firmly on her shoulders. She began to cry openly and lay her head on his chest in defeat. "Wickham is like the vilest of curses, a foul spell cast over both our families. Can we ever be free of him?"

Darcy stroked his wife's hair gently and whispered, "Come now, I cannot have you distressed, what are you afraid of? What can be so grave? Let me help you, ask anything of me, my love."

Elizabeth lifted her face to meet his eyes which were full of love and concern. "I ask nothing of you for myself, but my mother... " she became quietly angry, "*my mother*, who knows nothing of your past experience of Wickham, demands the impossible of you."

"In what way? If I can help then I shall, Elizabeth. What can be so impossible?"

Elizabeth wept quietly now and settled herself wearily on a lovers' seat by the window, her face was pale as she gazed out over the grounds. Darcy took the letter from her and read it. When he had finished, he sat next to his wife and took her hand. She smiled but it was a weak smile. "You do not wish to reject me, even now, when I seem always to bring you trouble?" she said quietly.

Darcy shook his head, never moving his eyes from her face. "I do not wish to reject you, Elizabeth," he said firmly, "and these troubles we have must be shared, they are the result of unfortunate circumstance, they are not brought about by you."

"Then you are not angry?" she asked, searching his face for signs of rage.

"Oh yes, I am angry, Elizabeth, but not with you, nor with Lydia or your parents. Your father displays a decency in his letter that I can only respect. He valiantly attempts to hide behind the image of cowardice, when in fact he is showing understanding and wisdom."

"But you are angry with Wickham," she said quietly.

A determined expression came suddenly like a fire across his handsome features and set a blaze in his eyes. He spoke quietly but with conviction. "Yes, with Wickham," he spat the name, "always with Wickham, but I will defeat him, one day I will, I will not have him hurt those dear to me."

He stood and paced the room again, stopping by the fireplace, the letter still in his hand, he raised it to look again at the paper as if some answer or enlightenment lay therein. Still staring at its content he spoke. "Write directly to Longbourn, I will arrange a carriage to collect your sister in seven days," he said.

Elizabeth went to stand but he was by her and guided her back into the seat, taking both her hands he said resolutely, "You see, I do not wish to reject you, you are innocent in all this." He swallowed hard and thought for a moment before continuing. "Innocent, like a blameless child, I could not reject innocence and claim to be a man. Tell your parents and Lydia we will take the child, Lord knows there is room in our house and our hearts." With that, he left the room and went to his groom to have his mount made ready.

What a man he had become, so softened by Elizabeth. Ruled only by passion and, despite his better judgment, he would accept and raise Wickham's child as his own. As his father had done before him with Wickham himself. The coincidence did not escape him, it alarmed him but he was beyond the point in his life where appearances or impropriety were his main concerns. His concerns now were his wife's happiness, their own child and Lydia's. He rode the grounds and stopped to look back at the house, memories of his past dealings with George Wickham came rapidly to him. "History will not repeat itself, I shall make sure of it." He rode off into the woods; the powerful, rhythmic pounding of his stallion's hooves on the forest floor momentarily drowned the rapid beating of his angry heart.

CHAPTER 14

"I have faults enough, but they are not, I hope, of understanding. My temper I dare not vouch for. It is, I believe, too little yielding, certainly too little for the convenience of the world. I cannot forget the follies and vices of others so soon as I ought, nor their offenses against myself. My feelings are not puffed about with every attempt to move them. My temper would perhaps be called resentful. My good opinion once lost is lost forever."

———◦◦◦◦———

Before too long events became more complicated at Pemberley; Darcy and Elizabeth made arrangements for Lydia's arrival to take place the day after Lady Catherine's proposed departure on the ninth day of May. But the evening before their leaving, Anne de Bourgh's health deteriorated and Lady Catherine announced that they would remain in Derbyshire until such time as a significant improvement could be seen.

"The physician is adamant that she should not be moved, tell my nephew I shall be staying another two weeks at least, Anne will travel better once the climate has improved," she told Mrs. Reynolds.

Lydia was to arrive on the tenth.

In private Elizabeth spoke to Darcy. "Do you suppose Lydia's condition will be noticeable yet?" She looked down at her own figure. "I am not showing and, at worse, Lydia cannot be far advanced, I doubt Lady Catherine will notice."

Darcy smiled. "You are applying your own morals to your sister which is unwise, Lydia has had the advantage of living with Wickham in London prior to their marriage, she may be further advanced in her confinement than we imagine."

"If that is so, then let us hope Lady Catherine is only concerned with Anne at present." Elizabeth looked weary. "It is all so complicated, how to explain things, the surgeon, have you spoken to him?"

"Yes, he will be seen to come and examine you to confirm your condition, then we will make an announcement."

"Our happy announcement, forced upon us by such unhappy events," said Elizabeth quietly.

"He will also examine Lydia to determine how long it is until the birth."

Elizabeth looked thoughtful. "And I shall have twins?"

"It is the only way, the child must be as our own, there can be no difference in rank or connection or fortune. Wickham's resentment and vicious character were forged by the extremes of such division, I will not let it be so again with two more young lives."

Elizabeth shook her head. "But the temptation, the natural feelings of preference towards one child, how does one combat the most genuine of feelings, how does one love another's child? I believe I can love my sister's child with relative ease and a good deal of real feeling. The infant will be of my own blood and I comfort myself that I have something of a start towards loving properly. But you, will you be able to look into the eyes of your enemy's child and still give love?"

"I have to, Elizabeth, I have no choice, you must let me deal with this my own way, trust me, there can be no interference from Wickham in this, that he knows nothing of her condition is vital."

"He knows nothing at all, for once Lydia's childish and flirtatious attitudes have had a good result, she was not going to tell Wickham until it could be hidden no more." Seeing her husband's inquisitive expression, Elizabeth paused and then went on, "she probably thought she would not be allowed to go dancing."

"And neither shall you," said Darcy stroking his wife's abdomen gently. "Love and duty you see, Elizabeth, we will raise one child through love, another through duty, but the treatment and the outcome shall be the same, none shall know the difference."

Elizabeth was tired and could not find the strength to raise any argument to her husband's points. She felt neither playful nor angry but stayed in that most distressing of states, indifference. Her own condition meant she grew fatigued easily and it was in both her mind and Darcy's that the decision they had made was to have a lasting and dramatic effect on all their lives.

And so it came about that Lydia arrived and was soon after visited by the physician, though great lengths were gone to to ensure that this fact remained concealed. Always, in the back of her mind, Elizabeth puzzled over the identity of Wickham's collaborator. But the subject was not raised by her or Darcy, even Jane did not refer again to it and Lydia, who perhaps could not bear the insult of recalling it, showed no inclination to do so. To speak of the matter may serve as an incantation, the mention of Wickham's name may conjure him up from invisibility. It was not wanted by any of them to have him back again and all preferred to mislead themselves in the belief of his nonexistence. Besides which, the matters requiring immediate attention provided ample distraction. It was a thankful discovery that the sisters' confinements seemed to coincide in progress, though the physician stated that there was no guarantee that delivery would take place concurrently. "The child determines these things itself," he declared. "But I would say we do not have long to wait, five weeks short of a score should do it."

Darcy shook the doctor's hand. "Thank you again, Mr. Drummond, I know I can be assured of your confidentiality."

The old man nodded. "Glad to help in any way I can, my boy, I attended your mother when she brought you and your sister into the world. This is the natural sort of progression a surgeon relishes."

Darcy smiled; the old man's almost paternal affection did not go unnoticed. Looking fondly at Darcy again he said, "I shall arrange for Mrs. Quinn as nurse when the time is near. Good day to you, sir."

The announcement was made, resulting in heightened feelings of one sort or another in the house.

Georgiana was thrilled. Caroline Bingley feigned goodwill but spoke privately to Lady Catherine. "I would not insult you, ma'am, by offering congratulations or claiming any personal delight at the news."

Lady Catherine nodded gravely. "I appreciate your candor Miss Bingley, I do not take kindly to falsehood, this is vexing but inevitable news, *this* is how the strain is weakened. It heralds the destruction of all that is right and proper, to think I should witness in my lifetime the mingling of such very different bloodlines, it lays a disquiet deep within."

Caroline smiled sympathetically. "And you must endure the indignity of suffering everyone else's misplaced pleasure while Anne is so unwell."

"Indeed you are right," said Lady Catherine, "it is unfortunate that we cannot leave and get away from all this tiresome celebration, but Anne's well-being is my priority, I shall bear it as best I can until she improves." She added viciously, "Though I do not know that I shall be able to tolerate too much of this other sister who is just arrived, I know of her, of course, but then who does not?"

"I believe she is unwell, your ladyship, the physician visited her last evening after seeing Eliza, though I do not know what it is that ails her."

Lady Catherine seized the opportunity to voice her dislike of the Bennets once more. "The same thing that infects the rest of the wretched family, rampant disregard for their superiors and ill-manners of every kind, the most severe of diseases. I am only thankful it is not contagious outside their own susceptibility." She sat back and lifted her head in order to view the grounds out of the window, looking down her nose she narrowed her eyes and said, "Dear Pemberley, such sullied activities are an insult to its elegance, that such scandals and impropriety should take place within its distinguished architecture is a disgrace."

Lady Catherine was kept occupied, if not amused, by the latest revelations, and on finding Elizabeth alone in the grounds one day made to join her and take a turn on the lawn. She commented first on the fact that she could only walk in shade, going on to mention how the sun should be avoided at all costs.

"For it is most unbecoming to see a woman's face made brown by over-exposure." She eyed Elizabeth archly. "The ladies of our family have all had exceptionally delicate complexions, made all the more pleasing by abstaining from the elements."

Elizabeth detected Lady Catherine's disapproval of the high color that overspread her own features. Embarrassment, her unrelenting love of the outdoors, and a recent tendency to feel flustered all, in equal part, had caused the bloom in her cheeks. To defend herself she could manage no more than a few words.

"I dearly like a walk in the sun, but I choose shade now, I have more than my own well-being to consider," said she.

This was too much for Lady Catherine. "Expect no felicitations on my part, your condition will be greeted with despair by our family and while I cannot change the situation, do not think me accepting of it."

"Your feelings and considerations are of little consequence to me, Lady Catherine, you must know me well enough to realize that. As for your family, it is now my own and contrary to your expectations and wishes, I believe my news will be greeted most kindly."

Lady Catherine angered quickly. "Should my nephew hear you speak to me in this manner he would be most perplexed, you are devoid of manners, young lady."

"If my husband heard you speak to me thus he would be equally perplexed for you appear to be as lacking in social graces as you deem me to be."

Lady Catherine quickened her pace as Elizabeth made to walk away, she called out harshly, "Hear me out, you discourteous creature. I have said before that you mean to ruin him, and it seems you shall. This child, your offspring, will dilute the history of which our family is proud. That weak progeny of your kind should spring from such admirable origins as our own is quite detestable."

Elizabeth stopped and turned abruptly to face her tormentor. "Lady Catherine," she said, "if those are your rules then in making such judgments you surely lay censure at your own late husband's feet. Anne is, and always has been, a sickly girl, I dare not suggest that you take responsibility for this inadequate inheritance, therefore I must ask, did you marry beneath you, ma'am?"

Lady Catherine stared at Elizabeth; her tone was harsh with incredulity. "How dare you speak ill of my husband, if you knew your history better, if you had taken the time to research the family you have had the good fortune to secure yourself in you would know that Sir Lewis de Bourgh was a respected man. He was well-connected in every conceivable way. My daughter's physical fragility is not a sign of ill breeding, contrary to your insulting suggestion, it is a sure indication of the purity of her lineage."

Elizabeth smiled. "It is a confusing game that you engage in, Lady Catherine, I cannot understand the rules, on the one hand frailty and weakness are the result of poor breeding, on the other a sign of nobility. I have discussed with you before the equality of my marriage to your nephew. Surely I need not elaborate upon it, only to say that these connections you speak so highly of are now my connections, whether you like it or not, but at least I have the satisfaction of knowing I made those connections because of love, not duty nor the happy chance of a fortunate birthright. I doubt you have known love in the way I do, and I am sure you never will and I pity you for it. You can dislike me all you wish, your ladyship, but you will not break me." Elizabeth walked away quickly. Her heart was pounding fiercely in her chest and the feeling threatened to overcome her. She did not desire altercations with Lady Catherine, but she was too forthright to stand by and hear her without reasonable defense. She knew she should not allow herself to become so impassioned, so furious, but felt unequal to the task of controlling the vehemence of her feelings.

CHAPTER 15

"Unhappy as the event must be for Lydia, we may draw from it this useful lesson: that loss of virtue in a female is irretrievable, that one false step involves her in endless ruin, that her reputation is no less brittle than it is beautiful, and that she cannot be too much guarded in her behavior towards the undeserving of the other sex."

───◦◦◦───

From the time of her arrival Lydia had kept to her bed, the travel having taken what little energy she had, she was oblivious to the startling array of feelings that pervaded Pemberley. In her new state of womanhood, she seemed more childlike than ever. Her Aunt Gardiner took charge of her care and, as was the woman's manner, proved to be discretion itself. Elizabeth concealed her own misgivings about Lady Catherine when she visited her sister.

"You are comfortable, Lydia?"

Lydia nodded and huffed impatiently. "To think how I've longed to be back at Pemberley and now here I am, and I cannot enjoy any of the fun."

Elizabeth shook her head. "You must bear it as best you can, we must be adults about this, besides there are no balls or special occasions, this must be a time for rest, for both of us."

Lydia groaned. "You sound like Mary. Where is Mary? You would think she could see me, her own sister, she spends all her time with Anne de Bourgh and never thinks of her family."

Elizabeth smiled. "Come now, Lydia, you never actively sought Mary's companionship before, petty jealousy is not reason enough to seek it now, you will have to make do with me. Besides we have a secret and must keep it so."

"Do you not trust me to keep quiet, Lizzy?"

"I must trust you, Lydia, I have little choice, but I would have you admit that you have been guilty in the past of revealing confidences when you should not. You must not berate me for fearing you may do so again."

"I shall not expose myself," Lydia exclaimed. "I do not want the truth known, I do not want to know it myself, I want the business done with and finished so I can have a chance at life again, I have had a dreadful time, it simply is not fair."

"Then I shall rely on your silence," said Elizabeth.

"Yes do, I can do no more than have this child and hand it to you for a chance in life, it is a great sacrifice, Lizzy, I hope you know that."

"Oh Lydia, believe me, I know of sacrifice," said Elizabeth sadly.

Elizabeth, as ever, was astonished by her sister's apparent lack of proper feeling. That she could be so cold about the most serious of matters and so impassioned by frivolity was a mystery to her.

"My sister thinks little of the child," she said to Darcy when they were alone together again.

"She is but one herself, there is your explanation," said he with gravity.

"But it pains me to hear her indifference."

"I say be gladdened by it. Would you prefer that her heart break when she abandons her own baby? No Elizabeth, that would be more than you could stand, her immaturity is preferable, she will recover quickly and seek the pleasures in life with scant thought for her son or daughter. We have that as reassurance, my love."

"And little else," said Elizabeth with conviction.

"You do not regret our decision?"

Elizabeth thought for a while. "I cannot regret doing what is right, and I shall do so without resentment, but I wish it had been different, I wish there was not this repeated need for you to rescue my family."

Darcy looked at his wife, his eyes fixed upon hers, the resonance of his voice stirred her emotions. "You have been my salvation, Elizabeth," he said, "therefore I shall stand by you or rescue you or your family whenever the need is there."

"But I did not save you from anything so desperate," she protested.

"Ah, but pride creates distance and distance in turn causes loneliness which breeds its own desperation." He looked directly at Elizabeth. "You showed me the possibility of experiencing proper feeling, you reminded me that I was set out in life to be a gentleman above all else and you proved to me, when no other could, that I had failed. I will not fail again and I will not fail you."

Elizabeth put her head in her hands, her emotions soaring from deep within, her husband's strength and power humbled her almost to tears, but she lifted her head and with eyes just moistened she looked at him and knew that between them all the wrongs in the world could be made right no matter how often others might attempt to put them asunder.

CHAPTER 16

*"But the wife of Mr. Darcy must have such extraordinary
sources of happiness necessarily attached to her situation,
that she could, upon the whole, have no cause to repine."*

Mr. Bennet had always accepted that he must endure his wife's
rantings, and when they first had Darcy and Elizabeth's announcement she flew about the place in a state of euphoria.

"You see, Mr. Bennet," she said boastfully, "this is all working
out just as I planned, indeed it is better. Oh, that is just like Lizzy to
be sly and keep her news a secret. But there we are, her confinement is most convenient for Lydia."

Mr. Bennet looked at his wife over the rim of his spectacles. "I am
glad to know you greet Lizzy's news with such heartfelt affection."

"Mr. Bennet, if I was in the habit of letting my emotions run
away with me I do not know what would have become of us all.
Someone has to keep a level head you know! You should be thankful I am not given to silly outbursts like some women," she said
firmly and with a change of expression she went on, "but listen to
me! Of course I am delighted, to think we should have grandchil-
dren born of such status, it will be Jane next you know, now there
will be a child set for great things."

Mr. Bennet sighed. "Indeed, Mrs. Bennet, I am sure you are
right, and what design do you have for Jane's infant, shall you begin
by choosing the crib or the style of its bonnets before we have the
necessary confirmation, or do we rely on your well-tuned instincts
to predict yet another child's arrival?"

Mrs. Bennet was at once affronted by her husband's remark.
"Oh, Mr. Bennet," she reprimanded, "you would have everyone

believe me simple and meddlesome, I know you would, you mistake my meaning. I merely behave with the intuitive nature of any good mother or *grandmother* for that matter, I am only suggesting that Jane will follow Lizzy shortly, it is the way of things."

Mr. Bennet nodded. "I see, Mrs. Bennet, you would have it that no woman in the family is safe if conception be so contagious, perhaps you might call a physician to your own bedside for reassurance."

Mrs. Bennet gave her husband a look of exasperation. "You think it highly amusing that I demonstrate a natural care and understanding toward my daughters."

"Oh, I would not mock you for that, Mrs. Bennet, it is good news," said her husband, "but dare I suggest your maternal concerns might include Kitty? The child is not herself you know, I do believe she feels peeved that no scandals surround her."

Mrs. Bennet looked at her husband expectantly. "And what am I to do, shall I suggest she find some trouble or other? No indeed, she is only vexed that she misses out on Pemberley, she has the idea that it is all lightness and entertainment there. No! I am afraid she will just have to bear it. Besides, I need someone here to steady my nerves, you have not the first idea what anxiety all this has caused me," she said with exasperation and then, her mood lifting suddenly, she exclaimed, "oh! I must tell you, Mr. Collins is eager to be considered as a suitable clergyman for the baptism. I have told him to write to Lizzy directly if he is serious about the position before she has the opportunity of appointing an alternative."

"Mr. Collins, eh? He shows himself quite readily at the slightest scent of dilemma, he has quite a talent for it."

"Mr. Bennet! Our Mr. Collins is a decent man; it has not been easy for him or for Charlotte. Much as I resented the way she took him right from under Lizzy's nose, it is past, why should they not be given another chance? A baptism of such note would be just the thing to reestablish his position within the church."

"You are all kindness, Mrs. Bennet."

"Indeed I am, often to my own detriment, but there it is."

No sooner had Mr. Collins had the notion that he may have the chance of baptizing the Darcy heir than he began to regale his father-in-law with the marvelous possibilities this represented.

"You understand, Sir William," said he, "the great import of my securing such a position, and I flatter myself that I stand a substantially good chance of being selected as the appropriate clergyman due to my potent connections with the family."

Sir William Lucas looked bemused but nodded.

Mr. Collins went on, speaking fast and barely pausing for breath. "Confidentially, sir, I have, in the past, had reason for resentment, but my natural integrity and that demanded of me by the church dictate that any previous grievance on my part has resulted only in forgiveness. If that were not the case, I could not be so benevolent as to offer myself thus. It is my belief that every child is deserving of the full advantage of God's recognition, it is a sad fact that this vital ingredient of a proper upbringing can often be overlooked even by the most dedicated parents." He stopped briefly for breath and smiled smugly. "It is part of my crusade as a minister to ensure that these oversights are amply compensated for. You see, I take the view that should I christen the Darcy child, I should thereafter devote myself as much as possible to making its spiritual development my own mission."

"Well, I wish you the best of luck," said Sir William who meant what he said with complete sincerity, for should his son-in-law happen to secure such an involvement in Derbyshire, he himself would be relieved of the intrusion of the odious man's presence at Lucas Lodge.

Charlotte met her husband's idea of taking it upon himself to visit Pemberley with a little astonishment. "I think you should write, as Mrs. Bennet suggests, to enquire about making a convenient appointment, would it not be considered discourteous that you offer no announcement of your arrival?" she said with concern.

Her husband gave her a condescending look. "My dear Charlotte, so often you seem to forget the very particular rights offered to clergymen. Certain rules and guidelines that apply to society on the whole do not always restrict a man of the cloth, I may travel where I see fit, when I see fit, for I believe that the Lord guides me to go where I am most needed."

Charlotte raised her eyebrows. "But the news from Pemberley does not hint at crisis, all is well I believe, I urge you to await a proper invitation."

Mr. Collins looked flustered. "Charlotte, though it always does damage to my affections for you when you find occasion to disagree with me I fear I must defy you in matters where I have the greater understanding. I shall make my arrangements to travel to Derbyshire tomorrow afternoon, if you are prepared to accompany me willingly then you may use the opportunity to visit Elizabeth, I am sure, now that she also is married that you will find you have a great deal in common."

"Indeed, it would be my greatest pleasure to see my friend again," his wife conceded, "but are we not imposing ourselves too readily, the birth of the child is some way off, the baptism more so. Would it not be prudent to avoid visiting prematurely?"

Mr. Collins showed further agitation at his wife's persistent questioning and his words of protest were heightened by the effect of his face becoming flushed and his speech more urgent. "Charlotte," he said nervously, "it is not too soon to offer our gracious felicitations, from which I shall divert matters to the question of the necessary blessing of the child. I must implore you to try to comprehend that, in this, I cannot be too hasty. The matter, if left unattended, could result in an alternative, and dare I say, less worthy appointee taking charge. No, my dear, it is your place to accept the wisdom of my decisions without protest, if you resist then I shall sadly have to consider making my journey alone. I feel I must caution you that this would be a poor indictment of the sanctity of marriage."

Unable to accept the adverse reflection on herself and her choice of husband that her absence might imply, Mrs. Charlotte Collins consented to accompany Mr. Collins to Derbyshire despite her innermost feelings that her husband was making a grave mistake.

CHAPTER 17

"I have been used to consider poetry as the food of love," said Darcy.

———◦◦◦———

News of Anne de Bourgh's improvement was gratefully heard by Darcy and Elizabeth. Lady Catherine, with a tone of disproportionate gravity, informed the latter that her daughter's health, although far from restored, was steady enough for the party to consider returning to Kent before the sixteenth. This came as glad news for Elizabeth whose spirits were further lifted by an express that arrived from Netherfield for Caroline Bingley informing her that her sister Louisa requested she return to Hertfordshire as Mr. Hurst was in very poor health and her presence would be a great comfort. To be rid, almost in one instance, of all disagreeable guests was fortunate indeed.

Caroline was not properly impressed by the news of Mr. Hurst's ill-health; her feelings for her brother-in-law were of an unremarkable kind but she was not loathe to leave Pemberley either once she heard the news of Lady Catherine's imminent departure. For what would the place hold for her now other than the cruel and constant reminder that Darcy was most definitely impervious to her charms? She had endeavored, on several occasions, to test her allurements and his susceptibility to them, but found him unmoved by her leaning in close to him or looking at him in a way she thought beguiling. Her esteem depended on his attention, for she was that make of woman who judged her worth by the success of her flirtations. She was attractive and elegant to be sure, certainly not devoid of feminine charm but Darcy was too smitten with Elizabeth to notice Caroline's teases and too honorable a man, if ever he did detect them, to respond.

There lay the matter, with Darcy going about the world in apparent ignorance of the strength of Miss Bingley's desire for him. Elizabeth could not help but be made aware of Caroline's craving and although she could not claim to like Miss Bingley or admire her personality, on this point she consented to understand her. For who could avoid, on close and repeated acquaintance, becoming besotted with him when it was, it seemed, an involuntary result of knowing him? She pitied Caroline. Wretched being! Poor animal indeed! What torment to have the pleasure of looking at him, of hearing him, but never touching his hair or feeling the warmth of his embrace. The agony that must come from watching him talk, seeing his mouth move and fix into one of his reluctant smiles and only know his kiss and affections in dreams. The lovesick covetous cat would steal him away if she only could, I shall wave her goodbye with civility but I am not sorry to see her go, thought Elizabeth.

And so it was that Darcy and Elizabeth were quietly pleased to be ridding themselves of the most tiresome of their guests, they spoke nothing of their sentiments openly but they anticipated the departures eagerly.

"We shall have some peace at last," said Elizabeth quietly to herself that night and how she longed for it, depended upon it for the full restoration of her character. Oh, to exist again with the unguardedly natural, uninhibited way that so defined her.

To birdsong and light she awoke the next morning making the joyous calculation that another day heralded the departure of Lady Catherine and Caroline Bingley. It had been impossible to remain indifferent to their abuse. But in knowing that they would soon be gone, she was better able to tolerate them than ever she had been; for all troubles and ailments are infinitely more endurable when their relief is in sight and even the sourest of folk are made, in retrospect, so much more acceptable, if not faultless, by their absence. It soon seemed to Elizabeth that alleviation of any kind was to be short-lived, for before she had the chance of enjoying respite from her unfavored guests' departure, she was forced to endure the arrival of unexpected visitors, Mr. and Mrs. William Collins.

She was naturally happy to see Charlotte, her behavior in every way affirmed this, but even so, the Collins's unforeseen arrival made her wary. Mr. Collins, whose confidence in the success of his plans had inflated somewhat during the journey from Kent, found all his overblown feelings of assurance quickly deflated when he learned that Lady Catherine was still present at Pemberley.

"Resist the urge to reproach me for this oversight, Charlotte, I had surmised from my last correspondence from Mary that the de Bourgh party would be returned to Rosings over a week ago," said he.

His wife was quick to reveal what she had learned from Elizabeth. "Reliable though Mary is, Anne's constitution is not, that explains the extension of their stay. Thankfully their departure is imminent, I for one do not look forward to reacquainting with Lady Catherine, I shall avoid it if I can."

Avoidance of Lady Catherine proved impossible, it had not escaped her notice that Mr. Collins had arrived and she deemed it a necessary part of her duty to summon the clergyman and his wife for a discussion. She observed the pair with a harsh expression in her eyes. Presently, the examination complete, she concluded that the deterioration of their character, since losing her patronage, was markedly obvious. Finally she spoke. "Mr. Collins, I dare not imagine that you contrived to visit Pemberley in order to orchestrate your way into my path."

In Lady Catherine's company Mr. Collins quickly lost sight of any sense of pride and reverted without hesitation to his former subservient style of address. He bowed his head in an attitude of apology. "Indeed no, your ladyship, I was unaware of your presence here." He made an attempt at commiseration. "May I take this opportunity to say how very sorry I was to hear that Anne was taken unwell?"

Lady Catherine turned immediately to Charlotte. "Your husband seems unable to conceive that I do not intend to accept his sympathy or any offer of a renewal of our acquaintance. Is he so foolish as to misunderstand the reason for my demanding your presence?"

Charlotte replied, "No, ma'am, I am sure he is not, indeed, would not make such a presumption, we came here merely to offer congratulations to Mr. and Mrs. Darcy on their glad news, I can assure you we will make every effort to avoid inconveniencing you while you are here."

"I have endured inconvenience enough from my acquaintance with you, I do not intend to suffer further insult. It is most unfortunate for me that our paths have crossed once again, though I see no reason why they should." Now she turned her gaze on Mr. Collins. "On what grounds do you reconnect yourself with your cousin Elizabeth? I imagine notions of personal advancement govern you."

Mr. Collins swallowed hard and made an attempt at composure, but he felt at that instant that the woman had read his mind and could see his strategy. "Madam, whatever your opinions of me, as a worshipful woman you will understand that I come purely to offer my blessings on this happiest of occasions."

Lady Catherine was unimpressed. "You have no permanent position with the church as yet, I understand? You should know, Mr. Collins, that I am greatly respected by my nephew, if you are thinking of trying to win his approval for your own advantage I shall ask you now not to attempt it. You will merely be wasting your time. I have considerable influence over family matters." Before Mr. Collins could make any further comment Lady Catherine demanded that he and his wife, discomposed by embarrassment, take their leave.

Elizabeth learned this latest of Lady Catherine from Charlotte, but she was not surprised by it, she smiled at her friend's grave expression. "Do not worry yourself unduly, Charlotte, Lady Catherine's influence is not so powerful as she claims." She spoke playfully to cheer her companion, "After all, I am mistress of Pemberley, am I not? That she could not prevent although I believe her efforts to do so were unrelenting. No, let me urge you not to be worried, for what privileges can Lady Catherine take from you?"

"You are right, Lizzy, we have long since lost her patronage."

"Then you see, Charlotte, she cannot take what is already gone."

Charlotte thought for a while. "I hope you do not mind us coming here unannounced, I feel it was so inappropriate."

Elizabeth laughed. "Indeed it was! I was surprised I admit, but I am not insensible to the fact that it was not the way you would have it."

"Oh, Lizzy, you know Mr. Collins too well for his own good," said Charlotte wistfully, and, looking at her friend in earnest, she said, "and that is why you could not marry him."

Elizabeth tried to hide her concern. "I could not have married anyone but Fitzwilliam."

"You are indeed happy, Lizzy, I can see it."

Elizabeth smiled and wished she could feel the same or at least say the same for Charlotte but it was impossible.

Darcy greeted the news of Mr. Collins's arrival with resignation and his discourse verged on resentful. "Are we to have court jesters appear next, Elizabeth?" he protested. "I can hardly think that Pemberley is an inadequately appointed house, but it lately feels overcrowded with all the comings and goings." He sat by Elizabeth who was becoming ever more sensible of the fact that, once more, the improprieties of her family might result in making her husband wary.

"I agree, it seems we have had little peace, and little chance to enjoy Pemberley for ourselves."

Darcy smiled fondly. "The tranquillity of the earlier weeks of our marriage was a blessing though, Elizabeth." He ran his finger gently across her cheek. "We will have such times again, my love," he said, his voice was as determined as her feelings were unsure.

By noon the following day, Mr. Collins had requested an address with Mr. Darcy who was reluctant to indulge the man but saw fit to oblige him as a means to ensure his imminent departure. Elizabeth consented to attend the address and sat quietly with the intention of allowing her husband control of the discourse. In every way that Darcy was handsome, Mr. Collins was ill-favored. Where one man's features were fine, the other's were markedly undefined and weak. It was not a contrast that went unnoticed by Darcy and, although he rarely consciously called on his much admired physical attributes for gain or playfulness, he did not resist the temptation to stand at his full height when he addressed Mr. Collins. Darcy's correct, elevated air was further enhanced by Mr. Collins's own stooped and subordinate bearing and it afforded him the advantage of looking down at the clergyman when he spoke to him.

"I will get straight to the point by asking the purpose of your visit, sir," said Darcy. His voice was measured and calm, with an undertone of superiority.

Mr. Collins held his hands together as if in prayer, had he maintained this posture it would have fared better for him but he could not contain the inner feelings of expectation that fueled his thoughts and began to rub his hands together as if anticipating some reward or favor. Darcy noted the man's affectations with derision and impatience. "Mr. Collins," he said firmly, "I must tell you I have many pressing matters of business that demand my attention. That I am affording you this address in turn means I am depriving other matters of my concentration, please do not repay my generosity by wasting my time."

Mr. Collins smiled. "Oh, Mr. Darcy, sir, that was not my intention at all, my procrastination stems only from a desire to convey, in a manner of utmost reverence, my deepest felicitations to you and your wife on the news of your happy forthcoming event."

Mr. Collins looked at Elizabeth, and seeing her catch his eye, gave her a sheepish smile. The dissimilarity between the two men could not escape her attention. Her thoughts briefly settled on the startling realization that had she been a girl more influenced by her mother's wishes she would have been in the unhappy position to be married to the unhandsome man that stood before her, a man who repulsed her fiercely, instead of the distinguished and desirable man who had won her heart. She was no longer truly listening to the conversation but observed the two men in discourse. Darcy's excellent features seeming more so now to her than ever. Mr. Collins's appearance was shown, in the company of such superiority, to be a curious mix of hideousness and stupidity.

When at last Elizabeth emerged from her reverie, she found that her husband was addressing Mr. Collins once more. "I speak for myself and my wife when I say we shall not be considering your proposals, Mr. Collins. Matters of this kind are traditionally dealt with by the longstanding members of the clergy affiliated to my family. It would be remiss of me not to point this out to you at this earliest opportunity, my doing so, I hope, will have saved you a great deal of trouble. There can be no reconsidering the subject; any children of mine will be christened at St. Giles. It is historically known to be the case. I am surprised you were not aware of it."

Elizabeth was all astonishment. Mr. Collins cannot seriously have thought he would be appointed to baptize the Darcy heir! The clergyman's embarrassment was clear; his face was flushed and flustered. Lost for words and altogether fully aware that he had been rebuked he stood to leave the room but his departure was halted by Mr. Darcy's saying, "I am most grateful for your offer of congratulations on the anticipated arrival of our child, Mr. Collins, please do convey my thanks to your good wife."

Mr. Collins nodded as graciously as a red-faced, rejected man could and departed without further comment.

Elizabeth raised her eyebrows at her husband, her spirits lifted. "You could not have spoken plainer, I admire you for it, but Fitzwilliam I confess to feeling a small measure of diversion at your reproaching my cousin and I am ashamed to admit to relishing it. He is such a silly individual!" she cried. "Oh, if I could only be as good as you. I confess I should not have thought to thank Mr. Collins for his good wishes, that you deigned to do so humbles me."

"Good manners were made a priority of my upbringing, Elizabeth, but one cannot thrive on courteousness alone, I often wish less attention had been paid to the honing of acceptable conduct and more study made of nurturing my compassion."

Elizabeth knew too well where he was leading; she was accustomed to her husband's habit of berating himself for any previous harsh behavior. She knew that it concerned him that his past conduct might be viewed as cold and he was always eager to display to her the dramatic changes in his character that had taken place. She looked at him with affection. "I find nothing lacking, you speak as if you had a cool heart or an unfeeling temperament, but I know this is not the case. Those that matter to you know of your generous and loving nature, you must not compare your own dignity with *my* freedom of spirit. Such comparisons do not bear scrutiny, I fear one or both of us will come out seeming deficient if we make too severe an examination of either of our characters." She swiftly put her hand to his cheek in a playful manner. "Besides which, I believe our opposed histories and personalities make for a particular kind of exhilaration in our relationship."

Darcy held his wife's gaze with a passionate stare. The more serious and brooding the set of his expression, the more she was enticed to tease him, she took in the firm line of his mouth and his captivating eyes and began to jest.

"I am surprised you have any time for even an ounce of compassion for any living soul when you have been so unfortunate as to procure such an ill-favored wife."

Darcy bristled at Elizabeth's comment although he knew she only mocked him. "What joke are you playing now, Elizabeth?" he asked.

Elizabeth stood tall and effected an expression of superiority, she lowered her voice and in a poor imitation of her husband she said through suppressed laughter, "She is tolerable, but not handsome enough to tempt me."

Darcy had her hands in an instant, he held them firmly, the anger in his eyes as much in jest as her teasing had been. "It is beneath you to mock an affliction in another, it is not your character."

"I have heard it said that you are without fault so what affliction of yours is it that I mock, sir?" Elizabeth said flirtatiously.

Darcy pulled her closer to him. "The blindness that prevented me from seeing what you really are."

Elizabeth relished his closeness and set out to further antagonize him. "Pray tell me, what is it that I really am?"

Darcy would not relinquish his grip, he pulled his arms further and tighter around her then raised her face to his and said, "What you really are is handsome, no, you are beautiful beyond the realms of imagination."

Elizabeth, as always, was stirred by their embrace and she said quietly, "Your words are worthy of Crabbe, sir."

Darcy spoke passionately. "You would inspire poetry in the coldest of hearts."

"Then I *can* tempt you, Mr. Darcy?" she said mischievously.

Her husband smiled knowingly. "Mrs. Darcy," he whispered, "the temptation is such that no other could imitate it." Then he kissed her with unbridled intensity and though he was ever conscious of Elizabeth's delicate condition, his desire recognized no limitation but the love in his heart meant that his every caress was one of tenderness.

CHAPTER 18

"I am grieved, indeed," cried Darcy, "grieved—shocked."

———◇◈◇———

Darcy's rejection of Mr. Collins's proposal was rebuke enough to inspire Charlotte in the pursuit of encouraging her husband to arrange their return to Lucas Lodge as soon as possible. William Collins was enraged but displayed none of his displeasure to anyone other than his wife. Charlotte bore the tedium of his grievances with admirable patience. No sooner were they seated in their departure carriage than his lament began. "Position in the church, it seems, governs more than mere dedication, my dear Charlotte."

Charlotte attempted to placate her husband. "George Holcombe is indeed graced with a high appointment in his parish, but it is not merely his status which secures the ceremony as his own, he is a devoted and respected man who, I understand, has been involved with Pemberley and the Darcy family for years."

Mr. Collins took his kerchief to mop his brow, he could not deny the truth in his wife's words, but he was all the same consumed with resentment at his own thwarted progress. Although it was Charlotte who had insisted upon their departure from Pemberley, on this point, the husband and wife were in agreement. William Collins wished to retreat from the site of his rejection as speedily as possible in the hope that he could forget his humiliation. Their carriage drew away from the house just moments after the de Bourgh party had done so. Lady Catherine had decided that no matter what fluctuations occurred regarding her daughter's health, she could bear no more of Pemberley. "I am grievously distressed by the theatricals therein," she said, casting her eye over the house as her carriage pulled away. "I am not sorry to take my leave."

Caroline Bingley, who was to travel some of her own journey in Lady Catherine's barouche, could only sympathize. "You share my sentiments, your ladyship," she said, "and did you notice Mr. Collins's ridiculous neckcloth? I do believe it was tied horse-collar style."

Lady Catherine nodded in agreement. "A most vulgar adornment, but unaccountably fashionable with the lower classes these days, I daresay due to their inability to tie one in any other style," she snapped.

Having offered the politest of farewells to their departing guests Elizabeth kissed Mary upon the cheek then she and Darcy watched as the carriages drew away. Neither husband nor wife waved, but once the parties were away, they turned slowly and walked hand-in-hand up the steps to the house. In the hall Elizabeth remarked upon the quiet.

"I have begun to fear peace, not for itself, but I am apprehensive of the discord it so often precedes," she said quietly.

On the road away from Pemberley and towards Lambton Mr. Collins's equipage closely followed Lady Catherine's barouche. The former privately enjoyed the status afforded to him by traveling not a quarter of a mile behind such a notable carriage, although he was not about to own the fact. It was universally known that Anne de Bourgh did not travel well; she seemed not to tolerate anything particularly well, but travel was deemed the greatest hindrance to her health and it was therefore expected that Lady Catherine would order her horsemen to halt frequently to allow her daughter the remedy of taking the air.

By the time the parties were not five miles from Pemberley and had reached the village of Lambton, Anne de Bourgh had taken the air three times. On each occasion the Collins's progress was delayed also, for although the road out of Derbyshire was good and wide enough to allow two carriages to pass, Mr. Collins thought better than to assume his equipage might take precedence over Lady Catherine's. His own horsemen had been duly informed of this matter and the subsequent delays made the journey tedious. On hearing his man call the horses to a halt for the fourth time Mr. Collins could not contain his exasperation.

"Oh, surely the girl cannot wish to take any more air, we have little chance of getting out of Derbyshire in reasonable time with these constant hindrances." He moved awkwardly to rise from his seat and extended his hand to his wife. "Come, Charlotte, we may just as well take the opportunity of God's pure air ourselves seeing as the chance is forced upon us." He stepped down from the carriage himself offering his wife little assistance. Narrowing his eyes to focus his view of the de Bourgh party he went on, "Oh, what is this all about? Some trouble on the road ahead, I cannot make it out, Anne is not taking a turn, no.... Oh, that is Miss Bingley getting out and...who is *that* person?" Charlotte was watching the scene with as much fascination as her husband, but her sight was better and she was, without difficulty, able to note that a figure on horseback was engaged in the office of talking with Caroline Bingley. She could see the man's features clearly and was able to ascertain his identity with as much conviction as was to be had at such a distance. Mr. Collins continued his objections.

"What is going on?" cried he. "Are they to slow everyone's progress with their partiality to giving directions to every lost traveler?"

Charlotte touched her husband's arm guardedly. "I do not think they give directions, Mr. Collins, you are mistaken." She paused and watched the man dismount and lean into the carriage and exchange words with Lady Catherine. She sighed and declared, "That man is not a traveler lost, I do believe he knows exactly where he is going."

Mr. Collins strained his eyes to focus his view of the man. "And what knowledge do you have of this stranger and his business, Charlotte?"

Charlotte's face was pale. With reluctance she professed, "That man is not a stranger Mr. Collins, he is Mr. Wickham. Mr. George Wickham."

Mr. Collins, satisfied that his wife had correctly identified the man as no other than George Wickham, again observed the scene played out ahead of him. This subsequent viewing confirmed all to Mr. Collins. Yes, it was Mr. George Wickham, he could see that now. For how much easier it is to see specifically when we are told exactly what it is we are looking at.

In watching the actions of those persons ahead of him, Mr. Collins could glean no details that might give indication of what the purpose of the meeting might be. Clear though the day was, it was impossible to judge if the brief discourse that ensued was one with angry overtures or if the exchange was a pleasant one. Before very long, he saw that Mr. Wickham had re-mounted his horse and the wheels of the de Bourgh carriage were once again set in motion to take them homeward. Charlotte could not bear to look from the carriage as the sound of hooves passed them but Mr. Collins pulled the curtain aside in time to see that the gentleman was, without doubt, George Wickham and he was heading in the direction of Pemberley with a look of grim determination upon his face.

CHAPTER 19

"When my eyes were opened to his real character—Oh! had I known
what I ought, what I dared, to do! But I knew not—I was afraid
of doing too much. Wretched, wretched mistake!"

With Lady Catherine and Caroline Bingley gone, Georgiana
Darcy was more inclined to show herself outside the music room,
for she too had quietly welcomed their departure. It must be
remembered that Miss Darcy, despite being naturally constrained,
was still young and appeared markedly so as timid girls often do.
Her manners were elegant and pleasing, and she was all that her
brother had ensured she would be, ladylike and accomplished. But,
like him, she was not naturally disposed to put herself forward to
those she did not know. The girl, like her brother, did not converse
easily with people with whom she was little acquainted, so when
she took it upon herself to go to Lydia's rooms to visit it was as
unexpected an occurrence for the recipient as it was for the visitor.
But Miss Darcy had been told the girl was sick, although she had
not the first notion of what ailed her, and felt very strongly that a
visit might help the invalid suffer the tedium of bed rest with some
fortitude.

Lydia was confined to her bed, a course of action that had little
to do with the physician's advice and more to do with the girl's
own determination to be as miserable and sorry for herself as
possible. She was emotionally frail from circumstance but rosy
enough in appearance. She sat up in bed; she had removed her
chemise and sat quite comfortably. She found herself very glad of
Georgiana's company for she was beginning to find her Aunt Gardiner's conversation and children tedious and exhausting respectively,

and although Lydia was not always intentionally unkind, she was often cruel by error. "Oh La! I am pleased to see you Georgiana, my aunt has no understanding of the kind of things that interest young women. I know I am a married woman, but Heavens, I am still closer to sixteen than I am seventeen." She looked at Georgiana. "The lace on your sleeve is very pretty."

"Thank you," said Georgiana. "I am trying to copy the style myself. I hope to fashion a large enough piece by September, if am successful I should like to make a gift of it to Elizabeth for the baby."

Lydia sighed heavily. "It is so boring being unwell, I should like to sit by the window, my aunt is determined that I should stay in bed for eternity, but I do not want to," she said defiantly pulling back her bedspread. She wrapped a shawl around her shoulders, and gave a brief examination of her arms. "I'm grown so blemished these days. I am sure I have not had such abominable freckles before. I shall tell Lizzy to give me a good dose of Gowland's lotion for I shall not be fit to be seen." Lydia's conversation was oft of little worth, unless complexions or bonnets are to be taken as serious subjects, but she was never lost for a topic, mostly she spoke about herself, therefore, with her vanity thus catered for, she could talk unchecked at length about everything that concerned her. When she had settled herself in a seat with a fine view of the grounds she turned to Georgiana. "You must be having as dull a time as I am, do you not long for a ball or some other amusement?"

Georgiana shook her head. "I am not at my best in large gatherings, I have not your confidence."

"Oh, my confidence is all very well, but it has not afforded me a great deal of luck." She looked again on Georgiana and said, "I wish I had been a quieter sort of girl, like you, perhaps then Wickham would not have singled me out as his favorite. Yes, I would infinitely prefer to be you, Georgiana, for I daresay my husband has scarcely ever noticed you exist."

Lydia Bennet was and always had been a girl too taken up with her own thoughts to really notice a great deal about those around her. The fact that Georgiana's countenance had paled dramatically had no effect on her; she went on regardless of her companion's obvious discomfiture. "You know my husband, of course," she continued, "but none knows him so well as I." With an eagerness to impress Georgiana with an appearance of worldliness, she rather falsely referred to her married state with a small measure of pride and a definite tone of superiority. "I should not even be speaking of it, but I have been treated very ill by Wickham and it is supposed I shall never see him again. Not that I anticipate it. I should not wish to see him," she said sourly.

Georgiana tried to divert Lydia by beginning a conversation about music, a subject in which she was well-informed enough to espouse, but it was to no avail. Her companion was set upon reminiscence.

"He is fearful handsome, as you know," she said remorsefully, "you cannot imagine, Georgiana, the joy when I first fell in love with him."

Georgiana gave a weak smile. "No, I am sure I cannot," said she. Her expression was downcast, for she did not need the assistance of imagination to allow her to know what it felt like to think herself in love with George Wickham. With distress and no other sentiment she recalled, in the privacy of her mind, her own infatuation with the man and wished heartily that she had not been so unfortunate to be reminded of it. She prayed Lydia would follow her lead and talk of other things, but the girl was determined to give Georgiana every detail, both good and bad, of her marriage.

This detailed account of Wickham was more than Georgiana would have wished to bear, but she was obliged to endure it and she feared the renewed picture of him she had in her mind would stay there a long time before fading. Still intent on reflection, Lydia took pleasure in her descriptions and seemed to gain some relief from them as if such recollections exorcised her demons. She gazed out of the window, but took in none of the impressive view it framed. She saw only the images in her mind's eye, only the visions created therein by the color of her words. And so, blinded with passion in equal part resentful and yearnful, she gave scant regard to the appearance of the well-featured gentleman who rode his horse with urgency into the grounds of Pemberley. He could have been any one of a hundred foreigners for all the regard she paid him, yet it *was* her husband George Wickham, and despite her own failure to recognize him, his arrival was noted by Georgiana Darcy with very real feelings of alarm and despair.

That George Wickham saw fit to present himself at Pemberley goes a fair way to give illustration of his character, of the deficient nature of his conscience, for he went through the world feeling neither guilt for his own misdemeanors nor gratitude for others' generosity to him. But, as ever was his manner, he carried himself with an air of decency that would only truly befit far more gentle-manlike fellows than he could ever contrive to be. This expert guise allowed him into people's affections and society alike. He gave such a convincing performance of honor and affability that not many were ever alerted to his true evils. Those who knew him well were few, and those who knew his history were fewer.

When Mrs. Reynolds noted Wickham's arrival her expression and her color changed all at once, she took on the look of a woman who had experienced the apparition of a specter. Quickly she sent the butler to receive him at the door with strict instructions to maintain him in the hallway to afford the master time to decide on appropriate action. She ran to the drawing room to her master and mistress, arriving, established etiquette abandoned, without knocking upon the door, and came upon them in a such a state of sickness as they had never before seen her in. Her words fought with her breath. "Oh, Mr. Darcy, sir," she cried, "*he* is come, sir, *Mr. Wickham*, here to Pemberley, Brooks has him in the hall."

Georgiana arrived now, her state of distress being far in excess of the housekeeper's. Elizabeth gestured for the girl to sit by her. Darcy stood abruptly and left the room. Elizabeth had never seen such a display from him; his face had turned white with fury. He was beyond that stage of agitation that colors a man's complexion red. Georgiana was pale and afraid, Elizabeth wished to comfort the girl but could not find the words to do so, she held her hand but it was not long before her thoughts ran to Lydia and what the consequences of seeing her husband might be.

"What of Lydia, what of the effect if *she* knows he is come?"

Georgiana shook her head. "I do not think she knows, we have been talking in her room, she tires now."

Elizabeth summoned Mrs. Reynolds and turned back to Georgiana. "Then we must ensure she sleeps. Take a draft to my sister, Mrs. Reynolds, make haste. Drink a glass of wine yourself, Georgiana, excuse me, I will return as soon as I can."

Elizabeth left the room but did not go far outside it; staying in the vestibule, she could clearly hear a confrontation. Darcy was enraged; his voice was not raised but was somehow deeper, graver, more determined.

"How dare you seek further assistance from me, I am long since done with you, Wickham," he said.

Now Wickham's voice was heard. "Indeed?" asked he with unfitting confidence. "Then you are foolish, do you think I should ask your help without first being confident that I had some way of guaranteeing it?"

"The vilest conduct is not beneath you!" cried Darcy, "I, above everyone else, am wholly aware of that, but what is this insurance you claim? What possible power could you have that would force my hand to your deliverance? Do not base your expectations on the assumption that I would be so susceptible to bribery as you are."

Wickham smiled. "Come now, Darcy, my old friend, no man is invulnerable, not even you. Hear me out, I do not wish to reveal truths that would damage you anymore than you would wish me to. You get me entirely wrong if you think I seek to injure you. I do not. My motive is the opposite; my intention is to conceal those truths that would be unflattering to you. You see, I have no resentment, I speak honorably."

"There is no honor in the supposed protection of a man if his defense must be bought, you make the mistake of judging my character by your own. I have nothing to conceal and therefore no reason to buy your silence."

"I concede, Darcy, your own conduct is rarely cause for scandal. I confess when compared with my own it seems you have not lived. Do not think I claim misdemeanors on your part, only a fool would suppose *you* defective. But in all things that matter in society we are judged by association and thereby your own impeccable conduct may still be sullied by another's less desirable behavior. You have sought perfection in all things and I daresay you have achieved it to some degree but if those connected to you are less scrupulous you may be subject to derision also."

Darcy's anger was shown in his expression and his stance was everything defensive. "I can think of no connection of mine, other than that which I have with you, that would be the cause of shame to me! You do not trouble me with your threats, you merely anger me with your presence. I demand an end to this conversation and suggest you take your leave."

"You resolve not to hear me out?" said Wickham. "Yet I am quite persuaded that you will wonder to what it is that I allude when I say that a certain lady near to you is manipulative, I might even say she is corrupt, the term is harsh but deserved, I believe this person to be a good way more dishonorable than you think me capable of being."

Darcy's eyes darkened and he stepped toward Wickham, his urge to strike and his instinct to refrain from doing so creating a fairly matched battle within him.

"Oh!" exclaimed Wickham, "you wish to attack me, Darcy, is that it? Why? Do you think I insult your Elizabeth or perhaps you worry that I harbor some depraved detail of our dear little Georgiana?"

Both men were pale, one with rage the other with fear. Wickham stepped back a pace but Darcy would allow no such escape and he strode toward the retreating coward so that the distance between them was once again uncomfortable. It was the first time Darcy's voice became significantly raised and the impact of it was not ineffectual. "Damn you! That you dare to speak of my wife and sister gives me reason enough to strike you, that I refrain from doing so is in your favor."

"I have it on good regulation that you are afraid of nothing, is your control the result of strength or cowardice?"

Darcy stared Wickham in the eye and caught the man's collar in his fist. He examined him with contempt; the tone of his voice was raw, passionate, and angry. "I am not afraid of you, Wickham. I am more afraid of myself, be warned, if you further antagonize me to brutality I will kill you without question," he said and, mindful of the ladies present in the drawing room, he lowered his tone again and demanded, "step outside, I do not want you or the continuation of this dispute in my house."

Wickham, visibly unsettled now by Darcy's fury, headed for the door but he cast his gaze around the features and elegance of the hall. "Your house," he said with emphasis, "is a distinguished property indeed, I fear a murder would scandalize both Pemberley and its master."

Once outside Darcy spoke again with disgust. "Your theorizing is pointless, but since you insist on the subject let me give you my view of it. The reward of such disgrace would be your removal from those I love, my own castigation would be a small price for such relief."

Wickham's composure had only briefly returned but now waned again and he turned to sentiment for his attack. "Darcy, we are old friends, boys grown up together but now apart, I confess to mourning the loss of our camaraderie."

"If you had truly valued it as you suggest, we should still be as brothers. But you abused, in every sense, the relationship you now lament the loss of. Any scant remainder of goodwill I have toward you exists as a result of your father being as fine a man as you thought mine to be. But you are a very long way from being worthy of their mention."

Wickham bowed his head, his stance indicative of remorse, but his appearance was so often the reverse of his feelings that Darcy was determined not to be deluded by it, though he felt his wrath to be significantly tempered by his adversary's look of helplessness. To the appearance of any passing observer, should there have been one, the two men who walked the park at Pemberley that afternoon could just as well be friends as enemies. Both men cut elegant figures as they strode through the woods and despite the tone of their discourse being less violent now, its content was disturbing.

Elizabeth, in Darcy's absence, could do little more than offer comfort to Georgiana who, more than half an hour after its occurrence, was still shaken by Wickham's arrival. Oh to be so helpless! If any consolation could be found in the whole affair, it was that Lydia slept. Though it may be supposed she saw her husband in her dreams it was certain she was not aware of his presence in reality, nor did he, in his conversation with Darcy, indicate that he had any knowledge of Lydia's being at Pemberley at all.

The possibility of vicious confrontation hung ominous over Wickham and Darcy, but the latter condescended, with the full intention of dismissing it, to hear the former's story. It was thus that Darcy learned his enemy's intentions, resolved to hear the allegations with disbelief and he listened with incredulity and no small degree of disgust as Wickham revealed his collaborator to be none other than Lady Catherine de Bourgh.

"Before coming into Derbyshire today I ventured first to Rosings Park," said Wickham. "My initial intention was that of having out my grievance with Lady Catherine, but on arrival I was informed by Mrs. Jenkinson that her ladyship was detained here at Pemberley. I made haste but was not, as was my hope, afforded the opportunity of addressing her here."

"I am glad of the fact that she had gone before you arrived," said Darcy.

"Do not take too strong a relief from it, Darcy. I met, through fortune or mischance, depending on your view of the matter, with Lady Catherine on the road near Lambton, our exchange was brief I confess, but it had length and content enough to allow me the satisfaction of reminding her of her debt to me, which remains, as yet, unpaid."

Darcy stiffened. "Despite all you say and despite all I know of my aunt, I cannot readily accept the existence of this deficit. Do you expect me to believe that she designed to award you with favors and fortune for marrying Lydia Bennet? I suggest that in inventing this tale you have overlooked the fact that she would never have desired such a union, your connection with the Darcy family is a tenuous one I admit but it is link enough for Lady Catherine to accept some small association with your name. I know well enough that her disapproval of my wife's family would prevent her encouraging the alliance."

"Your perspective of the matter is awry, Darcy. I concede she made no mention of marriage, her instruction went only as far as elopement, nay, seduction. Surely you cannot be in any doubt about her motives, had Lydia's demise proved to be as scandalous as Lady Catherine intended the Bennet association would certainly have been one you would not have wished to further."

Darcy's expression and tone were serious as he considered the implications of Wickham's claims. His reluctance to credit him was firm but at the same time he felt compelled to learn more. He went on, subdued by the ramifications. "If all you say is true, why did you not halt the association at the elopement? If there was this further fortune awaiting you with Lady Catherine, why then did you concede to accept my offer to settle the matter of the marriage and the clearing of your debts? Was not the fortune offered you by her an easier one to accept than my own?"

"Easier yes," said Wickham, "but of less significance, the sum you proffered exceeded the remainder I would have procured from the de Bourgh purse." He had a smug look about him. "Come, Darcy, you must surely admire my acumen, besides, here is something of a confession, Lydia is comely, is she not? And was always… "—how should such a delicate matter be approached?—" …very obliging from the first."

Darcy heard this with disgust. "You are no better than a beast, Wickham, if you sought to repulse me you have succeeded."

"I protest! Is it unnatural that I felt it preferable to marry Lydia than to not? I had lived the previous year in uncertainty and I knew loneliness. Oh, I flatter myself that I was rarely without the attention of some agreeable young lady or another," with this comment he observed Darcy closely, daring to speak again, "and of all my encounters, my memories of certain Hertfordshire ladies are particularly fond."

Darcy suspected an allusion to his own wife and was quick to retaliate. "Do not seek to anger me further, Wickham, I can assure your regret."

"Then as gentlemen we shall proceed, for you are as deeply entrenched in this collusion as your aunt, her investment bought Lydia's engagement and yours paid for our marriage. It is truly a family affair!"

Darcy did not hesitate to defend himself. "I have nothing to be ashamed of, I assisted in the guarantee of the girl's respectability, that is all, I can see no dishonor in that. If, as you suggest, my aunt's plan was to procure Lydia's disgrace then I am proud to have prevented it and I cannot see how you mean to coerce me into providing anything further. If what you say is true, let Lady Catherine suffer her own shame and buy your silence if she wishes, her evils, if they exist, are no reflection on my own character."

Wickham gave a wry smile, "But by association?" he asked.

"You have been away too long, Wickham, you do not know me," said Darcy. "Defamation by connection is not the most vital of my concerns. If you set out to ruin me, you will gain nothing more than your own destruction. These weak threats are of no consequence to me." With nothing further to say he turned his back and strode with purpose in the direction of the house. His heart was heavy with all he had heard, though his predisposition to distrust Wickham's words had been strong, there was about the tale a very strong tone of validity that his instincts would not allow him to discount. As swiftly as Wickham had arrived he now departed but in his absence his ill effects were still to be felt.

Darcy, Elizabeth, and Georgiana, relieved at Wickham's departure, dared not allow themselves the luxury of believing they had seen the last of him. Darcy's feelings on the matter were mixed; he dwelt on the fact that he ought not to find the man's revelations so easy to believe, but he knew his aunt's resentful character, her artfulness, and her convictions that her own ideals were beyond reproach and therefore worth pursuing no matter what price might be paid. Elizabeth knew, perhaps better than any other, Lady Catherine's vehement opposition to their marriage and had only a slight difficulty in crediting Wickham's claims although it pained her to think of them.

"My fear is of its being true, Fitzwilliam," said she when they next occasioned to speak on the subject. "Lady Catherine's determination where Anne's well-being is concerned is unconstrained, likewise her disdain for me. But still I am puzzled, if Wickham claims that in consenting to marry Lydia he fell short of Lady Catherine's expectations, how then does he justify his demands for the remaining payment?"

"He cannot," said Darcy firmly, "that is the point in hand, Elizabeth, he sought to threaten Lady Catherine with exposure and by that means procure further fiscal security. I have a suspicion that their brief discourse on the road at Lambton left him doubting that she would agree to buy his silence."

"So he sought to offer you the opportunity of purchasing it on her behalf?"

"He misjudged me, I am not of a mind to save Wickham from financial ruin or my aunt from retribution. It is my experience that repeated salvation of wickedness only serves to regenerate it. I am neither my aunt's nor George Wickham's redeemer. The bad will end bad if they decide upon it, no matter what attempts are made to save them."

"Then you do not concern yourself unduly? I am sure you have frustrated Wickham by being so impenetrable."

"He came here with the intention of alarming me, he has left in the full knowledge that he cannot. What he chooses to do now is his concern, I shall not seek to confront him. He will not reveal all as he threatens; he knows full well he would have no power if he does so. No, he is too covetous of wealth to discard his supposed key to it."

Elizabeth put her hand in her husband's. "I admire your strength and composure, I believe I am a good way to being twice as furious as you, even your tone is calm." She looked at him questioningly. "Does your coolness of temper derive from an affection for the boy Wickham once was?"

Darcy thought for a moment. "Those memories are fond indeed, but too much has passed between then and now to allow me the pleasure of happy reminiscence."

"But you berate him far less than I, you surely do not think there could be humanity in him?" she asked, incredulous.

"There is humanity in everyone, Elizabeth, the chance of repentance in every soul, I can pray for it without self-reproach, without hope we have nothing."

At once humbled and alarmed by Darcy's humility Elizabeth could not help but recall the severity of Wickham's conduct. "But Wickham is such a man!" cried she with urgency. "We two have young sisters who have suffered at his hand, his deviance I judge to be beyond reform, all feelings of hope in my heart are extinguished. You are naturally of a more severe nature than I; I cannot comprehend how you can keep faith where resentment would be entirely just."

It was thus their discourse ceased and though they spoke no more of Wickham, he was never far from either's thoughts.

CHAPTER 20

"He is just what a young man ought to be," said she, "sensible, good humored, lively; and I never saw such happy manners! So much ease, with such perfect good breeding!"

Necessity settled the state of things at Pemberley and thankfully Lydia remained uninformed of her husband's visit. How grateful Elizabeth was that this, at least, had been concealed from her and how fervently she abhorred the deceit. But it had to be so, there was no undoing it, he had come and gone and was to be forgotten. Georgiana was determined to put him from her mind, which showed great fortitude on her part, but her ability to remove Wickham so swiftly from her thoughts was in part due to the arrival of an excellent gentleman by the name of Mr. Edwin Hanworth. For even timid girls have an inclination to be distracted by handsome young men and Georgiana Darcy was no exception.

Hanworth, who by matters of business was brought to Pemberley a few days after Wickham's departure, was indeed handsome. He was no more than three and twenty and no less than six feet in height, a combination which gave him an air of youthful distinction. His manners were pleasing and the fact that he had recently inherited Great Fordham Hall, a large estate in Yorkshire, meant he was in a state of perpetual ease.

Those who had the wrong impression of Darcy may very well have viewed him as a man quite capable of feeling and showing instant dislike of strangers. His reticence to promote himself having generally been considered a mark of contempt, he might perhaps have astounded his critics by the immediacy with which his liking of Edwin Hanworth was formed and demonstrated. When formal introductions had been made, Mr. Hanworth revealed the purpose of his visit to Darcy after the latter had shown him into his study.

"You know of Fordham Hall, sir?" said he amiably.

Darcy nodded. "Yes, I spent some time in Yorkshire as a younger man, I know it in passing. Fine architecture, very fine. The sight of an elegant building is second only, for the pleasure it affords, to that of an elegant woman."

"Indeed, I should like occasion to keep it, but I already have an estate in Gloucester and a house in town," said Mr. Hanworth, adding, "alas, Mr. Darcy, there is no elegant woman in my view but I hope that my horizon will be so adorned some day."

"Of course, nothing enhances a vista like the presence of feminine beauty," said Darcy, "but, before this pleasing meditation leads us both to lose our purpose, pray tell me, sir, what is your business here?"

Mr. Hanworth settled more comfortably in his seat. "Ah!" said he with a pleasant smile, "I intrigue you, Mr. Darcy, but there is nothing mysterious about me. The purchase of Fordham is soon to complete, I have had many dealings with a certain gentleman of Hertfordshire whose dear wife is set on it, but I am to be gone out of Derbyshire in three weeks time, I return again six weeks thereafter. A business acquaintance put your name to me, I require an emissary in my absence, for the overseeing of negotiations."

Darcy nodded again. "But of course, I have business matters of my own to see to and feel myself quite equal to the task."

Mr. Hanworth smiled. "It is a great relief, Mr. Darcy, I thank you, sir, I shall have my attorney contact Mr. Bingley posthaste, he will be relieved to hear of developments, I am afraid there have been a few delays thus far."

"Bingley you say?" asked Darcy. "He is a dear friend of mine, Mr. Hanworth, I shall therefore be even more glad to assist."

"I am overjoyed, he is an affable man, and his wife is a perfectly pleasant woman."

"Mrs. Bingley? Yes indeed she is, my own wife is her sister," said Darcy proudly.

"Then may I congratulate both you and your friend on your fine choice in wives." Hanworth laughed and, further considering the matter, said, "I see now how you can speak with such authority on the beauty of ladies, Mr. Darcy, but confess, I have heard you described as a very different sort, purely businesslike. Your eloquence has been a welcome surprise. Well, well! It all connects somehow, does it not? This is a happy coincidence indeed, sir," he said and proffering his hand to Darcy he said, "I am very glad to make your acquaintance."

Darcy's judgment of the newcomer was not to be questioned. Edwin Hanworth was all that is charming and when he was invited to stay for dinner at Pemberley he was at first mindful to ensure that the offer was not merely a gesture of civility. When he was satisfied that absolute sincerity prompted Mr. and Mrs. Darcy's hospitality he condescended to accept their invitation with gratitude and looked forward to the evening with anticipation.

And so it was in the form of this welcome relief offered by the company of their affable new acquaintance that Elizabeth and Darcy were able, momentarily, to put their dealings with Mr. Wickham behind them. Lydia still fancied herself weak and was taken, with discretion, to stay with her Aunt Gardiner in their cottage. She made no resentful protests about this, as she was not disposed to acquaint herself with handsome strangers, no longer being in a position, or of the inclination, to flirt with them. She preferred to indulge in her misery in privacy.

Adjourned to the drawing room after an impressive dinner, Hanworth informed the party of many little particulars of his life, and in more detail, his inheritance of Fordham Hall, a house he expressed a deep fondness for. "I confess I have felt a small measure of reluctance over the business of parting with the place, I spent a fair portion of my youth there. I am undeniably fond of it." He looked at Elizabeth. "My visit here has been so fortuitous, Mrs. Darcy, for I begrudged the idea of relinquishing Fordham, but now I learn it is to be the home of your dear sister, I shall take leave of it with equanimity."

"You are very good, sir." Elizabeth smiled; her liking of Mr. Hanworth was as immediate as her husband's. "I know Jane will love Fordham Hall as much as I have come to love Pemberley."

"Without question," said Hanworth, "Derbyshire and Yorkshire are beautiful counties, I regret that I am soon for Gloucester." He looked at Georgiana, "yes, I regret it greatly," he said, "Derbyshire in particular has many pleasant attractions and I hope to enjoy the prettier of them before my departure."

Georgiana, shy at first to acknowledge Mr. Hanworth's delicate compliments, remained silent. Her blushes were noticed by Darcy and Elizabeth but as the evening passed and the little tributes continued she became ever more capable and willing to accept them without embarrassment. Her usual way was to speak without conviction and only make a comment when it was least likely to be noticed, but a pleasing and encouraging confidence hitherto unseen in her now replaced her natural caution and reticence. Elizabeth was glad to note this transformation in her reserved sister-in-law. Her fondness for Georgiana was genuine and she was relieved to observe that the girl was not disposed to be shy of affection though she might have had every cause to be so.

Due to frequent practice, Georgiana's proficiency at the pianoforte was evident and she elected, without provocation, to play for the party. Mr. Hanworth made the choice to turn pages for her, and was delighted not only with the music but also with her proximity. "Beautiful, simply beautiful," he said when she had finished playing. There was no doubt that his praise was all for her and little for Mozart.

CHAPTER 21

"I never saw a more promising inclination. He was growing quite inattentive to other people, and wholly engrossed by her."

Three weeks of quiet had passed slowly for Elizabeth and, as is the way when a woman awaits the birth of her child, many hours were spent in daydreaming or whiled away by her imagination.

For Georgiana the time went too fast and brought about Mr. Hanworth's departure for Gloucester and by the time of his leaving the two had developed a noticeable rapport. He had divided his time most unequally between Pemberley and Great Fordham Hall, choosing, by the inducement of his favorite, to be in Derbyshire more often than not. His temperament was as friendly and good humored as that of the object of his affections and none who had seen them together were left in any doubt that a natural progression from adulation would be matrimony. But business called him to Gloucester as was expected, and any proposals Georgiana might privately have wished for were to be postponed. Hanworth left promising to write as often as his occupation would allow. Georgiana, though sad to see her amour go, could not be aggrieved in his absence for her heart was infused with the thought of him and her fondness therefore increased.

There had been no word of Wickham, no sign of associated repercussion. Kitty, accompanied by Maria Lucas, had returned to Pemberley, Mr. and Mrs. Bennet having decided upon the idea of a tour of the Lakes. She made once more a happy companion to her favorite and closest sister and Lydia was glad of her arrival and equally pleased to see Maria. She was in the envied position of being a girl with an already rounded figure and her condition was not outwardly discernible, though she had little more than ten weeks until the child came. It is a truth that Lydia barely recognized this fact herself, her character had veered even more toward a tendency to self-absorption and at times she resembled her mother, always bedridden with some imagined malady. But with Kitty and Maria arrived and willing to visit her at the cottage, she held court happily from the comfort of her chaise lounge or bed.

Elizabeth anticipated Jane and Bingley's occupancy of Fordham Hall to take place in October once all documentation and corrections to the house had been attended to. In the meantime, the sisters contented themselves with their letters which had grown in both length and frequency by way of both women's happy ability to pay the high costs of the post.

Refreshed by more than a month's respite Elizabeth was once more disposed to have the house filled with family and friends. Her Uncle Gardiner was at last settled again at Pemberley and her husband's cousin had arrived. Elizabeth had always considered Colonel Fitzwilliam a most agreeable gentleman whose company she was not inclined to reject.

Now, so happily married to Darcy, she felt a little embarrassed to remember that she had at one time considered the Colonel a gentleman worth considering as a husband. He was not reputed as so handsome as Darcy but his gentlemanlike manners were the result of both good breeding and innate friendliness. She often wondered how such a man, now passed thirty and so respectable, had managed to go about the world and not yet secure a suitable wife. Ever a great observer of human nature she would amuse herself with thoughts of matchmaking the Colonel with some pleasant acquaintance of her own. With the summer weather now usurping the crisp spring days, many of the party were inclined to take turns around the grounds, the ladies covered from the shade with parasols. Elizabeth often sat upon a bench in the park, no longer disposed to or allowed long walks, those who sought her company would come to sit with her.

Maria Lucas, herself much matured in recent months, joined

Elizabeth one afternoon. She had always fostered much admiration for Elizabeth and she sometimes had the inclination to model her own behavior on her friend's.

"Pemberley is the most beautiful place, Lizzy, I cannot believe I am here. I look back to the visit we made to Rosings when Charlotte first married and can scarce believe how much has happened since then."

"Indeed we have seen a great variety of events," said Elizabeth affectionately. "I am glad you are pleased with Pemberley, but tell me, is Charlotte well?"

"Oh, very well, yes... and Mr. Collins is much the same as ever."

Elizabeth laughed. "I know what you are saying, my cousin may not be the cleverest of men, but your sister is well pleased with her alliance, you should be happy to have him as a brother."

"I am, Elizabeth, I do not find him dislikeable to any real degree, but I wonder at Charlotte, for she never showed any particular regard for him, to have made such a sudden choice."

"I should scold you, Maria," said Elizabeth playfully, "it is very wrong of you to judge your sister so, I daresay your needs tend more to the romantic and hers the practical, but neither of you are to be condemned for your dispositions."

Maria smiled. "I could not marry a man I was not in love with."

"Then you share my view of things, Maria."

"Oh yes, Lizzy," said the girl with enthusiasm and delight, "if there was another man so good as your husband I would decide to make him fall in love with me without hesitation."

Elizabeth was watchful of Maria. "I noticed you took a turn with Colonel Fitzwilliam this morning, how did you get on? You were not very much acquainted with him at Rosings I recall."

Maria smiled. "I got on very well indeed, but I do know him well enough from Rosings, you remember when Mr. Darcy and he came to take their leave at Hunsford, Mr. Darcy waited to speak to you, I became very much more acquainted with the Colonel then, he stayed for at least an hour you know."

Elizabeth sighed. "Be careful, Maria, he has nearly twice your years, that you may view him as desirable is not to be questioned, but an older man, more often than not, cannot see the woman for the child."

"I am not a child any longer, I am out, and at a marrying age which is all the age I need to be to secure any man's affections be he twenty or three times that."

Elizabeth looked fondly on her young companion. "Then let the man of your dreams be as ancient as you please," she said.

Maria whispered, "Though not so old as Mr. Collins."

"Mr. Collins is not *so* old Maria, he is merely one of those unfortunate men who gives the appearance of age without yet having the advantage of wisdom."

The two then walked the path in the direction of the house where they were met by Colonel Fitzwilliam himself, he bowed and doffed his hat to the ladies and offered to escort them. Elizabeth could not help but notice the bloom rise in Maria's cheeks and she was not inclined to think it attributable to the heat.

CHAPTER 22

"I cannot comprehend the neglect of a family library
in such days as these."

⟶⟶⟶⟶

Miss Georgiana Darcy, bravely enduring the absence of her beloved Mr. Hanworth, was invited, two weeks after his departure, to stay a month with a certain Lady Metcalfe in town. Lady Harriet Metcalfe, who was long acquainted with Lady Catherine, was more than happy to oblige her friend's niece. She kept a comfortable and exquisitely furnished apartment which she was always willing to exhibit to those friends and acquaintances she deemed worthy. Lady Metcalfe was considered by some to be a self-interested eccentric sort of woman, but she was affable and entertaining so for the most part her self-indulgent singular manner was forgiven. Her appearance was that of a caricature, the largeness of her head, which contradicted any notion that its purpose was that of housing vast intelligence, could only be put down to the extensive style of her wig. She had known Georgiana since infancy, was fond of her, and ensured that the young woman had a variety of dinners, assemblies, and plays to attend during her stay.

"One of the greatest pleasures in life," she said, "is pleasure."

Lady Metcalfe made an art of enjoyment. She had no time for practicalities and was fortunate enough to have in her employ a host of servants who attended to all those insignificant time wasting things for her. Her alliance with Lady Catherine was long-standing, though there were never two women so different in appearance or character. Lady Harriet, in contrast to her friend, was inclined to frivolous indulgence, she had none of Lady Catherine's severity either in her dress or her manner, but the two had maintained their close association despite this and possibly even because of it. Her favorite pastime was that of romantic fiction, both the writing and reading of it and she cared little for those who looked down at popular novels for women.

"I cannot see any reason for objection, novels are so enjoyable, my dear," she took a sip of wine, "that is why I enjoy them."

Thus Georgiana passed her weeks, but even with the abundance of entertainment and diversion Lady Harriet provided, the days seemed to pass slowly and the girl had the unmistakable pallor of love sickness. This did not escape Lady Metcalfe's keen eye for sentimental detail.

"Ah, the sweet pain of love," she said, "so painful and yet so sweet." She smiled at Georgiana. "I shall write you into my next novel, my dear, to be sure; for your exquisite suffering would make for a good tale. Oh, but do not be downcast child, I shall do you justice with my pen, I am always mindful to conceal the inspiration for my heroines, a little adaptation here and there, a change of name, color of eyes, and circumstance, you would not even recognize yourself, I assure you."

By this last Georgiana was relieved and the following discourse satisfied her immensely. Lady Harriet, once alerted to the girl's state of infatuation, would not rest until she knew all the particulars of Edwin Hanworth.

"Handsome and respectable," she cried. "I could not have fashioned him better, what a champion of fiction this young fellow shall make." She smiled, satisfied at her observation and went on, "Young women are never so eagerly drawn to literature except in such cases where a desirable man appears! But tell me, child, who is the villain of the piece? Such rays of light are never better appreciated than when the risk of shadow looms. I say there must be a scoundrel!"

Georgiana was amused by her companion's inclination to view the whole of life as a story. "I fear I must disappoint you, ma'am, there is no rogue, my life seems not to have the excitement of your sagas."

"My dear child, you are quite mistaken, do not be deceived into believing reality any less inspiring than fiction," said Lady Metcalfe shrewdly, "the truths are oft more scandalous than the fantasy, that is the delicious part of life." So it was, that Lady Harriet viewed human existence, with the naive conviction that events were played out in chapters, troubles sent to give color to dull days, and justice an inevitability so long as it was awarded to the handsome.

There was never a woman so in love with love itself as Lady Metcalfe and had she known of them, the developments at Pemberley would have been a great source of inspiration.

By July Elizabeth was delighted, despite her initial reticence, to note that Maria Lucas seemed to be achieving more than a small measure of success in her determined attempts to attract the attention of Colonel Fitzwilliam. Her plainer day dresses were now discarded in favor of her newest and most fashionable clothes and she seemed to grow prettier daily. The Colonel, succumbing to Maria's devotedly employed methods of feminine beguilement, regularly accompanied her on walks, sometimes by mutual design and at other times by his happening to chance upon her by the lake or sitting in the shade of the trees. He bestowed upon her the avid and charming attentions she had always dreamed of and she upon him unbridled adoration and devotion. Their manner of discourse was not fervent and did not challenge either's intellect, but was loving and considerate and had about it an innocent charm.

They made an engaging couple, he so tall and advanced in life and she diminutive, childlike, and consumed. At night she could scarce bear the deprivation of his company, the dark hours were so long to her, the sleeplessness a torture. She would retire to her bed with the hope that constant thought of her favorite would induce him to appear in her dreams and only by that means, would she would last the night until the sweet pleasure of seeing him once more came with morning. Her childish yearnings led her, on more than one occasion, to take up her quill in privacy and make a pastime of writing his name by hers and daring sometimes, though she blushed when she did, to sign herself Maria Fitzwilliam.

The Colonel, though not given to the self-indulgent fancies of his favored one, found himself, in her absence, quite consumed by thoughts of her. How astonished he had been to find her trans-figured in one year from girl to woman. The metamorphosis had pleased him and the bright butterfly she had become fueled his intrigue.

Maria was in every way her sister Charlotte's opposite; she was spirited, if not by nature, then by the determined modeling of her character upon Elizabeth's. For the latter was all that Maria dared hope to be, so much a mixture of beauty and intelligence. To imitate her was impossible, but to make small judgments on the nature of her character and undertake them as her own was within Maria's grasp. On this facsimile she depended, intent, with the knowledge of Colonel Fitzwilliam's regard for Elizabeth, to mirror her in some way so as to secure the unwitting gentleman as her own.

Two weeks into that hottest of months a young man called at Ros-ings Park seeking an address with Mary Bennet. This in itself was an occurrence of a unique type. Never before had her attention been sought so. The gentleman, a Mr. Robert Price, was known to the Bennets to be employed as a clerk in Mr. Phillip's offices at Meryton.

Lady Catherine was at once astonished and put out that anyone should think it their right to call upon Mary and when the young man was announced she said to her housekeeper reluctantly, "Very well, show him in." Then turning to Mary she said, "Are you acquainted with this Mr. Price?"

"He is known to my family, your ladyship, he is in the employ of my uncle."

"Oh I see," said Lady Catherine, "he is in trade, is he? Yes? Well, I am not surprised."

When Robert Price was shown in to the room he did not display the signs of reverence that would meet Lady Catherine's expectation. He presented himself with courtesy but made no false attempts at flattery or subservience.

"Mr. Price," said Lady Catherine, "you seem a sensible sort of young man, on what grounds do you come here?"

"I am only recently in Kent," he said, "I have relations who farm nearby, my annual leave affords me the opportunity of visiting them."

"Which farm?" said Lady Catherine, "the Houghton small holding or Newhams, the dairy people?"

"Newhams, your ladyship, Thomas Newham is my uncle."

"I see. They supply us of course, but that is no character reference," she said critically.

"I thought I would visit Mary," he said looking quickly at the girl, "being so close by."

"Oh indeed," said Lady Catherine, "is it the general manner of the farming community to visit wherever and whenever they see fit, it is highly unusual to my way of thinking."

Mr. Price smiled. "No indeed, ma'am. You may be assured of my regret if my unexpected arrival has inconvenienced you, as for the behavior of farmers I cannot speak for them, I am a clerk by trade."

"Oh yes, of course," said Lady Catherine. "Well I'm glad to see you have made some attempt at elevating yourself, you prefer the pen to the shovel do you?"

"Infinitely, ma'am," said the young man, "though I have not the experience with the latter to make too certain a ruling. I never picked one up in my life."

Lady Catherine smiled coldly at the man. "Well that goes in your favor I suppose." She turned then to Mary. "It would not do to have laborers calling! At Rosings? Highly improper!" she snapped.

Mary thought better than to respond to Lady Catherine and, despite her usual habit of complying with the de Bourgh dictates, she privately felt that Robert Price's appearance was something of a blessing. Without her observation being overt, she made a point of taking in all little details of Mr. Price. She saw that he was not handsome in the ways a man was often thought to be, nor was he so tall or elegant as others, but he had, she thought, a kind disposition and a well-meaning spirit. More importantly, she observed, he was unlikely to think her own appearance marred by her need of spectacles for he wore them himself and quite often that afternoon she found him peering over the top of them to look at her. In the week that followed, Mary was to enjoy Mr. Price's company on a further four occasions. As was her habit, she wrote a short account of her news to Mr. Collins in the usual expectation of his happiness at receiving it.

Rosings Park, Kent
21st July 1813

Dear Mr. Collins,
Forgive me for not writing sooner. I have, as you suggested, been reading to Anne from Fordyce's Sermons and have most recently been making a study of The Book of Common Prayer in order to procure an appropriate litany for her protection from recurrent ailments. The good Lord has blessed us with fine weather but I fear the climate is now too close for Anne, she has been very ill again. But, as we know, God gives out misfortune in equal measure to blessings. Last week I was called on by Mr. Price, you may recall he works for my Uncle Phillips in Meryton. It was a pleasant surprise to reacquaint with him. He remembers you and asks that I send you his best wishes in this letter.
I hope that Mrs. Collins is well, please give my kindest regards to her and all at Lucas Lodge.

Yours Sincerely,
Miss Mary Bennet

CHAPTER 23

How much of pleasure or pain it was in his power to bestow!
How much of good or evil must be done by him!

———◈———

"You have survived admirably, child," said Lady Metcalfe kindly to Georgiana. "I know the weeks have seemed drawn out for you."

Georgiana nodded. "And the remaining days will be as years."

Lady Harriet smiled. "But then, child, he is to come for you, I am as delighted as you, what a great advantage this will be for my writing, to meet the man. Oh! And what a gentleman, as you rightly said, to detour to town to take you back into Derbyshire. But then I have always noted that thoughtful men are so... thoughtful," she said succinctly.

Briefly diverted by Lady Harriet's nonsensical talk Georgiana again let her mind dwell on the thought of seeing Edwin again. On their last being together at Pemberley the two had not had the happy knowledge that Georgiana would make such a visit to London. Mr. Hanworth on learning her news from her letters made the immediate decision to include London on his itinerary with the express purpose of taking her back into Derbyshire with him. This welcome change in plans meant that the couple would reunite some three days earlier than anticipated.

The light relief afforded Elizabeth by the observation of Maria's happiness was not always enough to distract her from the more pressing and serious worries that loomed. With but a month until her own child and Lydia's infant came, she was less able to distract her mind with healthy pursuits like walking and often found herself dwelling on matters concerning Wickham and Lydia and the consequences of her own decision to foster their child. She detected that Darcy also grew reticent. He appeared remote, thoughtful, and preoccupied; his manner forced her to recall how she had perceived him before. She too, felt nothing like her old self, and marveled that Lydia displayed no signs of confusion at all.

"Can she be so coldhearted?" she asked herself. Her worries grew and preyed upon her. Fearing as the time drew near that their task would be difficult, she sought her husband's advice and reassurance on the matter of raising the infants as equals.

"I confess I am afraid," she said to Darcy, "afraid that you will not be able to see these infants as twins, as equals."

Darcy was quiet for a moment, he walked to the window. "I share your fears, but you must trust me, Elizabeth."

"If you do not trust that your hand will be even, how can I depend upon it?"

His voice was steady, resigned. "You cannot depend on my heart having a steady view. That is the material point. Only ignorance to the truth will ensure that my actions are impartial, only then can I vouch that my treatment of both children will be exercised with equanimity."

Elizabeth made no attempt to conceal her distress and she quickly became tearful. "Then you mean me to have our child and foster the other and conceal from you the rightful identity of each?"

"I believe it must be so."

"You have not thought that such a concealment will deprive me of being witness to your pride?" she asked incredulous.

"That you shall not witness it does not render it unreal. But pride, when misplaced, may endanger more than it protects."

"But surely pride in your own child cannot be judged improper?"

"In the course of a perfect life it may not be so, but in circumstances such as these I believe it may result in prejudice and above all else I do not want to risk that." There was anger in his voice.

Elizabeth, repressing her bitter tears, protested, "No you would not, *you* who know *so* much of improper pride and prejudice! I know it is your very great belief that where there is a real superiority of mind, pride will be always under good regulation. But you say nothing of proper feeling or kin, your refusal to acknowledge our own child, even to me, may have the unhappy outcome of depriving him of the love and fairness you so desperately wish to give in equal measure to both."

For the first time during their marriage, Darcy raised his voice. "Do not anger me further, Elizabeth, I assure you the consequence will be the exact opposite. I shall not know the truth; you will outline no such distinction to me. I forbid it, you must promise to suppress any desire on your part to subject me to even the merest whisper of disclosure."

Elizabeth had never known his voice to raise with such rapidity or to such a volume and she was aware in an instant that it had startled her and left her weakened but she resolved to speak calmly and hold back her tears.

"Then trust you may that my words shall never reveal the truth, but I defy your heart not to know it," she said. Her husband left the room; she remained there sobbing and did not know the heartbreak her cries caused him because he did not return to comfort her.

Within a few days, Elizabeth's spirits had lifted tolerably well, her husband's tone had softened again but he was not so demonstrative as he had been. She did not press him for discussion; her usual tendency to persistence seemed somehow weakened by her condition and the circumstances.

She was glad of Georgiana's return and was happy to see Edwin Hanworth again though neither had much time, beyond the normal courtesies, for anything or anyone but each other. Such an atmosphere of love surrounded Elizabeth. Maria and Colonel Fitzwilliam's mutual infatuation was plain and Hanworth and Georgiana's return further increased Elizabeth's awareness of the coolness that had come over her marriage. Kitty was rarely out of Lydia's sight, the two making an amusement of afternoons of girlish reminiscence at the Gardiners' cottage. Elizabeth's one consolation had been Lydia's apparent detachment from her expected child. But as the time drew nearer she detected a transformation in her sister, noted small but significant signs that led her to believe the girl was at last acknowledging the seriousness of the situation.

"What if I cannot bear to part with the mite?" said Lydia one day. "It is very likely, you know, Lizzy, that I shall have the sweetest baby ever seen. For all my husband's faults he cannot be condemned for his looks and handsome fathers, you know, Lizzy, make for handsome children. Oh Lord above, I hope the child is ill-favored, then I shall happily let you take it."

"You have indicated thus far that it is what you wish, Lydia," said Elizabeth with concern. "I am serious, there is gravity to this matter, there must be, we are not choosing bonnets which we may pull apart if we do not like them, we must honor our decision. Lives are not so easily stitched back again once ripped at the seams."

Lydia settled back on her pillow and sighed. "I'm grown so plump, I hardly know myself."

Elizabeth shook her head. "Oh Lydia, that should be the least of your concerns," she said.

"That is just like you, Lizzy, you would have me turn as serious as you are. And that would not do! You shall not make a somber mother to my child I hope?"

"It is not my intention and hardly likely, we are not of somber parentage, I daresay I shall be able to temper my so-called solemnity," said Elizabeth firmly.

"Good," said Lydia. "For I cannot bear to think of any child having a dull life."

Elizabeth could not help but feel angered. "Lydia, you insult me, the child will have as good and fulfilling a life as my own infant, depend upon it. Your circumstances are such that you are not in a position to dictate, you must trust me, sister."

"Oh, I do," said Lydia, "but I think I shall feel mighty jealous, if all goes well. I will be cross that you will have all the credit when half the work will have been mine."

Elizabeth was enraged by her sister's way of looking at things, but not surprised by it. "Lydia," she said quietly, "I certainly have no pretension to the kind of triumph you speak of, you must not think such of me. You speak as if we were only concerned with the trifling issues of winning at cards or singing well, you must attempt, Lydia, in spite of your youth, to apply some sober reflection to things."

As was Lydia's way, she went on to talk of having some tea and moaned that when she was well again she should deserve new clothes. "I am all drab these days, Kitty even says so."

When Mr. Collins received Mary's letter he afforded it close inspection, for though he was not clever, he saw therein a means to his own advancement that a less shrewd man would have over-looked. He called his wife to the study. "Charlotte my dear," said he, handing her the letter with a smug smile, "much as I feel we have been treated ill at Lady Catherine's hand, I cannot help but be alarmed for her daughter's situation. It would not, I am sure, be out of place for a clergyman of my standing to offer out a little warning to the de Bourgh ladies that their companion may not, if I am correct in my assumptions, always be so devoted."

Charlotte gave her husband a look of concern. "I think I know your meaning, sir," she said, "but forgive me, are you not a little hasty in your supposition?"

Mr. Collins laughed. "Your inexperience and ignorance are indeed in your favor, my dear Charlotte, but no, even if I am not to be proved right in my suspicions I think it would be remiss of me not to offer a small measure of advice to her ladyship. Imagine, Charlotte, the disappointment that would consume all at Rosings should Mary Bennet decide to marry."

"You read a great deal into this correspondence, I think you are quite wrong."

Mr. Collins became flustered. "Well perhaps I may be, but it is an indication of a side to Mary's nature that has as yet not shown itself, a warning, of the gentlest kind would not be viewed dimly, I am sure."

None of Charlotte's protestations could prevent her husband pondering these latest thoughts. For the next fortnight the ideas formulated in his mind until suddenly one morning he could resist the temptation no more and he set out with an air of urgency, to write a letter to Lady Catherine.

"Discretion, Charlotte, that is my dictum," he said as he took up his quill. He was engaged in the office of composing a letter for over an hour although the brevity of his missive did not reflect the copious time he had spent on it. If the thoughtfulness that delayed him so had been the result of sincerity it would have been commendable at least. But there are no such honors to award Mr. Collins; he was engaged only by the determination to write, as best he could, a letter that would cast Mary Bennet into a poor light. In turn, he hoped a glowing one would shine once more on him.

Lucas Lodge, Hertfordshire
12th August 1813

Dear Madam,
Allow me to begin this letter by offering you my sincere apologies for importuning you so. I pray that you will not be hasty and disregard its contents. My position as a clergyman and my own natural sense of morality prompts me to write. But let me get straight to the point; a few weeks ago I received a letter from young Mary, you will know I have, of all the Bennet girls, always favored the child for her devotion to and interest in those matters of doctrinal import that are my own speciality. She has indeed spent much of her time in studious toil and for this I maintain some small measure of admiration, but I fear that even Mary, for whom I had such high expectations, is not impervious to allurement. Of course, I understand the natural instincts that may prompt her to seek a partner in life and it is not this fact that causes concern.
Should the girl manage to secure a suitable husband then I would be most felicitous on her behalf, although I confide that such success would surprise me. I pray you do not misunderstand my meaning, your ladyship, I would not personally look down upon such a union, no I should not, but my concerns are thus; should Mary embark upon a relationship of this type I fear it would leave you, and more importantly your daughter, devoid of a companion.

My communication herein prompts you to perhaps look for those little signs, which young ladies are often ill-qualified to conceal, of an attachment. The young man in question has had the pleasure of your acquaintance and calls himself Mr. Robert Price. My sense of better judgment prevents me from confiding in you any personal sentiments about the gentleman, but my sense of loyalty to the de Bourgh name compels me to again warn you of a romantic involvement, which may, if I am correct in my suppositions, be to your own disadvantage. May I just add at this juncture that you must now, on receipt of this letter, realize that despite the unpleasant little incidents that are now passed I retain a genuine, dare I say, worshipful respect of your ladyship's excellence.

Yours Sincerely,
William Collins

CHAPTER 24

"Why, if he came only to be silent, grave, and indifferent," said she,
"did he come at all?"'

Although she had not been fond of him, Elizabeth was grieved to hear that Mr. Hurst had passed away.

"Poor Louisa," she said to Darcy. "Poor Jane! Imagine Netherfield in mourning and everyone in weeds."

"While my sympathies are with Jane, for all she will have to endure, I rely on you, Elizabeth, you know the form, send our regrets to the widow and the rest of the family," Darcy said. "I am for town on business this afternoon, I expect to be a few days at least."

With only this terse statement Darcy left her. How she yearned for the return of his warmth and his affectionate manner. He seemed to her so consumed with anxiety. How she longed for the approval in his gaze, the tenderness behind his firm touch, his breath on her neck. Oh ruinous imagination!

That he should return to her thus seemed at once a distant fantasy, a girlish dream made up of impossibilities, the more sensual her instincts the further the dream removed itself from reality. His recent address, so concise, bore no resemblance to the passion she had known and inspired in him. Where was his responsiveness? The detachment that now replaced it tore her heart to shreds. For his kiss, a thousand fortunes she would have paid, for that look of desire, so particular to him, she would have laid down her life. What rapture it was for Elizabeth to recall all this, and in that moment she was satiated by having the knowledge, by memory at least, of his appetite, of the unbridled want he was now restraining.

More still, her doubts were surfacing; the troubles with Lydia and Wickham must surely be viewed by Darcy as proof of the inequality of their own marriage, of her inferiority in breeding, connections, and fortune. All this she had considered inconsequential, yet now she felt on the threshold of owning defeat. One kiss could rally her spirits and set her up again to fight the battles she was facing. Was he regretful? How hard it was to read him. Painfully she recalled the words he had spoken to her on his first proposing. Oh, how clearly she could see their application now. How clouded her judgment then. The hurt she had suffered when he said, *"Could you expect me to rejoice in the inferiority of your connections? To congratulate myself on the hope of relations, whose condition in life is so decidedly beneath my own?"* Oh the bitter thought. But I am beneath him, thought she, we are not yet a year married and see how much he has endured for the sake of me. From passion to regret her heart lurched, the way to appease him eluded her. Turning her mind to practicalities, she took to the task of writing a small card to Netherfield but she felt ashamed that whilst expressing the expected sympathy she harbored more than a small measure of guilt at her own selfishness. "I fear this will prevent Jane's coming, and I long for her to be here."

Mr. Drummond had called with regularity at Pemberley to visit both expectant mothers and had most recently declared Mrs. Wickham to be in sound health and Mrs. Darcy fatigued and frail.

"Be careful, my dear," he advised, "now is a time for rest. I know you are a strong and active sort of young lady but with only a week to wait it would be foolish in the extreme to take risks."

Elizabeth sighed. "Strong and active?" she asked, for she felt in every way dissimilar to the description. "I cannot imagine I appear so now."

"You are a little pale, my dear, take fresh air by way of the window, but the walks must cease," he warned sternly. "I shall speak to Darcy about it."

"You spoil all chance of disobedience on my part, Mr. Drummond," said Elizabeth playfully.

The old man regarded her fondly and took her hand. "Your husband loves you, child, he is naturally protective, rejoice in it, I have seen many a man less caring. You have what you deserve in Fitzwilliam."

"Indeed I have," said Elizabeth thoughtfully.

When her husband's trunks had been put in the carriage ready for his leaving, Darcy came to bid his wife farewell.

"I shall hate it with you gone," she said. "I need you, the child is so near now."

Darcy held her hand and looked into her eyes, she searched his for signs of ardor but found only a look of resolve that was in no way equal to the affection she sought.

"I intend to return shortly, Elizabeth," he vowed. "I shall be here, depend upon it, until then you have Mrs. Quinn, she would sooner let a rat near a birthing mother as a husband, you know her starched notions."

Elizabeth managed to laugh. "Oh yes, if Mrs. Quinn has her way I shall never see you again."

He kissed her more tenderly than she had anticipated and within a few moments she was watching as the carriage drew away to take him to town. "How he must suffer," she said quietly, not far from tears.

Had they known it Colonel Fitzwilliam and Mr. Hanworth would have gained some diversion from the knowledge that both were eager to propose to their loved ones but both determined to wait until Elizabeth and Darcy had their child safely delivered and started in life. In delaying thus, both men's affections were increased, affirmed, and heightened.

So near to delivering herself, Lydia was moved back from the cottage and into her rooms at Pemberley though with reluctance. "I was quite happy where I was, it only vexes me to be so in the middle of things I cannot enjoy."

How swiftly spread ill feeling is. Lady Catherine, now in receipt of Mr. Collins's letter, had taken his allusions most seriously and began, without due subtlety, to make an investigation into Mary's intentions.

"So, you quite relish that young clerk's company, Mary?" she asked with disapproval.

Mary, although mindful not to give undue emphasis to her inner feelings of delight, could not contrive to control her smile. "He does seem a pleasant gentleman," said she in elation. It was rare for Mary's outward appearance to be altered by internal felicity. It has, however, long been acknowledged that expressions of joy worn on a face so unaccustomed to them have the effect of rendering the features almost unrecognizable. The marks of happiness, the smiles, the brightness of the eyes, and the natural glow of the complexion make beauty easily found in the plainest of women. For how much more pleasing unexpected loveliness is!

Lady Catherine observed the glow of Mary's cheek, never had she seen so rosy a threat. She remarked coldly, "Mr. Price may well be pleasant, my dear, but do you plan an engagement? Has he made any offer to you?"

Mary could not hide her embarrassment. "No, madam, he has not, I am afraid I do not understand where your questions lead to."

Lady Catherine narrowed her eyes and looked at Mary. "When I first agreed to your position here I thought I made myself quite clear about proper behavior. You do recall, I hope, that I outlined to you my dislike of flirtatious young women."

Mary nodded and remained silent.

"Then can you assure me," urged Lady Catherine bitterly, "that I am not to have the misfortune of seeing you stoop so low as your sisters have? I would be most put out."

"But I am not engaged, ma'am, and should I be so I would have expected your blessing, marriage is a sanctified union recognized by the church and in the eyes of God."

"Yes, yes," said Lady Catherine, "but it will not do. It would be most inappropriate... for Anne!"

Mary was at once disturbed by Lady Catherine's harsh tone of disapproval but felt flattered and hopeful about the possibility of marriage. But what had inspired Lady Catherine to assume an engagement? Robert Price had been attentive during his visits but they had not spent much time in each other's company and now he was gone back into Hertfordshire. He had made a promise of writing but Mary had, as yet, received no word from him. She wrote again to Mr. Collins, this time expressing her concerns about the possibility of losing Lady Catherine's patronage.

By the time her letter reached him her concerns were over, she had heard again from Robert Price and this communication so enraged Lady Catherine that the girl was sent immediately back to Meryton. Mrs. Jenkinson once more took to the task of being companion to both Lady Catherine and her daughter and tranquility resumed, there was no possibility of the former's loyalties being shaken by love and her employer considered this fact with great satisfaction.

Rational consideration of the indignity of her dismissal would have been mortification indeed for Mary, but her purpose was all lost! Lady Catherine, in the full belief that deprivation of her approval was the greatest tragedy any soul could endure, addressed Mary coldly. "I never expected you to betray us, Mary Bennet, I confess to being shocked but perhaps I should not be so. I had high hopes for you! I gave you the opportunity to prove yourself above your family and despite my generosity and kindness you have forsaken good sense and deceived me. You have done little more than to prove to me that you have the Bennet traits, the worst of them, in full measure. Believe me, young lady, they will be your downfall. To think," she lamented, "that I allowed poor Anne proximity to such a girl!"

With delightful sensations of liberation, Mary departed from Rosings Park, from its fireplaces, from its grandeur, and from its inhabitants. It was only Anne who felt the loss of Mary and it was only Anne who mourned losing her.

A little humbleness must come upon a girl who finds herself obliged, for any number of reasons, to return to her parents having left them, but the subtleties of submissive, conciliatory behavior that such a girl might be advised to display, might be overlooked if one or the other of the parents are not inclined to observe them. Mrs. Bennet made a great deal of her daughter's return and Mr. Bennet sought to tease. "So, you have upset Lady Catherine eh?" he said. "Well done, Mary, I would have believed it of your other sisters but never of you. You were always so intent on being good, I daresay now you will be more inclined to mischief!"

His wife could not approve her husband's suggestion. "Oh, Mr. Bennet, that is just like you to praise her for troublemaking," cried she.

"I did not make trouble, mama," Mary protested.

Mrs. Bennet shook her head. "Well Lady Catherine seems to think you did, not that I like the woman myself. No indeed, I find her most disagreeable," and quite forgetting Lady Catherine she leveled at Mary, "So, Robert Price has taken a fancy to you, has he?"

Mr. Bennet frowned. "Take heed! This young man's fancy for Mary may have been induced by nothing more than her having been the only girl in Kent, now he is back in Hertfordshire he may be inclined to desert her. Pray, Mrs. Bennet, do not marry Mary off before there is at least some certainty in the situation."

Mrs. Bennet looked at her husband with exasperation. "You do not know me at all, as if I would be prone to such rashness. You think me hasty, do you?"

"No, no, my dear," said her husband, "but let us look back over the previous year. I daresay you have forgotten what the expectation of our other girls' nuptials did to your infamous nerves."

"Oh! Mr. Bennet, you do not fool me with your concern for my poor health, I believe you think only of yourself and fear the expense of a wedding." She looked at Mary. "You see, your father would have you die an old maid to keep the extra pounds in his purse, that is his selfish nature for you."

"You are quite wrong, my dear," said Mr. Bennet. "I would be more than happy to see our little Mary married. Sillier girls have managed it before her, whoever the fellow may be he will be warmly welcomed here."

Mrs. Bennet became angrier. "Whoever he may be? What kind of talk is this? You know very well that he is Robert Price, my *brother's* clerk. You speak as if Mary had a queue of gentlemen to choose from. No indeed, Robert Price will do just right for Mary."

"I daresay he will and being in the enviable position of having no competitors, he will be confident, in recommending himself, of acceptance," said Mr. Bennet. "And you know both of them are rarely without their noses in a book. Neither are they handsome enough between them to invite unwanted attention, I should say it would be a perfect alliance."

Mrs. Bennet insisted on continuing the conversation although no formal offer or proposal had yet been made. This did not deter her. By tea time she had informed Mary that silk would be most suitable for a wedding dress although much ·depended on what time of year she married, in which case some of the finer cottons and muslins would be perfectly acceptable. "But I suggest, my dear, that you marry sooner rather than later, grasp the opportunity Mary, for you are unlikely to get another."

"I have had no proposal, mama," pleaded Mary.

"I am never wrong about these things, Mary, trust me," said Mrs. Bennet. "Oh, to think I should return from the lakes to find you in all this state, I do not know how I cope."

By the following afternoon, Mr. Price had indeed called at Longbourn to seek an address with Mary. With what trepidation did the young man approach Longbourn. He was there, at the door, smoothing his hair and straightening his waistcoat by eleven o'clock.

"See if I am not right, Mr. Bennet," said Mrs. Bennet knowingly, when a good while had passed. "They have been in the drawing room for a full half an hour. You wait, if he is not in your library asking for her hand in five minutes I shall retire to my bed forever."

Mr. Bennet smiled. "Then I hope, my dear, that he has called to comment on the fine weather we are having for this time of year and makes no more of the occasion than that."

"Oh, Mr. Bennet, you cannot vex me with your silly jokes, they are not in the least funny."

"Well, my dear, I am sorry you feel that way, but you do not discourage me, for I make sport for my own amusement and in that sense it serves me very well."

Mrs. Bennet ignored her husband and went to the library door. "Ssh!" said she. "He is coming, I hear him." She opened the door to leave but turned back again to her husband and said in a harsh whisper, "No jokes, Mr. Bennet, you do not want to put the young man off, if you do we may never get Mary settled."

Mrs. Bennet then went to sit with her daughter in the drawing room, while Mr. Bennet welcomed Mr. Price into his library. In a great state of excitement Mrs. Bennet instructed Hill to make some alterations for the evening's table. "For although it may seem presumptuous, I think we shall have one extra. Oh, hang it all!" she cried on glancing at the mantle clock, "we are too late to think of that leg of mutton! Still, Mr. Price is not so high that he will not be grateful for a piece of pie." She caught Mary's eye. "There is no need to look at me like that, Mary, the pie will do very nicely, this is not Mr. *Darcy* we are entertaining. I see no need to worry over the quality of the wine! I keep as good a table as the next person, better I daresay, and without the advantage of a French chef."

Mary, who could have eased her mother's suffering by confiding that Mr. Price had proposed and was indeed requesting her father's consent, elected to say nothing.

By dinnertime Mrs. Bennet could no longer have any doubts and she made no delay in telling Mr. Price how delighted she was at the news. Nor was she reticent about expressing her hopes for another of her daughters.

"Kitty next, Mr. Bennet, I flatter myself that not a single one of my daughters will end an old maid."

"You could be right, Mrs. Bennet, and what intricate plan do you have laid out for our Catherine?"

Mrs. Bennet, although eager to rebuke her husband, turned

instead to Mr. Price and made a great display of laughing the matter off. "You will forgive my husband, Mr. Price, he has a curious preference for absurd comments, he would have you think me calculating. Indeed he would! However, the joke prompts me to ask if you do have any brothers, Mr. Price."

The young man could not give a reply before Mr. Bennet had intervened. "Mrs. Bennet will never be easy until she has rid us of Kitty as well, I hope you will not disappoint my wife by being an only son?" he said.

"Sadly I think I shall, I have three sisters only," said Mr. Price.

"Oh what a shame," said Mrs. Bennet. "Never mind, all is not lost, I may make a little suggestion to Lizzy, when I write with this news, that she take on the assignment of introducing Kitty to some suitable gentleman whilst she is in Derbyshire."

Robert Price greeted Mary's offer to play with enthusiasm and turned pages for her.

"You see, Mrs. Bennet," said her husband in confidence, "this young man is either uncommonly kind or tone-deaf that he makes such a convincing portrayal of enjoyment."

Mrs. Bennet silenced her husband with a harsh look. For most of the evening she indulged in self-congratulation. For had not she known, and ensured to some degree, that her daughters would all end well? "Of course poor Lydia has had her share of troubles, but that is your fault, Mr. Bennet," she said in a whisper and having so shamelessly disowned responsibility for any familial ills and so greedily taken all credit for familial success she settled to her needlework with satisfaction.

Elizabeth was astonished to read of Mary's news. "This is all so sudden. Mary has quite surprised us all I am sure. But what of Lady Catherine? Poor Anne, they will waste no time in seeking out a replacement. Lady Catherine cannot be expected to exist without adulation," she said to Lydia.

"Well I hope he is fond of sermons," said Lydia of Robert Price, "for I do not imagine Mary shall think of giving them up."

"Certainly not! Oh, wait! Mama wants me to arrange a suitable match for Kitty now! That is just like her. I am barely strong enough to give time to all the particulars of my own life, but no, it is here, she wishes me to arrange Kitty's too."

It had been too long since the sisters had enjoyed light conversation and merriment and their mother's letter provided an ample source of diversion. Elizabeth entertained her sister with chosen excerpts. "Oh Lydia, listen to this, mama writes that he, Mr. Price, wears spectacles also, so he is perfectly acceptable to Mary. There Lydia, success in marriage is entirely due to both parties having poor eyesight!"

"Well it does not surprise me in this case," said Lydia mischievously, "a man with good eyesight would never marry Mary."

"Lydia, do not be cruel," said Elizabeth smiling.

"You only scold me because you think you should."

"It is the way of we older sisters, whether our knowledge be greater is debatable, but our age, which is certainly superior affords us the opportunity to reprimand you younger siblings as and when we please."

Lighthearted of mood the sisters passed their afternoon, as if no worry or trouble could touch them. They gave no voice to any serious concerns. They chose, one consciously, one not, to give way to frivolity and enjoy talk of an inconsequential nature. At the point in their conversation when it seemed their laughter would not cease, Lizzy became aware of the first signs that her child might come. Lydia did not, in all her rapture, see any difference in her sister though Elizabeth's face had paled and her laughter had stopped abruptly. She made an excuse of sudden tiredness. "Oh Lydia, you will excuse me, I fear our merriment has quite fatigued me, I must retire."

The girl watched her sister make to leave the room. "We were having such a lovely time though, Lizzy," she complained. "Can you not send Kitty or Maria to keep me company, or Georgiana?"

Elizabeth managed a quiet reply. "They are in town with Mr. Hanworth and the Colonel at Lady Metcalfe's pleasure."

On finding her mistress in the hall and seeing her so pale and shocked Mrs. Reynolds decided upon immediate action.

"I shall call for Mrs. Quinn directly, ma'am," she said.

"Oh no!" Elizabeth protested. "I am quite well, just a little tired, I have stayed too long with my sister."

Mrs. Reynolds took a long look at Elizabeth, knowing the truth but not wishing to alarm her mistress she said, "If you are sure, ma'am."

In that instant Elizabeth wished to declare her good health and settle the woman but she was taken up with the strongest of feelings. Quite overtaken with the suddenness of the discomfort she let out a cry of, "Oh Lord" and held herself against such pain should it come again.

The nurse was quickly called and after a moment's examination of her patient she offered assurance. "I shall be but a moment, ma'am, do not worry yourself." She left calmly but made rapid progress to find a manservant. On doing so, she gave her instructions for the surgeon to come. "Tell him to make haste, it is upon us so suddenly," she said.

Elizabeth had the feeling of being between worlds. The time had now come, her endurance was tested like never before but she was determined not to cry out or protest.

"This is no time for bravery, ma'am," said Mrs. Quinn on her return. "You let it out, my love."

All the while she cried, Elizabeth thought of Darcy. Oh, if he could hear her torment all the way in town he would surely return to her.

When Mr. Drummond had arrived the fullest part of an hour had passed. He sought a report from the nurse. "Mrs. Quinn?"

The woman, mindful of her mistress, whispered her account to the surgeon. "Very fast, sir, it will be very fast, she suffers so. It is a willful child to be sure!"

"Impatient! Like the father!" said Drummond in good humor. He approached his patient in a calm professional manner. "There now, madam, do not be fretful. You will have your child before very long."

"Can you help her, sir?" asked Mrs. Quinn. "She is a strong girl to be sure, but I cannot bear to see her in such agony, what have you brought that might ease her suffering?" she asked with a glance at the doctor's bag.

Mr. Drummond raised his eyebrow at the nurse. "Do not get flustered, Mrs. Quinn. Good Lord, you have done this time and time before, I did not expect you to be so gathered up in it. Mrs. Darcy will do very well as nature intends."

Elizabeth could only allow the pain to conquer her. Mrs. Quinn argued with the doctor. "Help her, sir, I *insist*. I have seen many a child into the world, as you rightly say, and this woman is tortured, relieve her, I beg you."

The surgeon looked kindly upon his patient. "*She* does not urge me, *she* does not create," he concluded.

The nurse was again willing to risk her position. "Help her, sir, I insist that you trust my judgment above your own."

Drummond now wiped Elizabeth's brow and spoke to his nurse. "But you see she is quiet, Mrs. Quinn, why can I not trust my own judgment, is my experience of thirty years insufficient? Must I instead rely upon yours?"

Elizabeth cried out again. Mrs. Quinn stayed devotedly by her but she implored the surgeon. "You could see a thousand children into this world and never have my experience, Mr. Drummond. I am a mother and I command you to alleviate this woman's pain."

The surgeon could conceal neither his shock nor his shame. He busied himself in the office of searching the contents of his bag.

Mrs. Quinn spoke closely in her mistress's ear. "Thank heaven, ma'am, he has henbane."

Darcy arrived back at Pemberley that afternoon. A man took his overcoat, hat, and cane and Mrs. Reynolds summoned him to the drawing room. "I am so glad you are returned, sir, Mr. Drummond wishes to speak with you, I shall get him directly."

Darcy found himself unable to stay in the room; he left hastily, brushed briskly past the housekeeper and ran up the main staircase. Drummond, hearing the master's heavy footsteps, met him at the top. "I am dulling the pain for her, sir, she has taken spirit of hartshorn and henbane, this is a mighty strong labor, the nurse is by her."

"Let me to her!" Darcy demanded, but the surgeon put a firm arm on Darcy's. "No, sir, it is no place for a gentleman, Mrs. Quinn would have a fit," he said, "besides, you would be best engaged by your *own* wife's bedside, Fitzwilliam."

Darcy took a breath and closed his eyes for a moment. "I thought you were talking of my *wife*, sir," he said with slight irritation.

The surgeon smiled. "Congratulations, Darcy," he said, shaking his hand. "You have a son, not a half hour into this world."

"Thank you," said Darcy coolly. "But explain, am I to take it that Mrs. Wickham is in labor also?"

"As we speak, sir. Quite a situation, is it not? One set the other off perhaps, it would not be the first time."

Darcy wasted no time and headed directly for the room where his wife rested, he turned to the surgeon. "What of Mrs. Wickham, can you assure me she will be well?"

"We are doing all we know. Oh sir, with Mrs. Quinn otherwise engaged should I call Mrs. Reynolds to attend Mrs. Darcy?"

"No, damn it!" said Darcy. "I shall attend her myself."

Drummond shook his head. "Singular."

Elizabeth at first thought she had a waking dream on seeing her husband by her bedside. He took up her hand. "Oh, my darling girl," he said, "I am here now."

"It is not a moment too soon," she said weakly, "but pray do not look at me, the nurse has not finished with me yet, she was called to Lydia urgently."

Darcy nodded. "We have a son, Elizabeth," he said.

"As you see," said Elizabeth, glancing to the crib. All the while she prayed he would go and take one small look at the infant. But he remained by her side.

"You are well? Do you need anything?" he asked.

"Little more than rest," she said, "for all my endurance and country walks I was ill prepared for this."

Never tearing his eyes from Elizabeth, Darcy stood and unfastened his cuffs and rolled the sleeves of his shirt to his elbows. He loosened his neckcloth and waistcoat, then discarded both on a chair.

"My love," he said, "let me take my kerchief and cool your face." He went to the washstand, took up the jug and dampened the cloth.

"You would have Mrs. Quinn out of a job, sir," said Elizabeth teasingly.

Darcy smiled. "Of all the times to be lively, Elizabeth, you choose now," he said, mopping her face tenderly.

"I am happy," she explained and daring to prevail upon him, she said, "and you, what feelings have you now? Knowing he is here, can you bear not to acknowledge him? You know, my sister may well have a girl, if so you already know the identity of your child."

Darcy bowed his head, daring not to look into the crib, tears came rapidly to his eyes and half due to anger and half due to pure emotion he spoke, his voice shaken.

"You know I could not have borne it, Elizabeth, that I have been such a fool causes me shame, I can no better hide him from my eyes than I could you." He stood now, relieved but vulnerable as if something of his soul had become raw and exposed. He looked again at his wife before walking to the crib; he stood a moment then bent gently to peer in. Their precious infant was sleeping. He leaned close over the crib. The child's soft sweet breaths were at once intoxicating and such a feeling of tenderness came over Darcy that his tears were unstoppable. For many moments Elizabeth watched her husband sob unashamedly, while their son slept peacefully.

Finally, he could cry no more. "Forgive me, Elizabeth, forgive me," he urged.

"What am I to forgive, Fitzwilliam? Have your tears wronged me?"

Darcy regained his composure. "The only wrong is that they were not your own, you have been given more reason to shed them than I. How you must have suffered, my love. How selfish I have been. I beg you to have mercy on me. I did not know what I was doing. I acted in an ungenerous way and I apologize."

Elizabeth smiled and held his hand tighter. "It is all forgot," she said through tears. The infant began to stir in the crib. "Bring your son to me, Fitzwilliam, I must feed him."

Without knowing how strong or how gentle his arms should be Darcy held his son for the first time and placed him tenderly beside his wife.

Then came a knock at the door and upon being summoned Mrs. Quinn entered. She looked surprised to see Mr. Darcy sitting comfortably on her mistress's bed. The infant suckled contentedly.

Mrs. Quinn made straight to the bedside; she looked at Darcy with astonishment. "Oh! If you do not mind me saying, sir, the usual manner of husbands on these occasions is to take a glass of brandy downstairs, this is no place for a man," said she.

Darcy did not move from his position but kept to it and fixed his eyes on Elizabeth, he addressed the nurse without looking at her. "What a silly notion. A stuffy view in my opinion. Of what are you afraid, Mrs. Quinn? Do you imagine that I have not seen my wife's breast before?"

The nurse was at once shocked and silenced.

Elizabeth saw on her husband's face a self-satisfied expression. "Fitzwilliam!" she scolded quietly.

Mrs. Quinn made another attempt at composure. "I came to announce, sir, madam, that Mrs. Wickham was delivered of a daughter not a quarter of an hour ago."

"Oh, I am happy," cried Elizabeth, "send her my love and congratulations, she will understand that I do not go to her."

"Of course, madam, mother and infant are both well. They rest now."

Darcy dismissed the nurse. "Would you return to attend my wife in a few moments, Mrs. Quinn?"

When the woman was gone from the room, Darcy turned to Elizabeth. "I must go directly to Lambton, my love, but I will, *I promise you*, be back before long."

Elizabeth sighed. "Well Mrs. Quinn will be glad to have you out of the way, you shocked her."

"Yes I did and I rather enjoyed it," said Darcy.

"But why must you go, is there unfinished business?"

Darcy shook his head. "This is not a matter of business, it is a matter of life."

Elizabeth was puzzled. "Should you not be here for our announcement, when are we to reveal we have a son *and* a daughter?" she asked.

Darcy held her gaze firmly. "I implore you, Elizabeth, do nothing until I am returned. Trust me." With that, he was gone. Elizabeth heard the carriage that took him, once again, from Pemberley.

"I do trust you," she whispered, but she wondered, for the first time since their marriage, if she was right to.

CHAPTER 25

"Pray do not talk of that odious man."

William Collins had received a letter from Lady Catherine. He at once summoned his wife. "Charlotte my dear," he said with superiority, "Lady Catherine de Bourgh has at last condescended to have us back at Hunsford." His wife was astonished. Her husband explained. "Yes, my dear, it is true, we must oblige her by returning posthaste. She writes that Anne is in a state of distress about Mary's departure."

Charlotte's response was to touch upon the happy circumstances of Mary's engagement. "When I called yesterday at Longbourn I admit I did not recognize Mary, she is so full of life, I am very happy for her."

"Charlotte, that is beside the point. The matter in hand is that we are once again to receive the gracious condescension of Lady Catherine. She has made a wise choice in requesting my return."

"A second choice is not always made through wisdom, Mr. Collins," said Charlotte with the immediate feeling that her observation would not be appreciated by her husband.

"My dear Charlotte, I think it will do you good to be reacquainted at Rosings, it seems you quite forget yourself these days. Lady Catherine would be astonished to hear you speak so, to your own husband. I shall pray for you, Charlotte, that this deviance in your nature will cease. To be possessed by such irreverence! For now though, my dear, it will not do to be at odds. I shall inform your father of our intended departure. He will, I daresay, be as happy as he will be sad. I flatter myself, but I think he has enjoyed my company and may well miss it when I am gone again to Hunsford."

As he had promised, and as Elizabeth had trusted he would, Darcy returned to Pemberley some hours later. He went straight to his wife and kissed her cheek. He looked weary but somehow free, confident, and assured.

"Elizabeth," he said softly, "I must make a confession to you now and pray you will hear me out."

Elizabeth, surprised by her husband's declaration, teased him. "Pray do not tell me you have taken a lover, for I have not the strength to berate you."

"I have a lover in you," he said tenderly. "I find nothing wanting."

"Oh, Fitzwilliam, please do not tell me you have embarrassed Mrs. Quinn again, I never saw a woman so red-faced."

Darcy stood. "Hear me out, Elizabeth, I do not speak in jest and beg you not to resort to doing so at present. I cannot easily find a way to begin my discourse but I must delay no more." He paced the room and was silent for a moment. Finally, he went on. "You know that you have been my redeemer, Elizabeth. I never acknowledged how much I needed salvation until you had saved me. Before that time I would not have thought redemption would have come in the form of a lively spirited young woman! But, there it is, from the unlikeliest of events a man is made. Not through his birthright or his proud manners, nor his mistaken beliefs in his own superiority."

Elizabeth laughed but was confused by her husband's sudden sentimental discourse. "You flatter me, Fitzwilliam, but I do not know why you do so, I know of the changes in you, but they are not all my doing, I could not have made you good if you had not the least capability of being so. I am honored to think you attribute all your compassion to me, but I cannot accept the accolade. I may have been the means of revealing your decency and that is all. I did not create it but perhaps uncovered it when you had kept it so well hid. There is no mystery to me."

Darcy shook his head. "There is a mystery to all things in life that love has touched. You must at least take credit for showing me that."

"Then in that I will oblige you if it makes you easier."

Still walking about the room Darcy implored his wife. "Oh, Elizabeth, can you not see, how much I have learned? I, who fought initally to conquer my love for you—I had not the vaguest idea that such passion cannot be defeated."

"But you confuse me, Fitzwilliam. Pray explain yourself."

Darcy began, sometimes sitting by her, at other times walking the room, to tell her all that he had concealed for so long. "When first we consented to help Lydia and take her child I was confident but only so because of my detachment. I had not the advantage of feeling our child grow inside that you have had. Forgive me that I had the audacity and ignorance to make such decisions in so impulsive a manner. It was not long before I began, with growing uncertainty, to notice the change in you. I became increasingly aware of the realities of what I had decided but I could not reverse the situation." He went over to the window. "Some may call it a softening of my character I suppose. I cannot explain it. When Wickham came here you detected it in me but I denied it to you and for that I am sorry. You were right, Elizabeth, that my approach to the man ended up kinder than your own. He has his respected and esteemed father to thank for that, you have heard him called an excellent man, he was my own father's equal in many respects. I held on to the faint hope that if a small measure of his father's character existed in Wickham I should have a chance to influence him, persuade him, if you like, to take the decent route in life."

He went to her side again and took her hand in his own. "I do not wish to alarm you, but for a long time I meditated on the very great difference in my character the prospect of my heir induced. From these reflections I came upon the idea that if I could be so transformed who was I to deny another man the same chance of redemption." Elizabeth went to speak but her husband silenced her and went on. "I began to feel as a thief might every time I considered taking his child and his chances. In vain I sought to conquer my feelings but could not let the matter rest. As the time drew near I could take no other action than to seek Wickham out. He was easily come by, I found him once more with Mrs. Younge in town."

"So you had no business in London?" asked Elizabeth.

"You see my deception, Elizabeth, but I could not reveal my premeditation to you then. I have done the right thing, I assure you. I found Wickham in a poor state, sick and tortured by more than the liquor. A confrontation ensued, I will not offend you with all the details of it, only to say we drew swords. Events became unpleasant until he was made to see that I could overcome him. I discarded my defense for I knew that I had weapon enough to subdue him, that my words alone would overthrow him. I told Wickham that he was soon to be a father, as I was. In doing this I know I risked more than my own reputation. I allowed him to be shocked and accepted his anger, but once his violence was spent I had all the assurance I could have asked for."

Elizabeth made no attempt to hide her shock. "In what way could he possibly assure you? You must know that he has the clever mastery to appear good when he is not. He is a man who gives that appearance easily."

"I know of his playacting, my love, I know he has the happy ability to speak words of love when his heart is consumed with hate. I did not make my judgment with my eyes, for they are just as readily deceived as the next man's."

"Then how did you judge him?"

"In the only right way, Elizabeth, with my heart," said Darcy.

When Elizabeth heard next of Wickham's tears and of Darcy's true conviction that they were shed in actual sorrow she did not know herself. To accept Wickham, forgive him even, in every way opposed her instincts. But how often had she misjudged others? That her convictions were always strong was unquestionable, but their strength did not ensure their accuracy. Oh, what to do? How to act? To know, if only by some small sign, which course would lead to the desired destination. Where was intuition now? All comprehension was lost to Elizabeth; trepidation marred her thoughts. "I confess I cannot easily think well of Wickham but my concerns, my fears are... oh, too many to mention, too serious to ignore. But what of Lydia? Pray tell me she does not know of this." And then, incredulous at all that Darcy had been about, she probed, "You cannot mean to tell me you have persuaded him to make amends there?"

Darcy paused then went on. "Until this very last I had my doubts, but I could not let them stop me doing what is right. When I first saw my own child I knew I had done right by being the means to bring Wickham to his."

"I cannot believe it."

Darcy was determination itself, his voice, his expression, and his stance all showed his resolve. "What is it that sits outside your comprehension, my love, that Wickham can be reformed or that I could believe it feasible?"

"Both I suppose, I had not dreamed either possible."

"You play with me, Elizabeth, you are more than capable of believing anything possible, you, a connoisseur of the human condition, will not recoil aghast, surely?"

"Fitzwilliam, pray allow me time for reflection, if I have the powers of observation you credit me with then you will afford me the time to use them wisely, I am inclined to keep away from rash decisions at present." She then expressed her desire to know all that had taken place between her husband and Wickham, thinking all the time that if Darcy had found some gentle spot in his heart for his enemy, then she should endeavor to find a similarly tender place in hers, however impossible it seemed.

Darcy continued, "Wickham traveled back from town with me as far as Lambton. I set him up at the inn there promising to come here and make clear my intentions to you and to Lydia. Believe me, my love, you had not the advantage of them but those hours from London in the carriage finally helped to settle our personal misgivings. There is little capacity in a barouche for men to solve matters with swords. Even words must be used sparingly, you know how conversation suffers on the less well-laid roads, but in that forced halting of talk lay some benefit, that of quiet reflection. Although in reality I can speak only for myself I believe those long moments when we sat face to face have since proved as restorative to the situation as any lengthy debate or duel could have done. We were eye to eye at some points, I would not let my gaze falter as his was at first inclined to—I held him with it—commanded him by looking as far as I imagined I could into his soul. It was not so charred as you might think."

Seeing Elizabeth taken aback, Darcy raised his hand at once to silence and reassure. "I know you, Elizabeth, you think I might be mistaken. Is it possible you intend to tell me I could not have looked deep enough? Pray do not. I have seen all I needed to. There is not a sight so naked as a man's soul bared and one so scarred and bruised as Wickham's I venture I will not see again, at least it is my hope that I shall not. You know the rest, my Elizabeth, upon arriving home I found that I was already a father and that he was soon to become one. In that instant I knew beyond any doubt that I must venture to restore faith and humility in Wickham. I went away directly, as you know, to Lambton, and have brought back my enemy in peace. He is in the drawing room. He awaits news of your acceptance before going to his wife and child. Will you let me tell him he has your blessing?"

Elizabeth was very aware that she was in no fit state to make rational choices. "It will be easy to give my blessing in words. Tell him to go to his wife and daughter, but afford me time to discipline myself. I must establish a means to re-educate myself to forgive him, to repel all thoughts of disdain and start anew."

"You are not resentful by nature, my dearest Elizabeth, I have every faith that on seeing your sister happy again you will find it in your heart to forgive him."

"She does still believe herself in love with him," Elizabeth conceded. "I imagine she could persuade herself toward happiness, but what of his feelings for her?"

"They have the very best chance of becoming stronger, Elizabeth, he may have taken Lydia as a wife for all the wrong reasons, but I believe he wishes to keep her as his own for all the right ones," said Darcy who watched as the great tears of relief, made all the more ready from abundant happiness, splashed onto Elizabeth's cheeks.

CHAPTER 26

"Oh," cried Elizabeth, "I am excessively diverted."

———

September brought with it the arrangements for Mary's wedding. Longbourn once again rang with the sounds of Mrs. Bennet's cries, sometimes euphoric but often panic-stricken. She found, once more, that she had ple3
nty of reasons to be boastful. Lady Lucas was one of the first recipients of her bragging. "Elizabeth has borne a son, thank the good Lord I say, for I cannot imagine Mr. Darcy accepting a daughter first time, people of his sort virtually insist on a son and heir to start with. I am only glad Elizabeth had the good sense to oblige him! Lydia of course has surprised us all and had a daughter and her husband is no longer detained by business so he is returned. And Mary's news you already know."

"You have every reason to be very pleased, Mrs. Bennet," said Lady Lucas.

"You are very good, Lady Lucas, very good indeed, I sincerely wish all your children equal felicity in marriage."

"I thank you," said Lady Lucas calmly, "and I accept your good wishes readily, for I recently have news of Maria, Colonel Fitzwilliam has asked Sir William for her hand, we are very pleased."

Mrs. Bennet let out a cry. "Oh well, there we are then, Lady Lucas, that will lessen the blow of Charlotte's departure for you."

Lady Lucas hid her astonishment at Mrs. Bennet's insolent manner. "Ah, but they are once again to be very well catered for at Hunsford, I console myself with that knowledge."

Mrs. Bennet lowered her voice and looked about the room as if to ensure the absence of eavesdroppers. "But Lady Catherine is not to be trusted, Lady Lucas, she can take away as soon as give, it would be best to advise Mr. and Mrs. Collins to err on the side of wariness. She is the most two-faced woman I ever came across. She treated my Mary very ill indeed! But I am not the resentful sort you know, I think I may just as well forget all about it and get on with the more pleasant things in life. Oh Lady Lucas, you must come to me with any little queries you may have about Maria's wedding arrangements. Heaven knows there is not a mother more acquainted with the matter than me. No indeed, when Mary is married I will have four daughters out of five settled within a year!"

"You are too kind, Mrs. Bennet, I shall not hesitate to seek your advice," said Lady Lucas without commitment. She took her leave with the sincerest belief that she would not, if she could avoid it, have Mrs. Bennet involved in Maria's arrangements.

Lady Metcalfe's party, which included Georgiana, Maria, and Kitty, returned to Pemberley. The latter feeling somewhat exhausted by her companions' affairs. It was the worst thing in the world, she thought, to spend so much time amongst lovers without having one of your own. Maria Lucas had annoyed her most definitely once the Colonel had applied to Sir William for her hand. Georgiana and Mr. Hanworth had made no such announcements but Kitty knew that it could not be long before they would. "Thank heaven I shall at least have Lydia for company," she said aloud to herself.

Elizabeth, finally accepting Wickham's return, agreed to her husband's suggestion of allowing the small family to have one of the larger estate cottages on the outskirts of Pemberley's grounds.

"I hope your sister will not think it insulting, it is certainly not meant that way."

Far from being affronted, Lydia had received the news with gratitude. All of her fears had been allayed and once again all her dreams were coming true. That she had a handsome husband, a sweet daughter, and the address of Pemberley was enough for her.

"I shall write to all my friends as soon as possible," cried she.

Wickham too was gratitude itself. Elizabeth noted that he did appear changed. She adopted a determination where he was concerned; that previous history would not color her present opinions, but it was difficult for her. She imagined that it was with some meditation that he came upon her in the breakfast room one morning. On entering the room he bowed to greet her.

"Mrs. Darcy, you are quite alone?" he asked.

Elizabeth looked about the room. "As you see."

"Forgive this intrusion, madam, but I beg you, devote a few moments of your time to hear me."

"Please Mr. Wickham, you need not be hesitant, I am not about to reprimand you."

Wickham smiled. "I am glad of it Mrs. Darcy. We have always been friends, have we not?"

"I prefer to think we gave the convincing appearance of being so, the basis of our friendship, as you define it, was never very sound, indeed, how could it have been when it was built on the infirmity that is deception?" said Elizabeth coolly.

Wickham knelt to the floor near where she sat. "I understand your caution but let me say this, if our relationship was based on falsehood of any kind I must own that I am to blame." He looked at her for a moment. "Let us begin our friendship from this moment and let its origin be genuine, Mrs. Darcy."

"I generally prefer that type of friendship to any other, falsehood makes enemies, not friends, Mr. Wickham."

"I sense your disapproval, I comprehend it absolutely and I pray we will not be enemies any longer."

"I have never been your enemy, Mr. Wickham, but you have been mine. Forgive me that I have not my husband's philanthropy. I cannot accept the idea of you being decent so easily as you might wish. There, it must be a cause of astonishment for you that I, the Elizabeth you once deemed so malleable, should prove harder to win than my husband. But," she ventured thoughtfully, "I am wiser by a small degree than ever I was and admit I have been made ever more cautious by the insincerity I have occasioned to witness in others. You might say it has hardened me, Mr. Wickham."

"Not too much I hope, Mrs. Darcy. Allow me the opportunity to beg you, do not lose your tenderness, it is this quality that so defines you."

"And causes my vulnerability. Mr. Wickham, I hope I am to be understood, kindly end all thoughts of my tenderness; it is a feature of my personality that I reserve for my husband. Allow me, in my own way, to come to terms with your rebirth, your reform or however you best define it. I hope with all my heart that you will prove me wrong and show yourself, by the means of unfailing decency, to be a worthy recipient of my husband's beneficence."

"This, I detect, seems impossible to you?"

Elizabeth laughed. "If you only knew what I have seen in my life you would not think so. No, I do not believe anything impossible. That my husband could have held a sword at your throat and refrained from cutting it seems to me an impossibility, yet it is not. Here you stand, Mr. Wickham. I am sorry, have I shocked you with my vivid depiction?"

Wickham shook his head. "No, no, I am not shocked, I am as humbled by your honesty as I am by your husband's integrity. I thank God that he was able to judge that the promise of life could overpower me far more completely than the threat of death."

Elizabeth could contain her misgivings no longer. "And what of Lydia, your intentions where she is concerned are honorable I hope?"

"Never more so than now, Mrs. Darcy, you may rest assured that I shall spend the rest of my days pursuing your sister's compensation. That she has deigned to forgive me fills my heart."

Elizabeth smiled. "You are a lucky husband to have as uncomplicated a wife as my sister, Mr. Wickham, her memory is admirably short where trauma is concerned."

"You are right, she is not resentful."

"No she is not, her purpose in life is to spend as much of it as possible in pursuit of enjoyment. Being resentful would only serve to deprive her of her own happiness, she has sense enough to see that, Mr. Wickham and, I say this with some reluctance, she does love you, though how you or I measure or define love may be entirely different, but make of it what you will. You have Lydia's regard and affection. I beg you do not abuse it further."

"I assure you, madam, I will not."

Elizabeth stood and went over to the window. "You came here for my forgiveness, I cannot give it easily in words. However I do not wish to cause you pain, I start with every intention of speaking of pardoning you." She shook her head and sighed. "In words at least it seems my desire to attack you is stronger than my need to forgive you, but it is not so. I have accepted you here, acceptance, Mr. Wickham, will do in place of any true welcome until such time as my heart dictates."

"Your acceptance, Mrs. Darcy, is as good as a hundred welcomes."

Elizabeth turned to look at him. "Oh, Mr. Wickham," she said in exasperation, "I do not seek your flattery, your compliments go a little way toward securing my faith in you but such easily bestowed praise does not prove to me your worth. Pretty words cannot persuade me of your good intentions."

"Then hear not my words but observe my actions and take this promise from me, madam, I will not fail you."

For some time Elizabeth was taken up by confusion; her brother-in-law seemed genuinely transformed. His intentions, his every look spoke of reform. But to trust him again, though her instincts urged her to, was difficult. How they had all suffered at his hands, how hard it was to keep faith in him, to forget his misconduct.

On each occasion, when she felt a small pang of hope on the matter, she was at once startled by her feelings of resentment, of suspicion. Oh, that he could be as good as he appeared by way of looks and manners. Elizabeth's frustration consumed her. Why do I worry so when my sister, who should be all taken up with concern, does not? She cursed the complexities of her nature. Too much thought, she concluded, was leading her away from her eventual goal of forgiveness. Other distractions were her relief, her child, of course, was her prize and furthermore her thoughts could not long be occupied solely by Wickham for she had other happy news to dwell on. She soon found her spirits lifted at the pleasing prospect of meeting Lady Metcalfe. This surprising, refreshing woman had accompanied her guests back to Pemberley.

At once Elizabeth wondered how Harriet Metcalfe had maintained so long an acquaintance with Lady Catherine when the two were so opposed in character. On the evening of the party's return from London a splendid dinner was arranged, the conversation was lively and by the time they had repaired to the drawing room Elizabeth was better able to witness Lady Metcalfe in full flow. She, Lady Metcalfe, was taking coffee by the fire and summoned Darcy to her side gesturing with her fan for him to join her.

"My daughter Cressida will be away at school in two years, Mr. Darcy. Let me insist, that you have Miss Pope for young Fitzwilliam. She is as good a governess as I could have wished for. Your aunt recommended her to me and I have never had a moment's complaint, Cressida's mastery of French has improved considerably under her tutelage. Oh please, tell me you will take my dear Miss Pope. It will save all the trouble of your putting a notice in the papers."

Darcy was, as ever, amused by Lady Metcalfe. "We have not yet baptized the boy, madam, I meet with the clergy tomorrow, let me keep my mind to that matter before I attempt to arrange his future education."

"Oh, you are right I know, I am hasty in all matters, but most particularly I simply cannot bear to consider that a good governess may go to waste, she is a treasure, you will like her a great deal but be cautious, she is young and may very well fall in love with you, sir!"

"I should hope not," said Darcy, astounded. "And in any case that hardly promotes her. If I thought her likely to do such a silly thing I would immediately deem her out of her wits and therefore an unsuitable governess. Lady Metcalfe, I was beginning to warm to the idea of your highly recommended Miss Pope, the reference is a good one, but now I fear my judgment is colored merely by the impression I have of her as a whimsical ninny with a predisposition to imagine romantic involvements where there is no chance of them." Darcy frowned sternly, and then there it was upon his face, a smile, a genuine expression of his amusement, which was caught by Elizabeth's having the chance to glance across at him.

He is teasing Lady Metcalfe! Poor creature, thought she, she has no idea he is all in jest, she will not know how to take him. Oh! What buffoonery and how very well it becomes him.

Lady Metcalfe was indeed quite shocked by Mr. Darcy's opinion and set about placating him. "Oh, sir, do not be affronted," she pleaded, "you will excuse my romanticism, it is a trait I cannot help. As a novelist I am always observing, taking little ideas here and there from life to draw my characters, you will forgive me."

"But of course," said Darcy, who bowed to bid the lady a farewell in order that he might speak with some of the others of the party. He did not get far. Lady Metcalfe again demanded his attention. "Mr. Darcy, let me thank you, if I may, you have been the means of a most sudden and unexpected inspiration." She saw his quizzical look. "My next romantic novel; a governess, born of poverty, falls in love with her handsome master, but the great divides of their separate backgrounds prevent their love. She leaves but is drawn back by a voice," said Lady Metcalfe dramatically. "Yes a voice!" she cried, "I shall add a little mysticism Mr. Darcy and make this tale ghostly, poetic license allows me that grace." She went on, "The governess returns to find the house burnt and her beloved gone, presumed dead. When she discovers he still lives her ecstasy knows bounds, but alas, he can never look upon her again for he has been blinded in the fire and quite tragically disfigured," said Lady Metcalfe quite clearly enraptured by her own narrative.

Darcy again tried to retreat. "That is quite a tale, ma'am. You should set about it with your pen without delay."

"Indeed I should, sir," said Lady Metcalfe, "before someone else has the idea and does it better!"

"Ah, madam you are too modest, no one could portray it more fervently than you, it is a tantalizing fiction," he said. He made his way across the room to Elizabeth who was talking with Colonel Fitzwilliam.

"I see Lady Metcalfe has consented to release you," said Elizabeth teasingly.

"Yes finally," said Darcy looking about the room. "I have apparently inspired her next work of fiction."

Elizabeth, even though she was newly acquainted with Lady Metcalfe, knew of the woman's literary tendencies. "Shall she model her hero on you?"

"Rather foolishly, yes," said he.

Elizabeth saw that he felt vaguely complimented and wished to mock him. "Alas it cannot succeed, you are entirely the wrong sort of man to be one of literature's desirables. You are altogether too difficult and complicated, I love you very much of course, but your personality would not be best portrayed in a book, readers would not like you at all," she observed.

Kitty, now further immersed in self-pity, engaged the next day in the girlish pursuit of playing a hopping game upon the flagstones of the hallway. Caring little for the ungainly appearance she created with her hopscotching, she continued to bob about the vestibule. With each hop her bitterness increased and with every skip it eased. Mrs. Reynolds soon came upon her. "Oh my dear girl," said the woman, "you cannot leap about here, the clergy are due for the master and mistress."

Kitty sighed, where was the excitement she longed for? If there was nothing more dour than the arrival of clergymen to divert her then Pemberley, she mused, was becoming decidedly tiresome. She assured the housekeeper that she had no intention of being involved in the clergy's arrival.

"I shall not get in their way, Mrs. Reynolds." At once she imagined Mr. Collins. "Oh Lord, if they be anything like him I shall pay especial attention to my invisibility," she muttered.

"Mind you *do* keep clear, child," warned Mrs. Reynolds, "they will think you possessed! Cavorting like that." She added hurriedly,

"Be out of the way soon child, they are expected any minute, you must find some other way to spend your afternoon—look sharp girl!"

Kitty indulged herself with one more go at the game then retreated into the breakfast room and sat by the window. "I am so bored," she said aloud to herself. Wickham's return had vexed her greatly for Lydia now had little time for her, and she had a baby. "Lydia is so stupid, how could she not have known? Lizzy is the same! Oh Lord, everyone has infants and husbands and lovers to fill their days."

Kitty Bennet sat and cried for a full ten minutes, not caring how she appeared, for who would pay any mind to her? She wiped her face on her sleeve. At last, she saw a carriage arrive at the front of the house. "Oh this will be the stuffy old priest," she groaned, "we shall have sermons until dinner and beyond."

But the decrepit creature of her mind's eye did not descend the carriage step. In his place was a young uncertain looking gentleman of about four and twenty. "Too handsome for a minister," said Kitty and suddenly mindful of her disheveled appearance, she put herself straight and decided that sermons may be just as interesting as lively conversation after all.

CHAPTER 27

"Now, Kitty, you may cough as much as you choose."

———◦◦◦———

"The reading shall naturally be from the Book of Common Prayer," said the young minister who had introduced himself as Jeremiah Cleary and proved to be, as far as one could judge within moments of meeting him, a pleasing, well-mannered young man.

"Yes of course," said Darcy.

"Have you appointed the godparents?" asked the minister.

Elizabeth spoke now. "Partially, sir, my husband's cousin Colonel Fitzwilliam takes the honor alongside my brother-in-law Charles Bingley," she paused, "the female selection is a difficult one to make, with so many sisters, sir, you understand I run the risk in delighting one and insulting three others."

Mr. Cleary smiled uncertainly. "Oh dear, if only I could advise as I know the Reverend Holcombe would."

Elizabeth reassured him. "Do not trouble yourself, we will come to a good arrangement."

The three spoke for a good while of the forthcoming event and the arrangements connected to it. With all the particulars detailed and the date set for the nineteenth day of September, there was nothing remaining. At last, Jeremiah Cleary stood to take his leave. "Until then, sir, madam," he said with a bow, "I shall look forward to seeing you in Matlock."

"Thank you," said Darcy returning the young man's bow, "but will you not stay for dinner? My wife and I have taken so much of your time and the hour is late now."

"This is an unexpected pleasure, sir, I am most grateful, I would be delighted," said Mr. Cleary.

That evening the dinner table was set to good advantage for the conversation. Darcy naturally had the head; Elizabeth his opposite at the foot, to her left sat the clergyman with Kitty directly across from him. Next to her Edwin Hanworth sat gazing across at Georgiana who was between Mr. Cleary and Colonel Fitzwilliam. Maria was next to Mr. Hanworth with as good a view of her favorite's face as she could have wished for. Mr. and Mrs. Gardiner and Lady Metcalfe completed the gathering at Darcy's end. Lady Metcalfe was as hungry for conversation as she was her main course.

"Your youngest sister Mrs. Darcy, she is not joining us?"

"No, ma'am, unfortunately not, she is not of a mind to socialize, she is recently reunited with her husband who has been away with the regiment. She has a new babe in arms. I think they prefer their own company at present."

"Singular, but admirably romantic," said Lady Metcalfe, then addressing Mr. Cleary at the far end of the table she said, "I am a great romantic, Mr. Cleary, I hope my overt opinions will not be too much for your sensitivities, sir."

Mr. Cleary looked surprised. "Not at all, madam," he said, "I am a great advocate of love myself."

"Oh how wonderful," said Lady Metcalfe. "And are you yet married?"

"No, ma'am I am not."

"Better and better," said Lady Metcalfe with a shrewd glance at Kitty whose face had become more than a little overspread with color.

Lady Metcalfe looked around at all present. "If I should pass away and see Heaven it could not be sweeter than this. I am surrounded by young lovers; it is indeed a treasure to see," she said with satisfaction.

When Lady Metcalfe at last afforded the others present a chance to have a share in the conversation, Jeremiah Cleary took the opportunity of talking to Kitty who, in order to keep his attention, showed an unexpected interest in, and knowledge of, Fordyce's Sermons. Elizabeth hid well her astonishment but recognized her sister's interest to extend beyond matters of doctrinal relevance. How clever she was and yet how ironical it all seemed, Elizabeth would never have dreamed she would see it, the spectacle of Kitty engrossed in conversation with a clergyman. But what a gentlemanlike manner he had and fine features too. Elizabeth knew full well that Mr. Collins could never have inspired so avid an interest in God as Mr. Cleary had the art of doing.

Later, in the drawing room Mr. Hanworth announced to Darcy and Elizabeth that the sale of Great Fordham Hall was at last complete and that the Bingleys should take residence by late October.

"Oh, I am so happy for Jane," said Elizabeth, "but, I confess, my felicitations are not at all generous for I relish the thought of having her nearer."

"I understand you are very close," said Mr. Hanworth.

"Oh yes we are, very close, but very different."

"You must understand, Mr. Hanworth," said Darcy, "that there is no one quite like Elizabeth, so she is naturally very different from everyone."

Elizabeth laughed. "You would have everyone think me a most singular person!"

Darcy smiled. "Not at all, Elizabeth," he protested. Turning to Mr. Hanworth he said, "Hear this, Hanworth, my wife, unlike other women, would not lie in after little Fitzwilliam's birth, the woman has every opportunity to take advantage of the best nannies and nurses in the land but she insists upon doing everything herself, she is quite determined."

"Oh, Fitzwilliam," cried Elizabeth, "how can you say that? I admit I like to do as much as I can, but I am not so obsessive, I am here enjoying this evening and quite happy to have Mrs. Quinn stay by William."

Darcy looked at his wife. "You are a terrible liar, Elizabeth, you are not accomplished at untruths at all. I would advise you not to attempt deception."

"My husband teases me, Mr. Hanworth, but he is much the same, he would not have you think it but he is just as likely to be found in the nursery as I am."

"Good Heavens!" cried Mr. Hanworth. "Pray tell me, what opinion does your nurse have of him?"

"Oh, she thinks very ill of him indeed, he has quite astonished her on more than one occasion, I can assure you," said Elizabeth merrily.

Darcy was adamant. "It is my house, surely I may go in any room I please, even if in doing so I risk alarming the nurse."

Hanworth laughed. "You pay no mind to convention in these matters, sir, it is admirable."

Darcy smiled. "I spent a great deal of my life concerned with petty principles and rules, I am a more natural being now, and proud of it."

"Heaven help the nurse!" said Hanworth.

Fitzwilliam Charles Darcy was baptized on the nineteenth day of September 1813. The couple's eventual choice for godmother was Kitty. This quite surprised Mary who had privately hoped for the honor herself. In the time since their first meeting Jeremiah Cleary and Kitty had formed an admirable relationship, and formed it with rapidity, he was gentlemanlike and attentive and she, quite surprisingly, responded to his reserved affections by returning them most fervently.

"I am happy for you, Kitty," said Elizabeth, "he is a truly good young man, you deserve him."

Mrs. Bennet was full of excitement. "Who would have thought it, Kitty to marry a clergyman, I could have believed it of Mary, but there we are!"

Kitty did not thank Lydia for reminding her that they had both laughed mercilessly at Charlotte Lucas for her choice of a clergy-man for a husband. "I wish you would not go on about it so, Lydia," she said, "I did not know then that clergymen could be handsome."

Mr. Bennet met the news with his usual astuteness. "They will do very well wherever they settle. He will excel himself in the church, I daresay. A good-looking parson could talk about the time of day in his sermons and still have a sizeable congregation every Sunday. I guarantee it. Young Mr. Cleary will make every girl in the land devout, just you wait. And Kitty, when she is Mrs. Cleary, will be jealous and smug all at the same time!"

September saw a burst of matrimonial activity, Colonel Fitzwilliam and Maria married in Derbyshire, Mary and Robert Price married from Longbourn, and Kitty and Jeremiah Cleary became engaged.

"What a happy month," said Elizabeth, "my mother does not know herself, if it were not for Jane's news of leaving Netherfield, she would be too happy for words. But alas, she is distraught at their moving. I confess I feel little sympathy for her, I am too taken up with pleasure at the thought of it myself."

"Ah yes, you will have your dear Jane back again," said Darcy.

"Indeed, and Caroline and Mrs. Hurst, we must not forget them, I cannot wait to see Jane and Bingley again but his sisters' company I can always do without."

"Mrs. Hurst, I understand, will not be making calls, she is still in mourning, remember. Take solace, Elizabeth, I have it on good authority that Caroline is to spend the winter with Lady Catherine."

"Really?" asked Elizabeth. "Poor Mr. Collins."

CHAPTER 28

"I am happier even than Jane; she only smiles, I laugh."

October brought Jane and Bingley to Derbyshire and much of that month was spent with the couple going between Pemberley and Great Fordham Hall. Jane threw herself wholeheartedly into the office of being aunt to baby Fitzwilliam. What a delight this cherub was, a solid, dark-eyed baby of an easy disposition.

"Like the master," observed Mrs. Reynolds. "Just the image of him! So good-natured. But I have always observed that they who are good-natured when they are children are good-natured when they grow up." The housekeeper's observation amused Elizabeth, at once for its being unfounded and for the fact that the woman had so often repeated it.

Jane and Elizabeth were so happy to be reunited and the friends likewise, for Darcy and Bingley valued each other's company. In happy reflection on the fortunate outcome of the previous year, Darcy and Elizabeth began in November to make plans for a ball at Pemberley.

"For Christmas! We shall invite everyone," said Darcy, "you will make up a list for the invitations, Elizabeth, and have them sent sooner rather than later."

Elizabeth was at once taken up with all the arrangements, the flowers, the food, the orchestra. All of her days for a great many weeks were filled with the organization of the assembly. "I have never in my life set about such a task," she said to Mrs. Reynolds who immediately set out to reassure her mistress. "Oh you are doing a fine job, ma'am, a fine job," she said. "Lady Anne would have been proud to see it. She was a great one for everything being perfect and you are just like her. No detail unattended. Her arrangements were always very much admired."

Elizabeth nodded. "So I hear, I am quite daunted by the prospect of attempting to equal her successes."

The housekeeper again gave her mistress words of encouragement but Elizabeth held firm the belief that she must not accept all the credit. "Oh I do not know how I would have seen to all my duties at Pemberley without your guidance, Mrs. Reynolds. I have taken so much credit for managing great affairs when really the accolade is yours if only those who have praised me knew it," said Elizabeth.

"Oh you flatter me, ma'am," said Mrs. Reynolds, "but you are not to worry yourself, it will be a wonderful evening, truly wonderful."

"And very interesting I am sure," said Elizabeth pointing to the guest list, "if Lady Catherine decides to grace us with her presence. And Caroline Bingley has been invited. What lively conversation we shall be favored with, there will be no shortage of cutting remarks, disapproving looks, and sly comments, all of which make for a certain form of diversion I suppose."

As the weeks passed and the replies gradually arrived at Pemberley Elizabeth went eagerly through them and divided the cards into neat piles representing those who graciously accepted the invitation and those who regretted that they could not. On finding Lady Catherine's card stating her regret, Elizabeth felt none. Caroline Bingley, however, was amongst those who would be attending.

"Oh well, I shall be as civil as possible," Elizabeth said, "but I am not sorry that Lady Catherine will not be favoring us with her company, I wonder how Caroline can dare to accept when the de Bourghs will not come, she is at Rosings for the winter. She has more audacity than I thought," said Elizabeth, studying the acceptance card from Miss Bingley. Examining it further she realized at once her oversight. "Oh heavens," cried she, "Lady Catherine will be seriously displeased, Caroline Bingley writes that she will be accompanied by Anne de Bourgh."

As Elizabeth rightly imagined Anne's decision to attend the ball had caused Lady Catherine the severest of displeasure. "This is Miss Bingley's doing I suppose," the latter said to her daughter, "well, I am not impressed, she pays no mind to your health or constitution, what can she be thinking dragging you off to Derbyshire for a ball?" For once Anne de Bourgh chose not the meek response her mother expected. She rose with quiet deliberation from her seat and said quite plainly, "You must not blame Miss Bingley, Mother, it was *I* who insisted upon going and I intend to enjoy every minute of it, I have even been learning to dance." This last was announced with so triumphant a lilt to Anne's voice that Lady Catherine found herself quite unnerved. "Learning to dance?" cried she in disbelief. "What kind of deviant influence has taken hold of you child?"

Caroline Bingley had entered the room and risking the loss of Lady Catherine's approval owned responsibility immediately. "I am afraid, madam, that the deviance you refer to is all mine, I believe it will do Anne good to be treated as most young ladies are and you will be overjoyed to know that she dances very well."

"Overjoyed? You are seriously misled, Miss Bingley, my daughter has never shown any inclination towards entertainments such as these you speak of."

"Oh, you are quite mistaken, your ladyship, she has every incli- nation towards the enjoyment of dancing, music and dare I say, eligible young men, all of which will be in plentiful supply at Pemberley."

Anne blushed slightly, which had the immediate effect of altering her sickly appearance.

"What have you done to my daughter?" demanded Lady Catherine with a harsh look at Miss Bingley.

Caroline Bingley smiled knowingly. "I hope, ma'am, that I have unwittingly found a remedy for her ailments."

CHAPTER 29

Every idea that had been brought forward by the housekeeper was favorable to his character, and as she stood before the canvas, on which he was represented, and fixed his eyes upon herself, she thought of his regard with a deeper sentiment of gratitude than it had ever raised before; she remembered its warmth, and softened its impropriety of expression.

On the evening of the ball Elizabeth remarked to Mrs. Reynolds that the time since she first came to Pemberley as mistress had escaped so quickly. She could scarce believe that Christmas was soon to be upon them. A light snow had fallen and made a magical scene of Pemberley. Pure white flakes fell like ivory stars and nestled on the branches of the wintering woods. The quiet sanctity of the chill days reflected the peace that had at last settled in her heart. She reviewed the year past in her mind but her present joy colored all previous resentment and washed away the pain of foregone tragedy. She looked from the nursery window over the park.

"So still and hushed," she whispered, "but soon we shall have carriages and guests arrive, it will not be so serene then," she said, leaning over the prettily dressed crib and kissing her infant. He did not stir at her touch or the rustle of her gown.

Mrs. Quinn said to Elizabeth, "You look beautiful, ma'am, perfect, this will be a great occasion, I do not believe we have had a ball like this since old Mr. Darcy's day."

Elizabeth shook her head and smiled. "No indeed, my husband says you have not. There are over two hundred guests expected, I must save my breath if I am to greet all of them." Leaving Mrs. Quinn to nurse young Fitzwilliam she went to walk the Long Gallery.

The strains of the practicing orchestra could be heard rising up from the ballroom. She paused for a long while to admire the fine portrait of her husband. She had been captivated by the painting from her first seeing it the previous August and her enchantment with his image was as complete as her adoration of the reality. How handsome a likeness it was, how cleverly it depicted his strength and everything that was good about him. For he was good, truly so, and her knowing him in the most intimate way had proven his excellence beyond doubt. It was so perplexing for her to recall that she had ever thought him even disagreeable.

But to remember that she had decided him to be wholly bad was at once a mystery to her. How painfully she recalled the naivety of her determination to dislike him. In her recollection, she made a study of her previous misplaced sentiments and was not happy to note them. I who credited myself as a great observer of human behavior, she mused. How foolishly I misled my own poor heart, she thought, and considering her old self to be opinionated and unforgiving she sought justification and amusement from her memories and so conceded; He was disagreeable it is true, I cannot reproach myself too harshly, we were both of us difficult creatures. Elizabeth spoke her reflections in the softest of tones. "To think how I once despised him yet could not admit to admiring him."

Darcy had walked the length of the gallery and reached his wife's side before her reverie was broken. He wore full evening dress with a cream silk trone d'amour neckcloth and though his fine features and figure required no improvement, his elegant attire dramatically enhanced his appearance.

"Elizabeth, may I ask, to what does your quiet discourse tend?" he said.

Elizabeth, surprised at first, then shy to have been caught speaking only to herself, turned to face her husband; her eyes met his. "If I do not tell you shall think me secretive and if I do I am afraid you shall think me very foolish," she protested playfully.

"I know you to be neither, so there is no great risk in revealing your thoughts to me," said Darcy.

Elizabeth turned her gaze again on his portrait. "You are not a bit altered, Fitzwilliam," she observed.

"You are mistaken, I am much changed," he said, himself observing the likeness. He pointed to it. "I am the better part of a decade younger here, Elizabeth."

Elizabeth could not disagree with him, for the painting originated from his father's lifetime; the subject could be no more than one and twenty. There was no dramatic alteration in him now, a maturity had set his features, he gave more the appearance of a man of the world than he had, there were indeed changes. But they were subtle. The Darcy in the portrait was neither a husband nor a father. She admitted that a certain youthfulness was shown in the painting that was no longer apparent in the man, but the loss of it was not to be mourned for in its place were qualities far more attractive and valuable than mere youth.

Darcy was still regarding the portrait. "I look at this man with detachment. I look at his eyes; they are eyes that have not yet looked upon you. His mouth hints at a smile but there can be no sure reason for his pleasure, his lips have not had the delights of yours, Elizabeth," he said softly and encouraged her to look again on his likeness. "It is certain he had a heart, this man, but it is empty because you had not yet filled it."

Elizabeth offered her hand to him; he raised it for a kiss. "I love you, Fitzwilliam," she said, "with all my heart."

"And I love you, Elizabeth."

They spoke then of matters past and Elizabeth confessed that she had stood bewildered before the painting, unable to reconcile her previous animosity to the man who she now adored.

"It is past, Elizabeth, we must let it be so."

"Yes, let the past die quietly taking its ghosts to rest alongside it, I cannot be haunted by them anymore."

Darcy was silent for a moment. "I must confess something to you my love," he said, producing some neatly folded sheets of hot pressed paper from his pocket. "Forgive me, I came across this when I was at your desk confirming details of the orchestra's instructions."

He gestured for Elizabeth to take the letter and she did so. She recognized her husband's hand and every word written, though not recently read by her, was familiarly painful to interpret.

The letter ran:

> *Be not alarmed, Madam, on receiving this letter, by the apprehension of its containing any repetition of those sentiments, or renewal of those offers, which were last night so disgusting to you. I write without any intention of paining you, or humbling myself, by dwelling on wishes, which, for the happiness of both, cannot be too soon forgotten; and the effort which the formation and the perusal of this letter must occasion should have been spared, had not my character required it to be written and read. You must, therefore, pardon the freedom with which I demand your attention; your feelings, I know, will bestow it unwillingly, but I demand it of your justice.*
>
> *Two offenses of a very different nature, and by no means of equal magnitude, you last night laid to my charge. The first mentioned was, that, regardless of the sentiments of either, I had detached Mr. Bingley from your sister; and the other, that I had, in defiance of various claims, in defiance of honor and humanity, ruined the immediate prosperity, and blasted the prospects of Mr. Wickham. Willfully and wantonly to have thrown off the companion of my youth, the acknowledged favorite of my father, a young man who had scarcely any other dependence than on our patronage, and who had been brought up to expect its exertion, would be a depravity to which the separation of two young persons, whose affection could be the growth of only a few weeks, could bear no comparison. But from the severity of that blame which was last night so liberally bestowed, respecting each circumstance, I shall hope to be in future secured, when the following account of my actions and their motives has been read. If, in the explanation of them which is due to myself, I am under the necessity of relating feelings which may be offensive to yours, I can only say that I am sorry. The necessity must be obeyed and further apology would be absurd.*

I had not been long in Hertfordshire, before I saw, in common with others, that Bingley preferred your eldest sister to any other young woman in the country. But it was not till the evening of the dance at Netherfield that I had any apprehension of his feeling a serious attachment. I had often seen him in love before. At that ball, while I had the honor of dancing with you, I was first made acquainted, by Sir William Lucas's accidental information, that Bingley's attentions to your sister had given rise to a general expectation of their marriage. He spoke of it as a certain event, of which the time alone could be undecided. From that moment I observed my friend's behavior attentively; and I could then perceive that his partiality for Miss Bennet was beyond what I had ever witnessed in him.

Your sister I also watched. Her look and manners were open, cheerful, and engaging as ever, but without any symptom of peculiar regard, and I remained convinced from the evening's scrutiny, that though she received his attentions with pleasure, she did not invite them by any participation of sentiment. If you have not been mistaken here, I must have been in an error. Your superior knowledge of your sister must make the latter probable. If it be so, if I have been misled by such error, to inflict pain on her, your resentment has not been unreasonable. But I shall not scruple to assert that the serenity of your sister's countenance and air was such as might have given the most acute observer a conviction that, however amiable her temper, her heart was not likely to be easily touched. That I was desirous of believing her indifferent is certain, but I will venture to say that my investigations and decisions are not usually influenced by my hopes or fears. I did not believe her to be indifferent because I wished it; I believed it on impartial conviction, as truly as I wished it in reason.

My objections to the marriage were not merely those which I last night acknowledged to have required the utmost force of passion to put aside in my own case; the want of connection could not be so great an evil to my friend as to me. But there were other causes of repugnance; causes which, though still existing, and existing to an equal degree in both instances, I had myself endeavored to forget, because they were not immediately before me. These causes must be stated, though briefly. The situation of your mother's family, though objectionable, was nothing in comparison of that total want of propriety so frequently, so almost uniformly, betrayed by herself, by your three younger sisters, and occasionally even by your father. Pardon me. It pains me to offend you. But amidst your concern for the defects of your nearest relations, and your displeasure at this representation of them, let it give you consolation to consider that to have conducted yourselves so as to avoid any share of the like censure is praise no less generally bestowed on you and your eldest sister, than it is honorable to the sense and disposition of both. I will only say farther that, from what passed that evening, my opinion of all parties was confirmed, and every inducement heightened, which could have led me before to preserve my friend from what I esteemed a most unhappy connection.

He left Netherfield for London, on the day following, as you, I am certain, remember, with the design of soon returning. The part which I acted is now to be explained. His sisters' uneasiness had been equally excited with my own; our coincidence of feeling was soon discovered; and, alike sensible that no time was to be lost in detaching their brother, we shortly resolved on joining him directly in London. We accordingly went, and there I readily engaged in the office of pointing out to my friend, the certain evils of such a choice. I described, and enforced them earnestly. But, however this remonstrance might have staggered or delayed his determination, I do not suppose that it would ultimately have prevented the marriage, had it not been seconded by the assurance, which I hesitated not in giving, of your sister's indifference. He had before believed her to return his affection with sincere, if not with equal, regard. But Bingley has great natural modesty, with a stronger dependence on my judgment than on his own. To convince him, therefore, that he had deceived himself, was no very difficult point. To persuade him against returning into Hertfordshire, when that conviction had been given, was scarcely the work of a moment. I cannot blame myself for having done thus much.

There is but one part of my conduct in the whole affair, on which I do not reflect with satisfaction; it is that I condescended to adopt the measures of art so far as to conceal from him your sister's being in town.

I knew it myself, as it was known to Miss Bingley, but her brother is even yet ignorant of it. That they might have met without ill consequence is, perhaps, probable, but his regard did not appear to me enough extinguished for him to see her without some danger. Perhaps this concealment, this disguise, was beneath me. It is done, however, and it was done for the best. On this subject I have nothing more to say, no other apology to offer. If I have wounded your sister's feelings, it was unknowingly done; and though the motives which governed me may to you very naturally appear insufficient, I have not yet learnt to condemn them.

With respect to that other, more weighty accusation, of having injured Mr. Wickham, I can only refute it by laying before you the whole of his connection with my family. Of what he has particularly accused me, I am ignorant, but of the truth of what I shall relate, I can summon more than one witness of undoubted veracity. Mr. Wickham is the son of a very respectable man, who had for many years the management of all the Pemberley estates; and whose good conduct in the discharge of his trust naturally inclined my father to be of service to him; and on George Wickham, who was his godson, his kindness was therefore liberally bestowed. My father supported him at school, and afterwards at Cambridge; most important assistance, as his own father, always poor from the extravagance of his wife, would have been unable to give him a gentleman's education. My father was not only fond of this young man's society, whose manners were always engaging; he had also the highest opinion of him, and hoping the church would be his profession, intended to provide for him in it.

As for myself, it is many, many years since I first began to think of him in a very different manner. The vicious propensities, the want of principle, which he was careful to guard from the knowledge of his best friend, could not escape the observation of a young man of nearly the same age with himself, and who had opportunities of seeing him in unguarded moments, which Mr. Darcy could not have. Here again I shall give you pain—to what degree you only can tell. But whatever may be the sentiments which Mr. Wickham has created, a suspicion of their nature shall not prevent me from unfolding his real character.

It adds even another motive. My excellent father died about five years ago; and his attachment to Mr. Wickham was to the last so steady, that in his will he particularly recommended it to me to promote his advancement in the best manner that his profession might allow, and, if he took orders, desired that a valuable family living might be his as soon as it became vacant. There was also a legacy of one thousand pounds. His own father did not long survive mine, and within half a year from these events Mr. Wickham wrote to inform me that, having finally resolved against taking orders, he hoped I should not think it unreasonable for him to expect some more immediate pecuniary advantage, in lieu of the preferment by which he could not be benefitted. He had some intention, he added, of studying the law, and I must be aware that the interest of one thousand pounds would be a very insufficient support therein. I rather wished than believed him to be sincere, but, at any rate, was perfectly ready to accede to his proposal. I knew that Mr. Wickham ought not to be a clergyman. The business was therefore soon settled. He resigned all claim to assistance in the church, were it possible that he could ever be in a situation to receive it, and accepted in return three thousand pounds. All connection between us seemed now dissolved. I thought too ill of him to invite him to Pemberley, or admit his society in town. In town, I believe, he chiefly lived, but his studying the law was a mere pretense, and being now free from all restraint, his life was a life of idleness and dissipation.

For about three years I heard little of him; but on the decease of the incumbent of the living which had been designed for him, he applied to me again by letter for the presentation. His circumstances, he assured me, and I had no difficulty in believing it, were exceedingly bad. He had found the law a most unprofitable study, and was now absolutely resolved on being ordained, if I would present him to the living in question—of which he trusted there could be little doubt, as he was well assured that I had no other person to provide for, and I could not have forgotten my revered father's intentions.

You will hardly blame me for refusing to comply with this entreaty, or for resisting every repetition of it. His resentment was in proportion to the distress of his circumstances, and he was doubtless as violent in his abuse of me to others, as in his reproaches to myself. After this period, every appearance of acquaintance was dropped. How he lived I know not. But last summer he was again most painfully obtruded on my notice.

I must now mention a circumstance which I would wish to forget myself, and which no obligation less than the present should induce me to unfold to any human being. Having said thus much, I feel no doubt of your secrecy. My sister, who is more than ten years my junior, was left to the guardianship of my mother's nephew, Colonel Fitzwilliam, and myself. About a year ago, she was taken from school, and an establishment formed for her in London; and last summer she went with the lady who presided over it, to Ramsgate; and thither also went Mr. Wickham, undoubtedly by design; for there proved to have been a prior acquaintance between him and Mrs. Younge, in whose character we were most unhappily deceived; and by her connivance and aid he so far recommended himself to Georgiana, whose affectionate heart retained a strong impression of his kindness to her as a child, that she was persuaded to believe herself in love, and to consent to an elopement. She was then but fifteen, which must be her excuse; and after stating her imprudence, I am happy to add that I owed the knowledge of it to herself. I joined them unexpectedly a day or two before the intended elopement; and then Georgiana, unable to support the idea of grieving and offending a brother whom she almost looked up to as a father, acknowledged the whole to me.

You may imagine what I felt and how I acted. Regard for my sister's credit and feelings prevented any public exposure, but I wrote to Mr. Wickham, who left the place immediately, and Mrs. Younge was of course removed from her charge. Mr. Wickham's chief object was unquestionably my sister's fortune, which is thirty thousand pounds; but I cannot help supposing that the hope of revenging himself on me was a strong inducement. His revenge would have been complete indeed.

This, Madam, is a faithful narrative of every event in which we have been concerned together; and if you do not absolutely reject it as false, you will, I hope, acquit me henceforth of cruelty towards Mr. Wickham. I know not in what manner, under what form of falsehood, he has imposed on you; but his success is not, perhaps, to be wondered at. Ignorant as you

*previously were of everything concerning either, detection could not be in
your power, and suspicion certainly not in your inclination.*

*You may possibly wonder why all this was not told you last night.
But I was not then master enough of myself to know what could or
ought to be revealed. For the truth of everything here related, I can
appeal more particularly to the testimony of Colonel Fitzwilliam, who
from our near relationship and constant intimacy, and still more as one
of the executors of my father's will, has been unavoidably acquainted
with every particular of these transactions. If your abhorrence of me
should make my assertions valueless, you cannot be prevented by the
same cause from confiding in my cousin; and that there may be the
possibility of consulting him, I shall endeavor to find some opportunity
of putting this letter in your hands in the course of the morning. I will
only add, God bless you.*

FITZWILLIAM DARCY.

Elizabeth sighed and Darcy took her in his arms. "We agreed that
this letter should be destroyed for it does neither of us justice to
chance upon it. I would have burnt it myself when I came across it,
but although I am its creator I am not its owner."

Elizabeth shook her head. "Oh you are too good, we shall burn
it together, one sheet each."

"And therefore rid ourselves finally of regret and condemnation?"

"Forever," she said, "the past and all cruel specters abolished."

Elizabeth and Darcy would, if given the choice to follow the
instincts of their hearts, have stayed content in the quiet of the
gallery sharing whispered sentiments, but they were mindful of
their duties and acknowledged that they must prepare for their
guests. It was no misfortune for them as they looked forward to
entertaining those family members and friends whose company
they had not enjoyed for some time. Downstairs they walked
towards the fireplace and without ceremony or mention of their
actions each threw a sheet of paper into the flames then turned and
continued across the hall towards the ballroom. And while the last

remaining evidence of their past conflicts became ash they conversed easily and happily on pleasant subjects.

"Mr. Hanworth is beside himself with worry that Georgiana may be asked to dance by some of the other guests, he has insisted she dance only with him," said Elizabeth with a satisfied expression. "I am not at all surprised, she is grown so pretty and confident this last year, their regard for each other is pleasing."

Darcy noted the pleasure his wife derived from his sister's happiness. "Yes it is sure, she will only stand up with him, but allow me to give you further cause for delight by telling you this; Hanworth has asked me for her hand."

Elizabeth was at once overjoyed and surprised. "Oh, Fitzwilliam, my love, she will accept him, it is a certainty! There is not a single reason she could find to refuse him. I will welcome him as the ideal brother, things could not be more perfect."

"Yes, we have much to celebrate, this assembly shall be reflective of all of our joy."

Elizabeth was still enraptured by this latest confirmation of Mr. Hanworth's regard for Georgiana. "I am so happy for them, I cannot find words to tell you, but poor Caroline Bingley, I am sure she will expect to dance at least one with Mr. Hanworth, she has an eye for handsome young men."

"Poor Caroline indeed."

Elizabeth teased her husband. "Could you not oblige her for the first dance, Fitzwilliam, even though it is common knowledge that you dislike the amusement."

Darcy at once saw his wife's mischief and loved her all the more for it, he pulled her closely to him and said firmly, "It is universally known that I rarely dance."

Elizabeth again alluded to Miss Bingley's misfortune. "Your good manners and judgment will surely lead you to make an exception and indulge dear Caroline," she said teasingly.

Darcy, as close now to Elizabeth as his breath to his words, looked lovingly into her eyes and said, "It would be a punishment to stand up with any other woman but you Elizabeth."

CHAPTER 30

"Heaven and earth! of what are you thinking?
Are the shades of Pemberley to be thus polluted?"

And so the year 1813 drew to a satisfactory close for Elizabeth and Darcy. Their first ball had been a resounding success; those who attended were many, those who declined few. Kitty was once again to be found standing, as she had done in September in the role of godmother to the Darcy heir, in the church of St. Giles in Matlock. This time Jeremiah Cleary stood beside her as both made the solemn vows of marriage. Mr. and Mrs. Cleary became well known and well loved in Matlock. Just as Mr. Bennet had predicted, Mrs. Catherine Cleary became the envy of many young women in her husband's congregation. Mary's husband Mr. Price retained his job with Mr. Phillips while Mary herself began a small but well-run library in the village. Despite disapproving of them herself, she devoted an entire shelf to Lady Metcalfe's popular novels for women. Her marriage and her unexpected venture made her something of a star in Meryton.

Mr. and Mrs. Bennet continued to live in familiar discord at Longbourn.

Lady Catherine was only once approached by her nephew regarding her involvement in Wickham's elopement with Lydia. Nevertheless, although she displayed signs of complete shame at Darcy's knowing her part in the scandal, she was too taken up with the shock of her daughter's newfound delight in socializing to reprimand herself too harshly. And there the subject was left by Darcy, for what could be gained, as far as he was concerned, in increasing his aunt's unhappiness? It was noted by Mrs. Collins that

Anne's health and disposition had undergone a miraculous kind of transformation, but Mr. Collins resolved to remain silent on the matter, tactfully agreeing with Lady Catherine that her daughter's sudden predilection for dancing was most definitely a cause for concern.

Colonel Fitzwilliam and his young wife immediately began a family. Mr. and Mrs. Bingley settled readily into Fordham Hall with none more delighted at their being there than Darcy and Elizabeth, and by the spring of 1814 their first and only son was born. Mrs. Georgiana Hanworth became the much respected and admired mistress of Glenhorn Park, her husband's estate in Gloucester, stunning society with her outgoing nature and confidence. Caroline Bingley never married but remained a devoted companion to her widowed sister Louisa.

Lydia Wickham had no sooner had her daughter than she was expecting once again. Her husband, under the watchful eye of Mrs. Darcy, proved, eventually, that love can indeed conquer all.

Elizabeth and Fitzwilliam Darcy, with the past behind them and a long and prosperous future before them, were thankful for their blessed lives. They continued throughout the rest of their time together to be as besotted and as adoring as young lovers long after their youth had gone. Elizabeth Darcy bore her husband a daughter, and two more sons. And although Darcy and his dearest, loveliest Elizabeth have long since departed this earth, their spirits alight upon the breeze through the trees at Pemberley, and tread, for the most part unnoticed, through its parkland. Reflected in its lakes and streams the careful observer may imagine they see the faintest outline of a fine gentleman and his fine lady, and in having so happy a fortune as to regard them will know, without doubt, that it is them, Fitzwilliam Darcy and his Elizabeth, united, entwined, inseparable as ever they were.

Oh, on remembering the young Elizabeth Bennet, who could not like her? And who could tolerate those who did not? Her portrait, a very fine likeness of her, can to this very day be seen alongside her husband's in the Long Gallery at Pemberley. She was once described by someone who knew her *very* well to have been as delightful a creature as ever there was.

Finis

OTHER ULYSSES PRESS BOOKS

MR. DARCY PRESENTS HIS BRIDE: A SEQUEL
TO JANE AUSTEN'S PRIDE & PREJUDICE
Helen Halstead, $14.95

When Elizabeth Bennet marries the brooding, passionate Mr. Darcy, she is thrown into the exciting world of London society. She makes a powerful friend in the Marchioness of Englebury, but the jealousy among her ladyship's circle threatens to destroy Elizabeth's happiness. Elizabeth is drawn into a powerful clique for which intrigue is the stuff of life and rivalry the motive. Her success, it seems, can only come at the expense of good relations with her husband.

THE WIT AND WISDOM OF JANE AUSTEN:
QUOTES FROM HER NOVELS, LETTERS AND
DIARIES
Compiled by Dominique Enright, $12.95

Drawn from her world-renowned novels, private writing, and extremely entertaining letters, *The Wit and Wisdom of Jane Austen* is an absorbing collection of the beloved author's insightful musings. Austen's social commentaries remain as fresh today as when first published. Featuring the best gems from *Pride and Prejudice, Sense and Sensibility, Emma, Mansfield Park*, and Austen's other writings, this compilation is a tribute to a writer whose work will resonate for centuries to come.

THE LOST YEARS OF JANE AUSTEN: A NOVEL
Barbara Ker Wilson, $14.95

There is a mysterious interval in Jane Austen's life, before any of her novels were published, when she disappears from sight. This book seeks to fill those missing months with a visit from England to the colony of New South Wales. It is a historical fact that Austen's aunt, Mrs. Leigh Perrot, was brought to trial on a charge of shoplifting black lace. Botany Bay, Australia, was the destination to which Mrs. Perrot might have been transported as a convict. Jane Austen and her uncle would have had good reason to visit the unfortunate in Sydney Town...where the dashing Mr. D'Arcy Wentworth has settled at Homebush, a convict revolt is brewing at Castle Hill, and no one is quite certain whether the Napoleonic War has ended or not.

ABOUT THE AUTHOR

Juliette Shapiro is an accomplished writer of both fiction and non-fiction whose work has been published by *Verbatim*, *QWF* and *Jane Austen Regency Magazine*. She also writes pseudonymously as Yolande Sorores and was one of the contributors, using that name, to Flame Books' *Book of Voices*, a publication produced in support of PEN, the Sierra Leone charity.

She has enjoyed an enduring and dependable love affair with Jane Austen's works from an early age, and re-reads *Pride and Prejudice* at various junctures in her life, always finding therein, something new to marvel at, laugh at, or take solace in.

Juliette Shapiro is the mother of two sons and two daughters. She takes laughable pride in being (to date) a grandmother to three glorious little girls and one beautiful boy, seeing as this achievement required no work or skill on her part. She thinks they are the most exquisite creatures on earth, but she is, of course, prejudiced. She was born in 1964 and named after a song.